Paul has interviewed many colourful individuals to add authenticity to his characters. Among them were a police psychologist, a Billionaire businessman who lives and works between London and Monaco, a homicide detective, artist Scott Greenwell also known as 'dARC Artz', a female escort, a lap dancer at a high end gentleman's club, a tattooist, a man who served time for murder, and notorious gangster Dave Courtney.

With over one hundred hours of body art hidden beneath his business suit, tattoos are his guilty pleasure and he once had a three page spread in well-known publication, 'Total Tattoo Magazine.' Whether he is writing about a steamy sexual encounter or a graphic murder, Paul listens to music before, and sometimes during a writing session to help set the mood.

Paul's work has been described by readers as Fifty Shades meets Silence of the Lambs.

For Blake Primo & Lex Massimo

Paul Michael Campbell

THE DEVIL'S TEA PARTY

AUSTIN MACAULEY PUBLISHERS™

LONDON • CAMBRIDGE • NEW YORK • SHARJAH

A CIP catalogue record for this title is available from the British Library.

ISBN 9781788781459 (Paperback)
ISBN 9781788781466 (ePub e-book)

www.austinmacauley.com

First Published 2022
Austin Macauley Publishers Ltd®
1 Canada Square
Canary Wharf
London
E14 5AA

My heart-felt thanks and blessings go out to my parents Ray and Jenny for your selfless sacrifice and unconditional love, my wife and soulmate Kerryanne, and my beautiful sons Blake and Lex for giving me a reason to smile every day, my little sister Sarah-Louise (keep shinning), Stephen, Irene and David, Johanna and Steph, Charles Oliver (an incredible English teacher), for helping to spark my love of literature, my good friend Manny Donaldson for his invaluable input on this project, Scot Greenwell for his stunning artistic creativity, Mandy Wilson for your help with my research, Darren Nullatamby Thomas 'Tommy Boy' Beach and David Parry (my QHS hombres), Jamie Russo and Sammy Dale for an insight into the high-life, Cedric and the Clarke family, the entire Glass family for always being there for me and making me feel part of something special, the rest of the Campbell clan (I'm proud to share your name), Grandma Hazel and Grandma Agatha (both gone but never forgotten), my Nottingham crew, Stephen Ardern, Tom Hine, Mike Freeborn, Joel Constantino, Martin McGuire (wherever you are) Danny McLaughlin and Kevin Downie (the legend who will always hold a place in my heart), anyone who has ever showed me love, I wish you blessings from above and anyone who has ever hated on me just know that your hate has helped to make me great, and of course, praise be to the great architect and divine creator of all things.

Chapter 1
The Hangman Tattoo

It's been exactly one week since the terrifying serial killer known as 'the Hangman', made a chilling 911 call. During that call, the Hangman, who has already claimed the lives of seven young children and evaded police capture for over three months, boasted that he would end the lives of no less than eighteen children at exactly midnight tonight. Over the past week, nineteen children between the ages of five and seven have been reported missing, and although there is no evidence directly linking any of them to the Hangman case, their disappearance has created widespread panic across New York. Earlier today, Mayor Golding met with the parents of one of the missing children, six-year-old Mimi Chandler, at the school she attends here in Brooklyn. During a heart-felt public address, an emotional Mayor Golding urged the people of New York to remain "hopeful, vigilant and united in these trying times." This afternoon, hundreds of brave law enforcement officers took to the streets, in a final attempt to find the Hangman and bring him to justice. Police Chief Edward Castilian is urging anyone who may have information to come forward without delay. In a month which marks the seven-year anniversary of the bloody Brooklyn Bridge Massacre, citizens of New York are once again holding hands and praying for the lives of more of its young sons and daughters. This is Belinda Bryce reporting for CWC News, Brooklyn, New York.

As Detective Jake Cannon stood shadowed beneath the canopy of a large tree staring up at Cecil House, he knew that he had reached the point of no return.

48 hours earlier, he had decided to ditch his partner and cut himself off from all radio contact. After three months of hell, there was not a cop in the city with a single credible lead in the hunt for the Hangman. Forensic teams had swept each crime scene following the discovery of seven dead bodies, and nobody had come up with a shred of evidence. Now the clock was ticking, and Jake could no longer run with the pack. A partner would slow him down, the Captain would demand answers, and Jake would need them both to look away while he took off his gloves and fought dirty.

Deep down, he knew that his insubordination would not go unpunished, and his conduct may even cost him his badge. Yet he remained resolute to the cause, determined not to worry about the consequences of his actions until the missing children were re-united with their families, and the Hangman was either behind bars or lying prostrate on the mortician's cold table.

Eager to avoid being seen, Jake crouched in the bushes and slipped further into the shadows as he observed the building. Cecil House was a five-storey apartment block in the Marcy Projects. All of the cars around the block were in keeping with their mediocre surroundings. All except for one 1967 Chevrolet Impala with cherry red gloss paintwork and butterscotch leather upholstery. It was sitting on 22-inch chrome rims, and Jake would be damned if the car did not belong to the very man he had spent the past two days trying to track down.

Samuel 'Porky' Sands was a former drug dealer-turned-pimp, who, like many of his slithering serpentine kind, traded street knowledge with cops, and in return, they turned a blind eye to his activities. Porky was a 'snitch', and as undesirable as it was to allow an enterprise like his to thrive, such alliances between law men and law breakers had become a necessary evil in the modern-day metropolis. But he was not just any street corner rat trading minor details for dollars. Porky was a central hub of information.

His stable of women was said to be the finest in the five boroughs—men would travel great distances and pay a premium for his girls. Inhibitions would loosen under the influence of liquor and soft music and in the heat of lust, tongues would slip. Mobsters, thugs, and even politicians and officers of the law would brag of their exploits, eager to impress their desirable female companions. Like loyal worker bees, Porky's girls would report back to him on a daily basis, with news of what moves were being made, when, and by whom. Street knowledge had become a powerful asset to Porky, enabling him to expand his empire.

However, his known affiliation with the 'pigs' had not only earned him his nickname, but also made him extremely unpopular with some of the major kingpins of the criminal underworld. So, when Jake learned that Porky and all of his staff had abandoned their high-end apartment complex in Manhattan and gone underground, he guessed that Porky was holding information that may finally blow the Hangman case wide open. Information that could also cost Porky his life, as one of the missing children was 5-year-old Nico Russo, the only son of Micky 'The Madman' Russo. Micky's cousin Tony was head of the infamous 'Russo Famiglia', and the feared Mob boss had promised to extract any information Porky was withholding by force, if he ever caught up with him.

With the men in blue and every Mob hand in the city on his scent, Porky could not afford to take risks, so he pulled his entire team off the streets and took refuge in the building where he had spent most of his childhood.

He had counted on Cecil House providing adequate cover, but he had not counted on the tenacity of the only cop clever and determined enough to track him down, Jake Cannon.

Before becoming a homicide detective, Jake had worked vice, so it was a world he knew well. From the top tier players to the base-line tricks and junkies, he had a catalogue of contacts and inside knowledge. And right now, he knew something that Porky did not.

Jake had discovered that one of Porky's women, a Cuban temptress who went by the name of 'Cookie', had been selling drugs on the side for her dealer cousin. After interrogating dozens of known pushers, he began hunting down new dealers in the hope of establishing a link with one of Porky's women.

Finally, he came across a known Junkie by the name of Billy Purvis by chance, as he stumbled out of a subway car at Marcy Avenue Station. Billy's demeanour was that of a man in dire need of a fix, so Jake followed him in the hope of discovering a dealer whom he could shake down for fresh information. When the dealer Billy met turned out to be Cookie, Jake knew that he had struck gold. He followed Cookie back to Cecil House, and although the car outside was not his distinctive Red Cadillac, the Impala parked close to the building had Porky written all over it.

Now, under cover of darkness, Jake stood contemplating his next move. Naturally he was armed with his Glock 17 pistol, but he also knew that somewhere in that block, Porky was sat surrounded by a heavily armed guard. Tensions would be high and everyone would be on edge. An unexpected knock at the door and half a dozen shaking arms would be held aloft, with index fingers poised nervously over cold steel triggers.

It would take a brave man to storm that building, and a fool to think that he could walk up and ask for an audience with Porky. Jake had to be more creative. He took another look at his watch. It was now 10:17 pm. "Deep breaths, Jake," he told himself. "Think, Jake, think!"

Inside an apartment on the top floor of Cecil House, Porky sat biting his nails and fidgeting nervously. A deathly silence had gripped the room. A week ago, he had been upbeat. The money he was losing did not weigh heavily on his mind, because he knew only too well that his troops would soon be back on their daily grind, making up for lost time and income. However, as the Hangman's deadline approached with no news of the killer's capture, the gang had become increasingly unsettled. The true terror lay in the threat posed by Tony Russo and his Mob. They knew that Tony would kill everyone but Porky, who would be tortured until he gave up all he knew, and then brutally executed.

As midnight drew closer, Porky rocked anxiously in his chair. Suddenly, his eyes shifted to the window. For the past hour, the sound of a basketball thumping on the court directly opposite the block had been a welcome break to the tense silence. Now, only the wall-mounted clock could be heard. The rhythmic ticking and tocking was a chilling reminder of Porky's present predicament.

Without warning he leapt to his feet and ran over to the wall, ripped the clock from its mount and smashed it against the side of a cabinet, sending fragments of plastic flying around the room. Nobody dared speak as he returned to the window. He carefully tilted the venetian blinds so he could see outside without being visible himself.

"Goddamn kids," he said bitterly, "don't they know there's a killer on the streets tonight?" From his vantage point, Porky could see three small boys, no more than 14 years old, peering through the fence in the direction of the cluster of trees that lined the nearby playground. It was pitch black, and despite the street lights, Porky could not see past the first row of trees. Seconds later, a fourth boy emerged from beyond the trees carrying a basketball.

That was it, thought Porky. One of the boys had clearly sent the ball looping over the fence and he had gone to retrieve it. In a few moments the comforting sound of children at play would resume, re-assuring him that danger was still at arms-length. But to his surprise, the youngster did not return to the court. Instead, he headed towards the other side of the street.

The boy walked over to where the Impala was parked before looking up, and scanning the rows of apartment windows. Porky was confused, and the expression on the boy's face suggested that he was both scared and uncomfortable. The boy glanced up at the block one last time before raising the ball high above his head. Then, shutting his eyes and wincing, he launched the ball at the windscreen of Porky's new prized possession.

"Oh, hell no!" shouted Porky, looking around the room for something that would cause this troublesome kid some pain. As the car alarm sounded off loudly, the boy kicked the driver side door repeatedly, and tugged the wing mirror until it came away in his hand.

"This little punk is looking to get shot out here tonight!" yelled Porky, as his girls and goons ran over to see what was going on outside. If there was one thing everyone knew, it was that Porky loved his cars above all else.

He picked up a belt that was lying on the bedside dresser and ran towards the door.

"Let me take care of this, Porky, you can't go down there," said one of his men, grabbing him as he made his way towards the exit, but Porky slapped his hand away.

"Nah it's cool, man, you guys hang back. This little punk is mine." He was spitting with rage as he spoke, "I'm gonna catch him and beat him like I'm his daddy!"

Porky expected a chase as he ran out of the block and into the street, but instead, the boy simply froze. He was staring at Porky with a look of wide-eyed terror, but he did not run. He just stood rooted to the spot, shaking with fear. As Porky approached him, the boy looked over towards the trees from which he had emerged moments earlier with his ball. Porky, who was now just a foot away from him, did not say a word. He raised his arm aloft, ready to crack the belt down on the boy who had vandalized his car.

"Hold it, Porky!" The voice was all too familiar. As Porky lowered his hand and stared out towards the darkness, the petrified boy ran back towards the court, and Jake Cannon emerged from the shadows, his gun held at eye level and pointed directly at Porky. Jake looked up towards the block and saw several faces peering down from one of the top floor apartments.

"I'm real sorry I had to get that kid to wreck your wheels, but it was the only way I could lure you out of that block. Now I need you to signal to your crew and let them know everything's cool, Porky," said Jake authoritatively.

Porky stared back at him with a look of defiance, but there was something about Jake's demeanour that made him uneasy. He was usually calm and calculating, but tonight his manner seemed edgy and slightly unpredictable.

"Let them know everything is cool or I swear I will put a hole in your head right here in the street!" yelled Jake.

Porky looked up towards the window and gave a strained nod.

"Now move," said Jake, ushering him down the path and around the corner to where his car was hidden away out of sight.

"What the hell happened to you, Cannon?" said Porky. "You look like you ain't slept for a week man."

He was not wrong. Jake looked like he was in a bad way. The man, often referred to as the 'Dapper Detective', was usually immaculately groomed, but tonight he looked like a man on the edge.

Jake did not respond to Porky's comment, instead he pointed at the driver's side of his car and urged him to get in.

"Wait a minute, man, you ain't even got no tinted windows," said the frantic Porky. "You want me to drive around in your ride with my ass on show tonight of all nights? You must want me to get shot, Cannon. But if this car gets shot up, you think the bullets will miss you?"

Jake ignored the warning. He had anticipated Porky's reluctance to be out in public.

"I'm pretty certain you're gonna be seen, Porky. So, let's just hope you tell me what I need to know before we hit the high street or like you say…we're both dead!"

Jake's sinister tone was enough to convince him that he meant business. As Porky eased himself tentatively into the driver's seat, Jake slid into the passenger side. "Now drive!" said Jake, tossing him the keys with his right hand, while the gun in his left remained trained on Porky.

"Now wait a minute, Cannon, just wait, man, I'm begging you," Porky pleaded for mercy; but Jake showed none.

"Talk, and you walk," said Jake, his face was void of emotion as he spoke, "stall, and I feed you to the dogs—it's that simple. Tell me what you know or it won't be Russo you have to worry about, I'll plug you myself!"

"Jake, I swear to you man, if I knew anything, I'd have come to you first," Porky's voice dimmed to a whisper, as if he feared that the street itself was listening.

"But I don't know nothin', man, I swear. I know I ain't no saint, Cannon. I've done some bad shit in my time, but this Hangman guy is pure evil."

Porky began to tremble, like a man about to break. "You gotta believe me, Cannon, I want this killer caught just as much as the next guy, but this time I ain't got nothin' to tell you!"

There was a moment of silence as Jake stared into Porky's eyes, searching for signs of sincerity.

"So why did you run, Porky? Why did you go underground? If you had no information then surely you should have just stayed put. By running, you just look guilty, like you know something that either the cops or worse still Russo could bleed out of you."

Jake had a talent for reading people. It was as though he had a sixth sense, and right now this sense was telling him that something was not right. Porky was lying and with time running out, he needed to crank up the pressure.

Without warning, Jake swivelled round and launched a heavy-handed right hook straight into Porky's ribs. As he yelled out in pain, clutching his chest, Jake's right arm drew back and shot out once more like a cannonball, landing flush in Porky's face, shattering his nose.

"Stop Goddamn it," Porky cried out. Blood was streaming from his nose and tears were running down his face. "What the hell, Cannon, not the face!" said Porky, confused by the ferocious attack. With his smooth ebony skin and hazel eyes, Porky had always relied on his good looks, yet Jake seemed determined to spoil them. He had seen Jake play hard ball before but this was different. This time he was serious.

"You and me have always been cool, Cannon. You're a good cop man, you don't do this kind of shit!" yelled Porky in desperation.

"Not tonight," said Jake, still showing no sign of mercy towards the whimpering pimp. "Tonight, I'm not a good cop,

I'm something different. Tonight, I'm tracking a monster, and if there's one thing I've learned in this job, it's that sometimes it takes a monster to catch one. You need to understand one thing, Porky. Four days ago, I looked the mother of one of these kids in the eyes, and I promised her I'd bring her daughter home. I'm not about to break my promise. I know you have information that can help me find these kids. That's why I've spent two days and nights hunting you down and I'll be damned if it's been in vain."

Jake was full of rage. The emotion that he had tried so hard to suppress had finally surfaced.

"We are dealing with a psychopath and he won't stop until he's ripped the soul out of this city. He's destroying us from within like a cancer and I have to stop him. I couldn't care less if it costs me my badge, your life, or mine for that matter. So, you'd better stop bullshitting me. Tell me what you know right now, or I swear to God this gun might just happen to go off in your face!"

Porky knew that there was no point calling Jake's bluff. He looked down at his feet, contemplating how little he could get away with telling him. Sensing that Porky was close to breaking point, Jake tried to re-assure him.

"Look, I know you think snitching to me will get you killed this time. So, you have my word that Tony Russo will hear from me first hand, how you came forward of your own accord to surrender the information, as soon as it hit your ears."

He looked up at Jake, who had lowered his gun for the first time. "You swear on that, Cannon?" said the blubbering Porky.

"My word is my bond," said Jake. "Now talk fast because we don't have much time."

"The tattoo kid, I think his name is Ronnie," said Porky. "He owns that tattoo studio called 'Bitter Skill to Swallow' down on Henry Street. He was runnin' his mouth off last week, he claims he knows somethin' big." Porky hesitated once more, prompting Jake to tap his watch with his pistol.

"Okay listen," Porky continued. "The kid reckons this guy came into his studio real late when the place was empty, and asked for a special portrait piece. Ronnie said the guy handed him a sketch, but the artwork was so good it could have been a photo. The guy told him he drew it himself."

Jake shuffled around in his seat, sensing that a breakthrough was imminent. "Where is this going, Porky?" said Jake impatiently. "I'm trying to connect the dots, but you need to give me something concrete."

"It was the picture," said Porky nervously. "Ronnie recognised it straight away. It was one of the missing girls, the one from right here in Brooklyn. Mimi Chandler."

"Are you certain?" said Jake. His eyes widened at the prospect of a solid lead.

"Ronnie was positive man," said Porky, who was pleased to see that Jake's anger had subsided. "Her face has been all over the news for the past week so he was one hundred percent certain it was her. The sicko wanted Ronnie to tattoo her face on his body. Ronnie said that when he took off his shirt, the guy had kids' faces tattooed all over his back. Every single face was black and white, except for blood red teardrops falling from each of the kid's eyes. They were cryin' blood man! Ronnie counted seven in total. Seven faces, Cannon! One for each of the kids he's killed so far!"

"Where?" Jake spoke with renewed intensity. This was the information he had been waiting for. "Where can I find Ronnie?"

"He lives above his tattoo joint, but you won't find him there," said Porky. "I hear he's posted up at some club owned by a friend of his down on Wythe Avenue. It's called 'Unchained'. It's a haven for the misunderstood generation. They all look the same down there, all piercings and glow sticks, but Ronnie stands out like a peacock cos of his ridiculous pink mohawk. If you're gonna find him tonight, the smart money says that's where he'll be at."

"I know the place," said Jake, pointing at the driver side door and gesturing for Porky to get out of the car. As he did so, Jake slid over into the driver seat and wound down the window.

"You did the right thing here tonight, Porky," said Jake. "Don't worry I will keep my word and square things for you with Russo."

As Porky stepped back onto the sidewalk, looking all around to make sure that he had not been spotted, Jake fired up the engine and sped off in the direction of Unchained nightclub, in search of the one person who could lead him to the Hangman.

Chapter 2
Unchained

Jake took a crisp one-hundred-dollar bill from his wallet and handed it to Amber.

"Now tell me again, Amber, who are you looking for?" She rolled her eyes at Jake. He had already explained to her twice that all she had to do was make a lap of the nightclub and report back on the whereabouts of a young guy with bright pink hair, and in return, Jake would give her another hundred dollars.

Amber was a working girl and her time was money. But two hundred dollars for less than ten minutes work made up for the inconvenience of been pulled from her regular perch on the corner of Kent Avenue and North 7th Street, by an unusually dishevelled-looking Detective Cannon.

Amber had developed a soft spot for Jake during his years working vice, and he knew it. His handsome features coupled with the animal magnetism of a dangerously passionate man, often left women hopelessly attracted to him. But it was his gravelly tone and broody intensity that had Amber hooked. She would have risked the wrath of her pimp for a brief and lustful encounter with Jake, so she accepted the task without hesitation.

As the sound of her heels clipped away down the alley behind Unchained nightclub and off towards the entrance, Jake paced back and forth impatiently, occasionally glancing at his watch, and playing all of the possible outcomes of the next hour and a half over and over in his head. Jake always thought several steps ahead. He had come so close to a major lead in the Hangman investigation, but he knew that one wrong move could blow everything.

'Wild Wednesday' as it was known in the city, was as popular as a Saturday night for the hardcore club fanatics. So Unchained would be packed to the rafters, making it the perfect sanctuary for Ronnie. It did not make sense that he was so afraid to come to the police with what he knew. Someone had put the fear of God into him, and he would be as nervous as Porky was about being located.

Jake's face was well known across the city. He was the relentless cop with a hawk's eye for detail and a reputation for catching his man. Right now, there were a couple of well-built doormen, half a dozen receptionists and hundreds of drunken rowdy revellers between Jake and Ronnie. If he waltzed in waving his badge like some overzealous bounty hunter who had finally caught a scent, then he was certain that Ronnie would be gone by the time he made it through the crowds to wherever he was nesting.

Thinking on his feet, Jake had decided to take a slight detour and pick up Amber before heading to Unchained.

He knew that a woman dressed as suggestively as she was would be ushered into the club by door staff without question, while others were made to wait in line. She would also be able to get right up close to Ronnie and his gang, and get a fix on their position without rousing suspicion.

Within minutes, Amber came bounding back around the corner in her impossibly high heels, smiling enthusiastically. Jake knew immediately that this was good news.

"Your boy is in there alright," said Amber, gasping as she tried to catch her breath. "He's slumped in the VIP booth right next to the stage, but he ain't alone Jake. There's about eight of them, all knocking back shots like there's no tomorrow, and grabbing every girl who walks by. As soon as your man with the pink Mohawk set eyes on me, he started picking ice cubes out of his glass and throwing them at me. He said I looked so 'hot' that I needed to cool down."

Amber's account of events was music to Jake's ears. It not only meant that Ronnie was inside the club, but his behaviour suggested that he was relaxed. Amber's presence had not raised any suspicion, so Jake's arrival would be totally unexpected.

"Thanks, Amber, you've been a real help." Jake took another two hundred dollars out of his wallet and handed it to her. "Here's what I promised you, plus a little extra for doing such a great job."

Amber neither smiled nor took the money. She had begun piecing everything together in her head, and she was concerned for Jake's safety.

"Is this guy dangerous, Jake?" she said. "Does he have something to do with those missing kids?"

Jake smiled back at her. "Don't worry, Amber, this guy ain't nothing I can't handle," he said reassuringly. "I've just got a few questions I need to ask him that's all. But he's the type to run if he knows I'm coming. So now I know he's in there, I'm gonna make an entrance that he won't be expecting."

Jake placed his hands-on Amber's shoulders, and leaned in, kissing both of her cheeks before kissing her on the lips. It was not the passionate kiss that she longed for, but enough to let her know that Jake cared for her deeply.

"We would have made a great team wouldn't we, Jake?" she said.

"The best," he replied. "Now you'll want to get out of here, because in a few minutes all hell is gonna break loose."

Amber took Jake's advice as well as his money, and marched off in the direction of Kent Avenue. As she disappeared into the distance, Jake took his pistol out of its holster and unclipped the magazine to count his rounds. Then he slid the clip back into the gun, pulled his badge from his pocket and began marching with intent towards the main doors. Jake had barely turned the corner when one of the doormen spotted him and immediately began muttering into his radio.

"Don't fucking move!" yelled Jake.

A group of women waiting in line spotted his gun and began screaming, forcing Jake to show his badge.

"Police officer ladies and gentlemen, please try to remain calm."

He turned to look at the two doormen, who were shuffling nervously in the doorway. "Give me your radios and your cell phones!" Jake spoke with authority, and the two men handed over their only means of communication with the staff inside the club. Jake snatched them, before dropping them on the concrete and smashing them one by one beneath his feet. He hoped that this would buy him enough time to get to the back of the club, before the men on the door had time to get word back to Ronnie.

"Get outside, now!" Jake ushered the doormen out onto the sidewalk, and ran inside the main entrance. He marched past the girls on the reception desk, waving his badge and holding his gun low and close to his right leg, trying to avoid anyone spotting it and causing a panic. He pushed his way through the double doors and into the nightclub.

The first thing that hit Jake was a wall of electronic sound. The thumping monotonous bass pulsated through him. Followed by the tusking clap of snare, rising higher and higher, thrashing its way towards a crescendo. As it reached its peak, there was a sudden pause before the whirling, zapping, fizzing synergy of the heavily synthesized production kicked in, whipping the crowd into a frenzy.

As he began making his way toward where Ronnie was sitting, dozens of inebriated bodies paced towards him, into him, through him, walking on auto-pilot in the opposite direction to where he was headed. He wrestled against the current of people traffic, but they were blissfully unaware of his purpose and simply slowed his advance, marching on as though they were spellbound by the contemporary Kraftwerk that boomed from the speakers.

The purple filtered strobe lighting flickered and flashed violently, momentarily blinding him every few seconds as he struggled to gain focus and assess his surroundings. He could make out a colossal iron framed Trojan Horse in the centre of the dance-floor, from which a woman dressed as a dominatrix and another as a burlesque dancer, swung, twisted and cavorted above the outstretched hands of the crowds below. Fifteen yards beyond the dance-floor, was a stage upon which a band would often perform. However, tonight the black and white chessboard tiled floor was empty apart from the resident DJ, bobbing his head as he twisted and prodded away at the mixer between two vinyl decks. There were two giant yellow cat's eyes spray painted on the wall above the DJ stand. Beneath them, in luminous purple paint were the words, *Oh, lovely Pussy, oh, Pussy, my love, what a beautiful Pussy you are!* Jake recognised the quote. It was from a story read to children before they went to sleep at night. On any other day he may have laughed at the obvious comical context in which it was intended to be read by the masses of drunk and sexually charged clubbers. But tonight, he was in no mood for humour.

As he glanced to the left of the stage, he could just about make out a head of spiked pink hair in the mid-centre of the VIP booth. "Bingo," said Jake under his breath. As he began wading through the crowd once more, he spotted a man dressed in the distinctive red and black uniform of nightclub staff approaching the table.

The man leaned over and grabbed Ronnie by the back of his neck and began speaking into his ear. Within seconds, the whole group was on the move. Ronnie leapt to his feet and slid over the table, sending glasses and bottles flying.

Ronnie had been tipped off and he was making a run for it. *There must have been a camera on the main door*, thought Jake. *Or perhaps the door staff had re-entered the club and grabbed a phone from behind the main reception desk.* Either way it did not matter now. He had to make a decision fast, or Ronnie was going to get away.

Without hesitation, Jake raised his gun above his head, and fired three shots into the air. Within seconds, the music was off, the main lights were on and men and women were either on the deck, crawling on their hands and knees, or running frantically in the direction of the exit. As the bodies on the dance-floor began parting like the red sea, Jake made a dash towards the booth.

"Don't move, Ronnie, just stop right there!" Jake shouted at the top of his voice, so that his instructions could be heard above the screams of fleeing clubbers. As he approached the table, he could see that the group of men were far from hardened criminals. They were skater kids and street artists. A couple of them barely looked old enough to be in the club. Every one of them was visibly shaken by the sudden arrival of a guy waving a gun at their friend, so Jake knew that he needed to re-assure them that he meant no harm.

"Don't worry, fellas, he's not in danger," said Jake calmly. "I'm a cop and your friend Ronnie knows that I'm just here to get some vital information from him, and then I'll be on my way."

Jake's words and his calm delivery did not comfort Ronnie. He flew into a panic, and began shouting and cursing. His eyes scanned every corner of the club as he contemplated making a dash for the exit.

"Screw you, man, I swear to God I won't talk, you can't make me talk cop."

Ronnie was having a meltdown. As his friends looked on in shock, he began heaving, before throwing up violently. Jake glanced at the table to see what the group had been drinking. Ronnie had gone into shock, and his body was rejecting an unpleasant cocktail of various liquors, and cheap champagne. As the distressed young man fell to his knees, sobbing shamelessly, Jake knew that he needed to take control of the situation before the fear that was consuming Ronnie rendered him totally unable to communicate.

"Listen to me, everyone," said Jake, addressing the rest of the group. "You all need to leave here right now. Your friend is in shock and he just needs a minute to pull himself together. But when he does come around, you can't be here, because he'll be embarrassed if you see him like this."

Without hesitation, everyone apart from Ronnie scurried off through the exit, and out of the club. Jake holstered his weapon. Ronnie was not a threat to him, and a gun would not help calm his nerves. He walked over to the table and picked up a bottle of mineral water. Then he opened it and took a large gulp, before handing the rest to Ronnie.

"Now look at me, Ronnie," said Jake assertively. "We really don't have much time, so I need you to clear your head and tell me everything you know about the man with the faces tattooed all over his back who visited your studio."

Ronnie was sat motionless on the ground, clutching his shirt so tightly that his knuckles had turned white. The look on his face sent a cold shiver down Jake's spine. He had seen this catatonic expression before, on the faces of traumatised witnesses.

Looking at Ronnie, Jake understood immediately why he had gone to such lengths to avoid being caught and questioned. Just like Porky, he was petrified. His encounter with the Hangman must have been a harrowing experience, and he was fearful of the consequences of uttering a single word about the incident. But he had done. Ronnie had confided in someone, and the word had hit the streets. It had found its way to Porky, and led Jake straight to him.

He no longer felt safe at his studio, or his home. He had sought refuge in his friend's club, surrounded by his people. Perhaps he had drowned himself in alcohol to overcome the guilt of withholding information that could save the lives of eighteen innocent children. Maybe he believed that the Hangman was too clever to be caught. If he evaded the police, the killer would come for Ronnie. He knew where he worked, and could easily find out where he lived. Ronnie must have believed that the Hangman would return to end his life in a manner too brutal to imagine.

"Okay, you have to listen to me carefully, can you do that?" said Jake. Ronnie nodded his head slowly, without saying a word. "I know you've met the Hangman," Jake continued. "I also know that you are afraid of what he might do to you if you talk. But you see Ronnie, you don't have to be afraid. You have to believe me when I tell you that the Hangman wants to be captured. He wants you to talk."

Ronnie was beginning to come around. The vacant expression on his face had been replaced by an attentive stare, but there was still caution behind his eyes. He needed more reassurance.

Sensing that he was close to a breakthrough, Jake went into more detail.

"I'm guessing that the seven faces tattooed on this man's back were all drawn by the same artist," said Jake. "An artist of your experience would be able to tell that with one glance wouldn't he, Ronnie? So, you have to ask yourself, why would the Hangman come and see you for his final piece? Why would he risk using an artist he didn't know, and bring you the image of a child whose face was all over the news? This is a man who has been clever enough to evade capture for over three months, without leaving a single clue, but then he came to see you. Now I'm guessing he left you with just enough info to lead me straight to him. So, I believe that I was meant to find you, Ronnie, and you were meant to tell me what you know. If you think about it for a moment, I'm sure you'll come to the same conclusion that I have."

"Yes...yes, I would," said Ronnie nervously. "His work was all done by the same artist. The ink on his arms, his chest and his back, all of it was the same guy." He took a sip of the water Jake had handed him, before continuing his sinister recollection. "His right arm was a tribute to heaven. There were angels, cherubs, clouds and the image of Christ. But his left arm was dedicated to hell! It was covered in demonic imagery, all engulfed in flames. I've seen this stuff before on guys who just wanted to look edgy, but this dude was different. There was darkness in his eyes, he was pure evil."

Ronnie began to rock back and forth on his knees, wringing his shirt in his clenched fists once more, until some of the buttons popped off and fell onto the floor in front of him.

"Relax," said Jake. "Take your time and tell me what happened."

"He took off his shirt," said Ronnie, still shaking. "Then I saw his back. Every tattoo was a black and white image of a child's face, and they all looked terrified. The only colour was the blood red tears running down each of their cheeks, and a small red inverted cross in between his shoulder blades."

"An inverted cross?" asked Jake. He had spent a lot of time expanding his knowledge on any subject that could help to make him a better detective, and he had often considered the possibility of religious extremity being a motivating factor in the behaviour of some of the more unusual homicidal maniacs he had investigated. So, he knew that an inverted cross was a symbol associated with the devil, and his defiant subversion of the will of God.

"Yeah," said Ronnie, assuming that Jake did not know the meaning of the symbol. "I've been asked to draw this type of shit before man. So, I asked around and I think it's got something to do with guys selling their souls to the devil, in exchange for power. I've always thought that people just had this kind of ink done to get a rise out of folks and stuff like that. But this guy was different. There was something real scary about him."

The hair on the back of Jake's neck stood up as Ronnie tearfully recalled his ordeal.

"What did he look like, Ronnie?" said Jake, sensing that he was now comfortable enough to go into more detail.

"He was a giant!" said Ronnie. "I mean he was huge. Like seven feet tall I swear, and he was all muscle. He was around forty-five I'd say, with long blonde hair tied back in a pony-tail and like I said, he was covered in ink. I remember feeling real nervous, so I tried to joke around with him about how he was running out of space for any new ink, but he didn't laugh, he didn't even smile, he didn't say anything. The dude just handed me the drawing. That's when I knew he was the child killer everyone's been looking for. I recognised the kid's face straight away. It was one of the missing girls that I'd seen like a million times on the news just that week, and that freak knew that I'd recognised her. So, I just froze. But the sadistic prick just sat there smiling back at me. Then he spoke."

"This is it, Ronnie, you're doing great," said Jake, weary that time was running out. When he had fired his gun in the air a few minutes earlier, he had not simply done so on impulse just to clear the club. Jake knew that any minute now a tactical team and other officers would be assembling outside. There would be snipers placed on the roof of the club and of the buildings across the street. A hostage negotiator would be shuffling through the trunk of his car for his loud-speaker. They would assume this was a standard hostage situation, but when the door staff and Ronnie's friends gave their account and confirmed that the guy inside was Cannon, the cops would be relieved. They would come bursting through the doors into the club and Jake would have the team that he needed to pursue the Hangman, poised and ready for action. So, he was gambling on Ronnie knowing more than just minor details.

If Jake's hunch about the Hangman was correct, he would have given Ronnie enough information to track him down. The only question was, would it be enough to find him in time to save the children, or would they catch up with him after his final murderous act?

"Tell me what he told you, Ronnie," said Jake. "But please be quick kid, we don't have much time."

"He was an artist," Ronnie continued. "The sketch of the girl was incredible. I didn't say anything. I just stood there staring at it while he spoke. He told me he was a janitor at a local school, but that he also drew portraits at kids' parties and stuff like that. Then he told me to get started with his new piece. I tell you man I was shaking like a leaf, but I was so damn scared of what he would do to me if I fucked it up, that I just kept drawing and got into my zone. I wanted to stop drawing so bad. I needed a cigarette, a coffee, anything to calm me down. But I couldn't stop man, I just had to finish and get this guy out of my studio. What freaked me out most of all was that he didn't flinch once. For three hours I sat there, sweating, drawing like crazy but he never moved a muscle. It was as though he didn't feel pain, or worse still, he enjoyed it. While I drew, I counted the faces over and over again. Seven! Seven! Seven! I wanted the number to change, but it never did. He just sat there, not talking, just looking back at me in the mirror. Every time I looked up, he was starring right back at me, taunting me with his evil grin. Like he was loving the fact that I was so afraid."

Jake stood, processing the information Ronnie had given him. Then it hit him, and all at once he knew where the Hangman's final massacre would take place. It had to be at the school! The Hangman had hung every one of his seven victims so far. He would need somewhere large enough to stage a mass hanging.

Somewhere that would be empty at midnight. If he was indeed a school janitor as he'd told Ronnie, he would have keys to a school that would be empty except for him and eighteen terrified children. Nobody would be able to hear their screams.

"Ronnie, that's incredible," said Jake. "You've given me so much, but I need to know if he gave you the name of that school."

"Yeah he did," said Ronnie, who was exhausted from answering Jake's probing questions. "Wallace Elementary. He told me his name too."

Jake's eyes widened. He was about to learn the identity of the merciless killer whom he had been tracking for so long, and the thought of finally capturing him hit him like a shot of adrenaline.

"He said his name was Sebastian," said Ronnie. "Sebastian Bronson." As the name left his lips, his last ounce of strength abandoned him, and Ronnie buried his face in his hands and wept. Jake got down on his knees and put his arms around him. It was a comforting gesture to a young man who had been through hell.

As Jake stood up and helped Ronnie to his feet, the double doors flew open Captain Abrahams came storming into the club, followed closely by three more uniformed officers.

"Cannon!" said Abrahams in his customary commanding tone, "your little disappearing act has landed you at the top of my shit list, but you can redeem yourself here and now by telling me that you have something solid on the Hangman."

Jake had not anticipated the arrival of Abrahams, and the shock was written all over his face. "Sorry, Captain, I didn't expect to see you leave your desk and cross the bridge," said Jake.

"No, I bet you didn't, Cannon," said Abrahams. "But it's times like these that we need all of our experienced men active in the field. I was in a patrol car with officer Jacobs here, on our way through Brooklyn, following up on a loose lead. Then we took a call to say some madman had just let off shots at Unchained nightclub. Cannon, I knew it was you the minute the call came in. Missing for over two days and one hour before the deadline you've resurfaced with our first solid lead in three months. Please tell me I'm right!"

Abrahams rarely stepped out from behind his desk, but his sudden appearance was more than welcome. He did not always agree with Jake's maverick approach, but at times like these, he was willing to excuse Jake's rule bending if it meant getting the right result.

"Yes, Captain," said Jake, pointing at Ronnie. "I've questioned this young man, and he's confirmed that he's not only met the killer, but he has given us a name. Sebastian Bronson. I believe that he has tattoos of all seven of his victims on his body. My guess is that he lives here in Brooklyn, and we are almost certain that he's a janitor at the Wallace Elementary school."

Jake had barely finished his sentence when Abrahams barked at one of the uniformed officers, ordering him to radio into headquarters with the name Sebastian Bronson, and pull up any information including his last known residence.

"Cannon, you've done some real good work here," said Abrahams, "now as soon as Jacobs pulls an address on this guy, we need to mobilise a team…"

"Just one minute, Captain!" Jake interrupted. He respected the zeal with which Abrahams now sought to wrap up this case, and he also appreciated that every minute that passed was precious. However, Jake guessed that the Captain was about to send every man that he could muster to whatever residential address they had on file for Bronson, and Jake was almost certain that this would be a huge error of judgement.

"I know we don't have much time Captain," continued Jake, "but we need to consider the possibility that Bronson has taken the kids to the schoolhouse. Not only will he have keys, but it will be empty at this time of night. It would be the perfect location for what we think he has planned."

Abrahams paused momentarily. He gazed pensively into Jake's eyes, weighing up his options before giving his response. "Well you're right, Cannon, it is a possibility," he said, "but I'm convinced that the Hangman would not risk transporting these children to a second location. Some of these kids have been missing for a long time, and I just don't see how he could have been hiding them within the grounds of that school. No, I'm positive that we'll find those children tied up in the attic or the basement of some house, and we will know where that is the minute Jacobs gets off that line."

Jake began to panic. Abrahams had made a valid point, but Jake was certain that Bronson had been very calculated when he had visited the tattoo studio. He had given Ronnie just enough information to enable him to be found, including the fact that he was a janitor.

Jake could not yet say why Bronson had decided to do so, but he was convinced that he had intentionally left a trail of breadcrumbs that would lead them to him. Abrahams, in his enthusiasm, was about to call the wrong play.

"Captain I disagree!" said Jake defiantly. "If we had spoken two days ago you would have tried to talk me out of ditching my partner and going dark, but look where following my instinct has got me. I am prepared to take the fall if I'm wrong, but my gut tells me that Bronson is at that school, so at least let me take some men and head over there to check it out."

Much to Jake's relief, Abrahams agreed to deploy him, Jacobs and a special weapons and tactics team to follow up the lead at the schoolhouse. Abrahams knew that his best bet was to divide his resources and cover all bases. As the group hastily marched out of the club, it became apparent to Jake just what strength lay in their numbers. Outside, it looked like every cop in the city had been called to the incident at the nightclub. Abrahams really had believed that Jake was at the club, and he had gambled on him delivering credible information that would set New York's finest in motion with force and purpose.

There was chaos outside, as crowds of onlookers were still being herded back by officers. Several news crews had arrived and were assembling their camera equipment, and the street was illuminated by the flashing lights of dozens of squad cars.

"Somebody get a barrier up and get these Goddamn reporters behind it!" shouted Abrahams. "Cannon, take the first tactical team led by Norton here, and get on down to that school. You can brief them on the way. I want a team of officers to coordinate the clean up here. We have a confirmed an address for Bronson, so I will take the remaining officers and the second tactical team there now. Let's pray to God we find this son-of-a-bitch in time. Move, gentlemen!"

As cops disbursed in all directions, Jake and Officer Jacobs followed Norton into the back of a large black S.W.A.T vehicle. Jake took one more glance at his watch, which confirmed that they had exactly thirty-seven minutes to reach the schoolhouse and locate the children.

"Haul ass!" yelled Norton, slamming the rear door of the van before turning to Jake.

"So, you're the legendary Lone Wolf Jake Cannon?" said Norton. He was a thick-set middle-aged man with grey hair trimmed in a short military style, and a dense grey moustache which completely covered his upper lip. "I hear you've stirred up a hornet's nest," said Norton, smiling affectionately at Jake. "Well I'll say screw any man who puts bureaucracy before the pursuit of justice. If your gung-ho police work means we claim the scalp of this so-called Hangman tonight and save all of those kids, then I'll shake your hand and call it an act of true courage, Jake."

Norton was an experienced field officer who had steered his men safely through many life-threatening operations. But as he placed a hand on Jake's shoulder and leaned in close, Jake could feel Norton trembling.

"I've heard the rumours about what he did to the first seven children," said Norton anxiously. "Be honest with me, Jake, what are we up against here?"

Jake clutched Norton's arm and held it steady. "A man," replied Jake confidently. "He's just a man, Norton."

Now was not the time to unsettle the men with tales of a devil-worshipping Goliath with a high tolerance for pain. He needed Norton and his men alert and ready for whatever lay in wait at the schoolhouse. But as the van raced off towards its destination and the inconceivable horror of what they may discover drew closer, every man on board, including Jake, was rigid with terror.

Chapter 3
Dark Nemesis

A deathly silence fell over the tactical team in the final minutes of their approach to the schoolhouse. As the convoy of police vehicles pulled up at the gates and the officers disembarked two-by-two, Jake was the first to observe the school bus parked near the main entrance. It was a chilling discovery, as it suggested that the Hangman had found the means to transport his infant victims from wherever he had been keeping them, to the scene of his vicious act of barbarism.

"Fortune favours the wicked," muttered Jake under his breath. He resented the fact that the bright yellow bus travelling through Brooklyn at night, could easily have been pulled over by one of the scores of police that were patrolling the streets, yet it had slipped through the net.

"There it is, officers," said Jake, trying hard to conceal his disappointment and lift the fading spirit of the group. "That's the sign we've been waiting for. That bus would not be here if my hunch wasn't correct. It means that the missing kids should be inside that schoolhouse. As long as Bronson doesn't deviate from his midnight deadline, it also means that we're not too late to save them."

One by one, the sunken heads of the officers began to lift. Jake was right. An hour ago, the fate of those children seemed like a foregone conclusion. But now they were on the brink of a successful rescue operation that would unite the city in revelry.

"This Hangman is nothing but an obstacle," continued Jake. "A real man doesn't prey on innocent kids. A real man protects the vulnerable and the weak. So, it's time to show this creep what real men are made of."

Norton, who was clearly lifted by Jake's speech, sprang into action and began firing instructions at his men. He deployed six officers to create a perimeter of the building and two more to inspect the bus, while Jake, Jacobs and the remaining men readied their weapons and made their way towards the entrance.

The school was a large two-storey structure to the front elevation, and attached to the rear was a further single-storey gymnasium with a large roof terrace. In front of the main entrance was a turning circle, enabling parents to drive right up to the front gates to drop-off or collect their youngsters each day. This was where the bus had been parked, just in front of a short flight of concrete steps leading up to the main doors.

The third team darted up the flight of steps with Jake at the lead, and stopped outside the entrance doors. Spotting that one of the doors was already ajar, Jake pushed it wide open and they entered in silence.

It was pitch black inside, but as their eyes re-focussed, they began to make out the details of the inner hallway. There were at least twenty doors on either side of the hall, no doubt leading to the many classrooms that were located on the ground floor. Hanging from the ceiling were several light pendants that would have shed some much-needed light on their surroundings. However, Norton was the first to flick the switches and discover that the power to these lights had been disconnected.

"Light it up," whispered Norton. Within seconds the hall was filled with long beams of white light, shooting out from the torches that were attached to his teams' automatic rifles. But as the men began to edge forward again once more, their silence was broken by the crackle of the wall mounted speakers, followed by the opening key notes of an eerie yet familiar piano melody.

"What is that?" said one of the officers, arching his ear up towards the sound.

"I recognise this music, but I just can't remember what it's called," said Jacobs, looking around at the rest of the team for answers.

"It's Beethoven," said Jake, deeply concerned by this sudden and unexpected twist. "It's called the *Moonlight Sonata*. He's trying to fuck with us guys. Don't let him get in your heads."

With a series of hand gestures, Norton split the team in three. With the haunting *Sonata* pounding through the speakers which lined the school walls, two groups began searching each classroom, while Norton, Jake, Jacobs and two more officers took off down the hall.

As they drew closer to the double doors at the end of the hallway, it became apparent that the room beyond was lit with a faint, yellow light. Jake stopped dead in his tracks. His breathing became deep and heavy, and his heart began to pound as if it wanted to break free from his chest. Through the small square window panes in each door, Jake could see several ropes hanging vertically, taut yet swaying gently in the flickering yellow candle light.

He burst through the doors and into the gymnasium, followed closely by the rest of the team. "Lord have mercy!" cried Norton, as their eyes fell upon the harrowing sight of the missing children. They were knelt on the ground with their legs bound at their ankles, and their hands tied behind their backs. Their mouths were gagged tightly with black rags, and their tearful wide eyes were filled with dread. There were nooses fitted around the neck of each child, and the ropes had been hoisted over wooden beams which were just below the transparent glass ceiling. Dangling above them, on the opposite end of each rope were large sacks which appeared to be filled with rocks.

Jake guessed that the sacks weighed more than each child and would have sent them hurtling up towards the skies by their fragile necks, had it not been for a second line of rope which was tied around each noose at one end and fixed to the ground at the other.

Resting on the ground, just beneath each of the secondary ropes, was a candle. Had it taken just a few minutes longer to find them, then the candles would have burned through the secondary ropes and every child would have been lifted off the ground. With the nooses constricting around their necks, it would not have taken long for the life to be drained from their small bodies.

The officers did not wait for orders. The whole team ran out among the cowering children and began setting them all free. Jake darted over to a small girl and kicked over the candle that had singed the fibres of her secondary rope down to a few threads, before gently removing her noose. He untied her hands and feet and as he removed her gag, she leapt into his arms, gripping him tightly and crying uncontrollably. As officers removed the gags from the other children in the room, the sound of Beethoven was almost drowned out by a sickening chorus of cries and screams.

Jake held the little girl close. "You're okay. You're safe now," he whispered. He was determined not to crumble, but as he looked around the room, he saw that many of the other officers had let their emotions get the better of them. Some of them sat slumped on the ground, weeping along-side the children they had just freed, while others paced around the room, shaking their heads in disbelief.

Suddenly Jake's thoughts shifted back to the Hangman. The children had been saved, but in the intensity of the moment, it appeared that everyone had forgotten that Bronson was still on the loose.

The thought frustrated Jake, but he drew solace from the fact that his name and description were no longer a mystery. Now it would be easier to track him down. It was only a matter of time until he was captured, and Jake would not give up the chase until Bronson was either dead or behind bars.

As Jake stood surveying the aftermath of the Hangman's scuppered attempt at mass murder, a terrible thought crossed his mind. *What if Bronson had not fled? What if he was still hiding somewhere in the building, aroused by their distress like some psychotic voyeur?*

It was completely by chance that Jake gazed up towards the glass ceiling of the gymnasium and stared into the moonlight that was streaming down into the room. It was at that very moment that his eyes captured the shadow of a gargantuan figure standing on the roof. Bronson had been watching them the whole time!

Had he been in total control of his rage, Jake might have given the war cry and rallied the troops to follow him to the roof. But he was not in a rational frame of mind and he knew that despite the vile nature of the man's crimes, none of the other officers would have the stomach to exact brutal vengeance.

Jake decided in an instant that he was going to kill him. He did not care whether Bronson was an armed threat or a picture of tearful remorse, it was his intention to unload an entire clip into the man's head and body before anyone had the opportunity to sway him from his course of action.

Eager not to rouse suspicion among the other officers, Jake slipped back into the hall, before climbing two flights of stairs and pausing outside of the door labelled 'Roof Terrace'. Gripping his weapon with both hands, he kicked open the door and ran out onto the gravel. But as he raised his gun to eye level, ready to let rip at the man now standing in his line of fire, he froze.

Standing just ten feet away was the colossal figure of Sebastian Bronson. He was an ogre of a man, who stood well over six feet tall, and had an unnaturally muscular physique. He had a hunched back that looked like the deformity of a man whose body had been tested by the burden of years of heavy manual labour, but it was balanced by his huge barrel chest. His arms looked as though they had been pumped to bursting point, while his waist and legs were disproportionately slender in comparison. However, it was his head that was Bronson's most shocking feature. It was too big, even for his enormous frame. Limp strands of long, blonde hair draped down over a large protruding forehead, and his eyes were like two horrid black slits, set deep in the central pit of his face. Two pursed pink lips sat lopsided on his small mouth, partially concealing his hideously uneven teeth, which looked like a row of rotting walnuts imbedded in his swollen gums. Bronson was a grotesque caricature of a man.

As Jake stood taking in his features and proportions, blood boiled in his veins. He had never wanted to kill anyone so much in his life. The very thought seduced him. He visualised the bullets fleeting from his pistol and peppering Bronson's Herculean body, tearing through flesh, shattering bone and puncturing organs until he was nothing more than a bloody mound of meat, quivering on the ground. But as Jake's index finger caressed the trigger of his pistol, Bronson smiled back at him, and began to clap his hands in applause.

"Bravo, Cannon!" said Bronson. "I knew that you would not let me down. You are even more determined than I imagined, and every bit as clever as I had hoped. Of all the cops who might have found me, I just knew it would be you. Now the game can really begin, but unfortunately there can only be one winner."

Jake was a flaming inferno of anger. His gun was still fixed firmly on Bronson and his arms were shaking violently as he fought the urge to open fire. But the giant of a man showed no sign of fear. Bronson knew that his words would be enough to protect him from harm. Jake's mind was far too inquisitive. He would crave knowledge and understanding. He would want to discover his motive for murder, but most of all, Bronson assumed that Jake would have to know why he had deliberately left a trail that would finally lead the city's most diligent detective straight to him.

"What do you mean, Bronson?" said Jake through gritted teeth. "What game? Tell me what you mean or I swear to God, I will end your life right here, right now!"

Bronson chuckled to himself. It was the condescending laugh of a man who assumed he held a position of intellectual superiority.

"Do not swear to God, Cannon—pray to him," said Bronson. "Pray that the trials ahead do not break your spirit, and pray that your soul is not lost in the battle. The truth you are yet to discover will shatter your heart and corrupt your mind. I am not your nemesis, Cannon, but believe me when I tell you that there are others far more worthy of that title."

Jake struggled to make sense of Bronson's cryptic words. There were too many questions, too much he needed to know, and not enough time. His thoughts had gathered such depth, that he did not notice the sound of a police helicopter approaching until it was almost upon them. Seconds later, the door flew open and Norton, Abrahams and a stream of other officers came charging out onto the roof terrace.

"We did it, Cannon, we got him!" shouted Abrahams, over the loud hum of the helicopter that now hovered directly overhead. "Read that asshole his rights and cuff him, Norton."

Abrahams ran over to Jake, and gripped him by the arms, forcing him to lower his gun. "It's okay, Cannon, you did good," he said. "But don't do anything silly now, kid, let Norton and the boys bring him in."

The killer did not struggle as Norton placed the handcuffs on his wrists. As he began to read him his rights, Bronson raised his voice above Norton's, so that Jake could hear his parting message.

"One more thing, Cannon," shouted Bronson. "It doesn't matter what you do to me now, I have earned my seat at the table, but you should have let the children hang. You think you've saved them, but you've only condemned them to hellfire!"

Jake, incensed by Bronson's words, made a charge for him, but was restrained by Abrahams and Jacobs.

"I'll kill you!" yelled Jake bitterly. "I swear on the graves of every child you've murdered, I will be there to look you in the eye when you take your last breath, Bronson."

"It's over, Cannon, it's over!" shouted Abrahams. "Nineteen kids have been saved and we've caught the Hangman, so pay no mind to that sick bastard." Jake had taken leave of his senses, but was not so stunned as to miss the glaring error in Abraham's statement.

"Nineteen?" said Jake.

"Yeah, you heard right," continued Abrahams. "While we were over at Bronson's house, one of my men pulled a small child out of the closet. It was Mimi Chandler! She was not one of the eighteen children you saved here tonight."

Jake was confused. The villain had been captured, but there were still far too many questions that remained unanswered. What was so special about Mimi Chandler? He had chosen to add her face to the images of his former victims tattooed on his back, yet now it had become apparent that Bronson had sought to spare her life. Then there was the most chilling question of all, who was the 'nemesis' that he had alluded to? Jake prayed that Bronson was just bluffing to buy time, and there was no new enemy lurking in the shadows, poised and ready to spark the fear of the entire city once more.

"I understand, Captain," said Jake, apologising to Abrahams for his ill-tempered outburst. "I'm sorry for letting my emotions get the better of me, but it's been a tough week. Like you said, we've saved nineteen children tonight. But you can be sure that when the sun rises tomorrow, there will be more bodies found and more murders to solve. So, I will do whatever it takes to put things right back at the department, but I need to get back out on the streets."

Abrahams put an arm around Jake's shoulder, before ushering him towards the stairwell. "Cannon, I need you to do exactly what I tell you," said Abrahams, taking on the role of father, as he often did with the men and women of his department. "You have been to hell and back, so I want you to go home and get some rest. I need you to be back on point by tomorrow morning."

As the two men walked through the building and out into the carnival of light and sound that was now taking place at the front of the school, Abrahams' words floated off into the air, and Jake found himself slipping into a trance like state. The adrenaline that had fuelled him for more than two days and nights was beginning to wear off. His mind and body were fading, like a junkie coming down from an epic high.

"Jake, are you listening to me?" barked Abrahams. "Jacobs will drive you home, and I'll get a couple of officers to pick up your car from the club and run it over to your apartment. I can see you're in no shape to drive."

Abrahams confiscated Jake's car keys, before packing him into the back of a wagon and instructing Jacobs to ferry him home safely. As the car rolled off, Abrahams tapped on the window, prompting Jacobs to slam on the brakes.

"One more thing, Cannon," said Abrahams sternly. "I want to see you in my office at eleven-hundred hours tomorrow, so for God sakes, get some sleep. We have a lot to talk about, and you ain't gonna like what I have to tell you."

Jake had no idea what time it was when he finally turned the key and opened the door to his apartment. Following a long vacation, a home often greets its owner with the dusty fragrance of neglect, and may at first seem unfamiliar. But although he had only been away for three days, Jake's apartment already felt foreign to him. He fumbled in the dark for a light-switch, before staggering across the open plan living space, towards the full-length windows which he had left wide open.

Jake strolled out onto the balcony and stood taking in the panoramic view. It was late, but drivers tooted their horns impatiently, while people marched with purpose up and down the sidewalk. His eyes focussed on a young couple as they walked hand in hand up the street, blissfully unaware that he and other cops like him had once again put their lives on the line to ensure that their journey home would be a safe one. It was a thankless task thought Jake.

During his time on the force he had endured every derogatory curse imaginable from the very people he sought to protect. He would lay down his life for the men, women and children of the city, yet many of them would spit in his face. But he was not in it for the kudos. Medals and public recognition meant nothing to him. He was simply performing his duty, as a guardian of his beloved New York.

Jake had become a cop to make a difference. But now as he looked out at the beautifully lit streets, the weight of the world he knew began to crush him.

The pressure of the Hangman case had broken his spirit and shattered him into a million pieces. Tomorrow, he would have to find his nerve and put himself back together again.

As he stood in silent solitude, Jake finally surrendered to the emotion that he had fought so hard to suppress. His eyes filled with tears and his legs buckled beneath him. He collapsed, and with his head buried in his hands, he quietly wept himself to sleep on the cold floor of his apartment.

Chapter 4
Dr Monroe

When Jake woke up the next morning, he was grateful that nobody had been around the night before to see him fall apart.

"Tears are for women and cowards, Jake!" His father had spoken these words many times, and they had remained indelibly imprinted on his memory.

Jake was only human. But he hated the idea of anyone seeing him in a moment of weakness. He wanted to be perceived as an immovable force, a cop with a high threshold for mental anguish who was both incorruptible and totally fearless.

After only a couple of hours' sleep, Jake still felt jaded. However, when he switched on the shower and the powerful jet of cool water drummed against his face and body, he soon began to feel refreshed and revitalised.

Once he was showered and clean shaven, it was time to refuel. He had been running on fumes for days, so the thought of a large breakfast excited him. He brewed some fresh coffee to wash down a bowl of oatmeal with honey and blueberries. Normally this alone would have satisfied his appetite until lunchtime. However, on this occasion, he followed the cereal with a round of toasted rye bread and three scrambled eggs, lightly sprinkled with salt and crushed black pepper. He finished up with half a glass of pineapple juice and a glass of mineral water, to make sure that his body was well hydrated, before walking into his wardrobe to select a suitable outfit for the day.

Jake picked out a bespoke tailored blue tonic suit, and a matching tie. He always wore crisp white double cuffed shirts, instead of patterned or coloured shirts. He believed that a man's shirt should be like a painter's canvas, a clear white foundation on which the remainder of the outfit, like a work of art, could be created. He completed the look with a pair of brown Italian leather apron tie shoes. Jake dressed more like a hot shot Wall Street stock broker or a real estate agent than a cop. He took his appearance very seriously, and by his own admission, he was incredibly vain.

Looking sharp and feeling more like his old self, he took the elevator down to the car park, where his Silver 993 Classic was waiting for its master. He smiled to himself at the beautiful growl of the vintage Porsche as he fired up the engine, before driving out into the busy street and off towards Police Plaza to face the

Captain.

The homicide department was located on the third floor of the building, and as Jake walked through the doors and into the open plan office, the atmosphere was sombre. He knew that many of his colleagues, even those who would usually curse the ground he walked on, would have loved to shake his hand and congratulate him on a job well done. However, because none of them knew what fate awaited him, nobody was willing to risk a show of support. Everyone's eyes were fixed firmly on the ground as he navigated his way past their desks and into the Captain's office.

As Jake walked in and greeted the Captain, Abrahams did not respond. He did not even look up at him. Instead, he finished reading a document marked 'urgent' in silence for almost a minute, before removing his reading glasses and launching straight into conversation.

"Cannon, I think it's safe to say that you were the difference between triumph and disaster last night, but…" The "but" that came after the Captain's opening statement of commendation reverberated through Jake's mind, and hinted that a brutal condemnation was about to follow.

"But," said Abrahams once more, "you know as well as I do that Chief Castilian has a hard-on for you. I am looking at a list as long as my arm here, Cannon. I'm talking about allegations of assault, forced entry without a warrant and let's not mention your stunt with your firearm at the nightclub last night. You broke all radio contact with the team and left a lot of people in the dark. Your partner thought you might have been slain in the field. Fortunately, most of us know you well enough to suspect otherwise, and the trail of battered and bruised leads that you left in your wake hinted that you were still very much alive and working the case in Brooklyn. But this whole episode is just another example of your insubordinate disregard for peers and protocol, Cannon. "

Jake sat and listened attentively. Deep down, he knew that Abrahams sympathised with him. Back in the Captain's days as a homicide detective, he would have done exactly the same thing if it meant catching his man. But while the force might turn a blind eye to some mild rule bending, Jake had set fire to the rule book. A book which Chief Castilian followed to the letter. Castilian had worked his way up the ranks as an exemplary officer for over thirty-five years, without a single black mark against his name. He wanted robots not rebels, and Jake simply did not fit in with his vision of a force built on rigid procedures and accountability.

"Cannon, you might just be the best Goddamn cop to grace this department since..." Abrahams paused. He was weary that his reference to Jake's mentor and former partner may cause old wounds to re-surface. "Well let's just say you're the best in a very long time!" continued Abrahams. "Unfortunately, you are also my mid-flight restroom nightmare."

Jake's confused expression forced Abrahams to elaborate. "It's like this, Cannon," he said, taking a long gulp of cold coffee before explaining in detail. "Imagine you are waiting in line to use the restroom on a plane. You can bet your bottom dollar that there will be a hot chick waiting in line right behind you. The guy in front of you steps out of the cubicle, you step in, and what's the first thing you see?"

Jake shook his head apologetically. He simply could not see where the Captain was going with this analogy. "I'm sorry, sir, but you're gonna have to help me out with this one."

"Piss, Cannon!" bellowed Abrahams. "A steaming pool of stinking yellow piss right there on the floor. It's a bitch of a dilemma because if you leave it, the fine piece of ass waiting to use the restroom after you thinks that you're the filthy animal who is responsible for the mess. So, you swallow your pride and you do the unthinkable. You clean up another man's piss!"

Now it was beginning to make sense to Jake. Abrahams, in his typically crude manner, was alluding to the fact that Jake had once again created an awkward mess. But Jake was not only his number one detective, he was also the Captain's responsibility. So, Abrahams simply could not afford to throw him to the wolves. He had no choice but to clean up after him.

"Don't worry, Captain," said Jake, assuming that the crass metaphor was his cue to respond with a wise crack. "When I piss, I never miss!"

Abrahams' face did not soften into a smile. He was not amused, and he certainly was not a man to lock horns with. So, Jake chose to keep his humour to himself, and remained silent while the Captain continued his rant.

Fortunately for Jake, he had friends in high places. Captain Abrahams went on to explain that despite the chief's disdain, Mayor Golding saw things a little differently. By capturing the Hangman, Jake had become as valuable to him as the rich sponsors who were bank-rolling his re-election campaign. So, Golding was not about to see Jake Cannon, the city's hero, unceremoniously dismissed from the NYPD.

Jake smiled with satisfaction at the news that he would keep his badge, and there would be no formal disciplinary action taken against him. However, as he prepared to thank the Captain and leave his office, Abrahams revealed that there was still one final twist.

It had been almost two years since Jake's last psychological evaluation. It was normal practice for homicide detectives to endure the interrogation of the police psychologist at least once a year. Given the often-extreme nature of the scenes that they were exposed to, it was important to make sure that none of the detectives who worked homicide displayed any signs of post-traumatic stress.

Jake hated these evaluations, and for the past twenty-three months he had successfully evaded the condescending tone of Dr Angelica Weaver.

"Do yourself a favour, Cannon," said Abrahams. "Sit still and smile back at her, talk when she asks you to talk, and try not to lose your cool. Especially when she recommends that you take a little time away from this place."

"Time away?" said Jake quizzically. It was clear that the Captain knew something about the evaluation that he didn't, and this was his way of preparing him for the bad news.

"Listen, Cannon, it's for your own good," said Abrahams. "This was Castilian's last throw of the dice, so don't give him the satisfaction of seeing you signed off for any longer than necessary. A short-term leave of absence is non-negotiable. You'll be back on the streets in no time."

"This is bullshit, Captain!" said Jake angrily. "You know that Weaver is Castilian's lap dog. She's always had it in for me, and now she's got a green light to assassinate my character and label me unfit for active duty."

Abrahams waved a hand at Jake, urging him to remain calm. He reached into his top drawer and handed him a business card.

"For someone who pays so much attention to the fine details, how has it escaped your knowledge that Weaver has not been with us for over three weeks, Cannon?"

"Felicity Monroe?" said Jake, snatching the business card from Abrahams and reading the name out loud. "Who is she?"

The answer to Jake's question was sat two floors above them in a small, dark office, quietly reading through his file.

It had not been long since Felicity Monroe had transferred from a big city firm specialising in private client work, to her new position as 'police psychologist', but she was already immersed in the fabric of her new role. She knew that it would not be a job for the feint hearted. It would mean tougher hours, a difficult caseload and less money than she had been used to. But the position was one that she had always wanted, and now that she had it, she was determined to rise to the challenge.

She glanced at the clock on her desk. In a few minutes, Jake Cannon would be sat in front of her for the first time. She assumed from the whispers around the office that he had split the opinions of his colleagues. The men in his department either hated him or respected him, but with the exception of Abrahams, none of them liked him.

The women on the other hand told a different story. To them, Jake was the focus of many steamy fantasies. He was incredibly handsome, but his manner was often so cold and unapproachable that the man himself remained a mystery to his female admirers. Felicity found it all very intriguing, and the rumours made her both exited and anxious about meeting him in the flesh.

As for Chief Castilian, she had already met him twice during her time at Police Plaza. However, their discussions had revolved around Cannon on both occasions. That same morning, he had called her to his office to brief her on what he expected to gain from Jake's evaluation. He stressed that while Jake's intentions may have been positive, his behaviour in the latter stages of this investigation had been both disruptive and potentially harmful to the department. He had asked her to pardon the pun when he described Jake as a "loose cannon."

"Two heads are better than one," Castilian had said, yet Cannon had chosen to abandon his partner, and not for the first time. His persistent rule-breaking had put the investigation and the general public at risk.

The unexpected meeting with the Chief had left her with little time to prepare for the evaluation, so when she returned to her office, Felicity decided to quickly scan through the notes in Jake's file, highlighting any important details.

Detective Jake Cannon, thirty-four years old, six feet two inches in height, black hair, very dark brown eyes, and athletic physique. Distinguishing features include a small scar above his left eye, a two-inch scar running down the middle of his left hand and tattoos on his left arm…son of the former WBC and WBA middleweight boxing champion

Shayne Cannon and musician Elsie Cannon, both deceased. One known sibling, no known wife or children…Jake Cannon was invited to attend the Whitlock School of Artistic Excellence at the age of 17, after displaying exceptional musical talent. He is a skilled pianist and is also competent in both violin and cello. Above average I.Q, scored a high 98 average on the detective aptitude tests. Cannon worked vice prior to being fast tracked to his current role as a detective in the homicide department. However, Cannon has persistently refused a promotion. Extremely intuitive and resourceful, but does have a tendency to display manipulative and sometimes ruthless qualities. Unfortunately, he does not work well with others and finds it extremely difficult to build personal relationships. My analysis of Cannon leads me to believe that he is a highly competent officer. My main concern would be his volatile temperament. I believe that this stems from the traumatic loss of his father as a teenager, followed swiftly by the departure of his mother. He has battled for years to overcome these issues, but they resurfaced three years ago when he received a letter from his mother confirming that she was dying of cancer. Since her death, I have noticed a significant change in his attitude and I feel that these tragic losses have contributed towards his very insular and sometimes aggressive nature. Jake is often guilty of a linear approach towards his work which borders on obsessive compulsive behaviour. I also feel that his reluctance to work with others and develop relationships inside and outside of work is unhealthy. Cannon must learn to channel his aggression and turn this energy into a positive and productive edge to his police work. While he clearly excels in his field, I would strongly recommend regular evaluations to ensure that Cannon does not go off the rails. Dr. Angelica Weaver, 28 July 2016.

While Felicity sat studying her predecessor's notes, Jake left Abraham's office, and headed back down to the main desk to find out when Felicity had booked in and out of the building over the past two weeks, before heading up to her office.

Although she was new, Jake was no less weary of her than he had been of Weaver. Castilian could be very persuasive, and he would no doubt have poisoned her against him, highlighting his negative traits and branding him as the black sheep of the homicide team.

As he arrived outside the office, he noticed that the name 'Dr Angelica Weaver' had already been replaced with that of 'Dr Felicity Monroe' in bold gold italic print on the frosted glass pane of the office door. Jake pounded the glass with the force of a man who often forgets his own strength.

"One moment please," said Felicity. As she stood up to fix her clothing and take one last look in her pocket mirror, Jake burst into the office. Their eyes met, and the spark instant. Jake paused for a moment and looked her up and down, before glancing around the room, desperately searching for an ice breaker to ease the sudden tension.

"I love what you've done with the place," he said, walking over to take a seat opposite her. Felicity laughed nervously as she sat down, assuming that his sarcastic remark was a jibe at her dull office. The dark, musty hole would have served a better purpose as a filing room.

"I know," said Felicity. "I asked if I could add a little personality to the place and hang a few pictures up. But the powers that be told me that would just provide a welcome distraction to anyone I was evaluating. In other words, psychologists are far too boring to compete with inanimate paintings."

She laughed nervously at her own joke. Felicity was a confident and assertive professional, and despite the fact that she was only twenty-nine, she already had a wealth of knowledge and plenty of experience behind her. She had dealt with many challenging individuals in her time, and put them all in their place. However, there was something about Jake that set her nerves on edge. She could tell that he was sort of man who would turn heads whenever he walked into a room, or make a powerful statement with his piercing stare without uttering a single word. Just as she had suspected, he was also fiercely attractive. His perfectly symmetrical face and smouldering expression were what most women would consider conventionally handsome. But it was his deep dark eyes that mesmerised her. They sat below two black brows that curved in a fashion that made him look devilishly mischievous.

As Felicity blushed, Jake gave a wry smile. He knew what effect he had on the opposite sex, and he often used it to his advantage. Women had always thrown themselves at his father due to his good looks and effortless charisma. Although Jake had not inherited his father's natural charm, he certainly had the same powerful sexual magnetism.

"So, Mr Cannon, I am Felicity Monroe and I am going to carry out your evaluation this morning."

"Please, call me, Jake" he said softly. "May I call you Felicity?"

"Yes, of course, Jake," said Felicity. She was pleased that he was not yet displaying any of the un-cooperative or hostile traits that she had been warned about.

"Now, Jake," continued Felicity, "I would like to start by assuring you that while the reports on your behaviour in the final days of this investigation do concern me, I am not here to judge you. I am not Weaver, and I promise to remain totally unbiased towards you, provided that in return you are honest and open with me. We are both on the same team here and I can only help you if you let me."

Jake felt his brows becoming heavy as he struggled to avoid frowning. Felicity's standard textbook talk frustrated him. The initial "I'm here for you," speech had been swiftly followed by the standard trade proposition. She was asking for insight into his nature and character and in return she would listen attentively, offering the occasional gesture of empathy while gently probing for more depth. She would no doubt stroke his ego and before long, he would feel comfortable. She would appear to side with him, and as his guard dropped and the conversation became more relaxed and familiar, he would begin to slip up. His detailed recollection of events and the manner of his delivery would come across as cock-sure, leading her to confuse his confidence with arrogance. She would perceive his selfless risk taking as nothing more than foolish thrill seeking. He would leave her office confident that the assessment had been a success, only to learn days later that she had branded his behaviour as another classic case of 'Machiavellian egocentricity', and sign him off indefinitely, pending a full psychiatric report. She would become another in the long list of people he did not trust, and all because she had simply misunderstood him.

Jake had endured enough of Weaver's folk psychologist sermons in the past, and was determined not to see this evaluation go down the same path. He took a deep breath, and with his eyes fixed firmly on Felicity, he began to speak.

"Felicity, I could sit here and give you the blow by blow account of what happened," he said calmly. "But you already know how and when it all went down. What you really want to know is why. Am I right?"

"I have to agree that understanding the 'why' in all of this would definitely be very useful to me," said Felicity. "Please continue, Jake."

"Have you ever read *The Origin of Species* by Darwin?" asked Jake.

Felicity nodded, suggesting that it was a text that she was familiar with.

"Great," he continued. "Then you'll know that Darwin believed that we originally came from apes, and that over time we have evolved, reaching higher planes of intelligence, spirituality, creativity and awareness." Jake got up from his seat and began pacing around the room, gesticulating excitedly as he spoke.

"Do you know what I think, Felicity?" He did not give her a chance to respond. Instead, he launched into his theory while she scribbled away on her pad, desperately trying to keep up with him. "I believe that we reached our apex a long time ago. The evolution of mankind has ground to a halt and we are in a state of regression. Do you see where I'm going with this?"

"I'm afraid I don't," said Felicity, who was confused, yet genuinely intrigued. Jake was extremely articulate, and clearly well educated, so she could not help but question why such a smart man often acted so recklessly in the field.

"What I'm saying here, Felicity, is that we are becoming less creative, less considerate, less innovative and less spiritual," continued Jake. "We are reverting back to the aggressive, uncontrollable beasts we once were. In a world where we now place very little value on human life, a killer who murders on mass and without a motive can become a legend, and the star of the next Hollywood epic."

Felicity clung to every word. Jake fascinated her and she was finally beginning to understand what made him tick.

"I want to make sure I am getting this right," said Felicity. "What you are saying here, Jake, is that society is somehow reverting back to its primeval roots. So, your tough, uncompromising approach to police work is simply your way of reacting to this decline in moral and social values?"

"Exactly," said Jake. "There's blood in the streets and killers are becoming more daring and more extreme. It takes a very special breed of cop to walk among the damned and enforce justice. I am that cop, Felicity."

Felicity had stopped writing and was now listening attentively. She placed her pen down on the table and gestured to Jake to take a seat. He accepted the invitation, and sat back down.

"Sorry, I get real passionate about my work sometimes," he said apologetically.

"I can see that," she replied. Felicity was pleased that it had not taken long for him to open up, but since she had begun working on his case, there was one thing that had puzzled her. Jake was a well-educated man and a talented musician. He was also the son of a wealthy sporting legend. So why had he chosen to become a cop?

"I have to admit, Jake, your enthusiasm is infectious," said Felicity. "But I must also say that I have heard many rumours about your background and your accomplishments outside of the job, some of which are detailed here in your file. Please forgive me for asking, but you could have gone anywhere in the world and been anyone you wanted to be. So why did you choose to join the NYPD?"

Jake smiled. This was the one question Weaver had never asked him, but he had hoped Felicity would. He placed both hands on the table and began to explain.

"Before coming to your office, I passed by the main desk," said Jake. "In just a few moments, I was able to work out that you and me are not too different at all, Felicity."

"Really, how so?" said Felicity. She picked up her pen once again, ready to jot down whatever gems of wisdom were about to follow.

"Last week you were here before 0800 hours every day," said Jake. "On Monday, Tuesday and Friday you were here until almost midnight." He looked her up and down, observing every detail of her appearance before continuing. "You're not married are you, Felicity? I'm guessing you don't have a boyfriend either?"

"I'm sorry, Jake, but I don't see how that has anything to do with this evaluation." Jake's assumptions were correct, but his inappropriate line of questioning had caught her off guard and left her feeling embarrassed. Jake sensed that he had hit a nerve, and immediately sought to explain himself, and get the conversation back on track.

"I'm sorry, Felicity, I didn't mean to offend you," he said. "It's just that you couldn't possibly find the time for a relationship, because you're totally wrapped up in your work. You have the same 'first in, last out' mentality that I do."

Felicity's expression softened. She had misunderstood his remarks and she felt guilty for cutting him down so aggressively.

"Okay, Jake, I see what you mean. I guess that's a fair comment. I definitely don't have time for much else besides my work at the moment."

"I can tell," continued Jake. "I am also guessing that's why you tie your hair in that simple pony tail, and you choose not to wear make-up. Not that a face and complexion like yours needs make up, of course, but you just don't have the time for any of that crap."

"Wow, you are very good at this," said Felicity. She was amazed at how accurately he had summed her up with so few details to go by, and her blushes indicated to Jake that his compliment had been noted.

"It's what all great detectives do," said Jake. "We take the smallest details and create a bigger picture. When I say that we are alike, it's because we share the same passion for what we do. You could be earning more money at some private firm uptown, but working with the NYPD is your calling. It gives you a sense of purpose. Being a cop is my calling, Felicity."

Everything he had said about her was true. Felicity loved her new job because now she was part of a team that really made a difference. As she sat listening to Jake, she realised that the callous and inconsiderate egocentric that she had been warned about was not the man sitting opposite her. Jake was the very epitome of selflessness. He put his life on the line each day protecting people who he had never met, from villains too dangerous to comprehend. Last night he had saved the lives of eighteen young children, and while others would be rewarded with medals and praise for their small part in catching the Hangman, the hour's true hero was to be punished for making the tough decisions that nobody else could.

Was this why he preferred to work alone? Castilian chose to believe that he did not want to share the credit for cracking the case, but Felicity now saw things differently. When Jake made the decision to give his partner the slip and break radio contact, he could not have known how things would end. If it all went wrong, Jake alone would have taken the fall.

"I'm sorry but there was something I really wanted to ask you, Jake, but for a moment I was considering whether or not my assumptions were correct."

"I know," said Jake. Like a chess player, he always thought several steps ahead, and had already figured out what she was about to ask. "You want to know why I prefer to work solo. Am I right?"

"Yes!" replied Felicity, impressed by his incredibly perceptive nature.

"A very wise man once told me that love can make a sharp mind blunt," said Jake. "Every bad guy knows that the best way to hurt a cop is through the ones he loves, so I have chosen not to have any ties. I'm one of the few detectives who doesn't have a wife, girlfriend or a kid to think about. That means that I'm one of the only detectives who can be selfish when it comes to confronting danger head on, and let's face it, catching killers is a risky business. Anyone I team up with will always have too much to lose, so they just can't take the risks that I can."

It all made perfect sense to Felicity. Jake was not an ego driven, reckless adrenaline junkie. He was a man on a mission to make a difference. At that moment, words were not needed to convey the fact that they both understood each other, and as they sat locked in a pensive silence, a tingling sensation surged through their bodies. It was like the cool chill of satisfaction experienced when a truly deep connection is established between two people.

"Well I have to tell you, Jake, I am impressed with what you've told me here today," she said. "I can assure you that my report will definitely be a positive one."

Felicity concluded the meeting by confirming that she had no choice but to sign him off for at least four weeks, and suggested that he use the time constructively. She also promised that she would do everything in her power to see that he was back to work as soon as possible.

"Take some time out, Jake," said Felicity. "Get out of New York and re-charge your batteries. Switch off your phone and disconnect from this place for a while. When you return in four weeks, you will feel like a new person."

Jake did not argue. He knew that this was the best outcome he could have hoped for. He had no doubt that Felicity would sing his praises in her report. Perhaps this would place her outside of Castilian's circle of trust, but Jake could tell that she was far too professional to side with the chief just to gain favour.

As the meeting concluded and Jake left the office, he smiled to himself. It would be some time before he needed another evaluation, but somehow, he would find a way to meet with Felicity again. He had always promised himself that he would never get close to his female colleagues, but there was something about her that would make that a very difficult promise to keep.

Back in her office, Felicity took a moment to clear her head, before writing a brief yet conclusive post-evaluation report.

Jake Cannon clearly does not work well with others and has a less than admirable attitude towards authority, regulatory procedure and departmental protocol. However, both his ability and his dedication to the cause are unquestionable. He is without doubt a fine officer and despite his numerous indiscretions in recent days, I believe that his intentions were positive. After a stressful conclusion to the Hangman case, I would strongly recommend a temporary break from duty and some much-needed rest. However, in light of his recent achievements in the field, I would not see this take the form of a punitive suspension. It is my belief that Detective Cannon's mental stability is not an issue. Therefore, his absence should not be excessive in length, and he should be allowed to return to active duty as soon as possible.

Felicity slid the piece of paper to one side, reached into her handbag and pulled out a little red leather backed book. She was a daydreamer, and keeping a diary of her most intimate thoughts and ideas was her way of clearing her head of anything that was occupying her mind. She opened the diary on a crisp new page, and immediately began scribbling fresh notes.

7th June 2018
I believe that it's in a man's nature to despise anyone who has the ability to make him feel both intellectually and physically inferior. Perhaps this is why Jake has so few male friends in the department, because there are very few men

here who would consider themselves equal to his physical prowess and superior intellect.

I also understand why so many women find him irresistible. I have never met anyone who radiates sexuality in the way that he does. He is incredibly handsome and engaging. He draws me in with his alluring magnetism, and makes me want to know more. Who is the man behind the broad vocabulary and the wall of bravado? What is it that drives him? I want to dig deeper and find out everything about him.

There is something very special about Jake Cannon. His image will be tattooed on my mind until we meet again...and I hope that day will come soon!

Chapter 5
The Poisoned Apple

The mysterious Mr Burgundy had the whole city talking. Was the young American-born art collector really a self-made billionaire? What did he look like and was it true that the name 'Burgundy' was a pseudonym he had adopted as a young artist on the rise? Was his new Manhattan gallery really as grandiose as the media had suggested? The spotlight was about to fall on Damian Burgundy, and many people hoped to have their questions answered at the unveiling of 'Labirinto', his ostentatious new art gallery.

Although it was now home to around a billion dollars' worth of art from around the world, the gallery at 36 West 53rd Street, was a truly magnificent spectacle in its own right. The exterior of the imposing skyscraper stood out from the neighbouring buildings like a shimmering obelisk. Its entrance was a tall black gloss door with a discreet rectangular plaque fixed to it which read 'Galleria Labirinto', in raised brushed steel lettering.

The lower floors of the prestigious midtown Manhattan building were occupied by several well-known business enterprises, while the middle floors consisted of luxurious private apartments. However, the upper most floors of the building were dedicated to the gallery. The 33rd floor housed an Italian restaurant by the name of 'Santa Lucia'. It was named by Burgundy himself, after an area located near the Bay of Naples. With its narrow-cobbled back streets and raw rustic charm, Naples had always captured his imagination, and inspired him to bring the taste of Italy to his native New York.

The 34th floor housed the gallery itself, while the exclusive 'buyer's lounge' was located directly above, on the

35th floor. This stunning Champagne bar was a comfortable waiting lounge for anyone who may have acquired some fine art at auction, and would no doubt become a venue for many high-end private parties. Finally, on the 36th floor capturing breath-taking views of the Manhattan skyline, was Burgundy's own penthouse apartment.

The grand opening was an invite-only affair. Celebrities, sports stars, political figures, and local businessmen were all in attendance, along with numerous journalists and reporters from a host of news networks and lifestyle magazines. Cameras flashed frantically, while the crowds that had gathered outside jostled for the perfect position to catch a glimpse of the fortunate few, as they were ushered across a small stretch of red carpet and into the stunning reception area which Burgundy called his 'liquid lobby'.

As guests entered the lobby, they found themselves completely surrounded by water. The walls, ceiling and floors were one big ice-white fish tank, filled with thousands of black molly fish. With their short fins and bloated under bellies, the tiny fish patrolled the crystal-clear waters like an aquatic battalion, and the soothing sound of flowing water created a serene ambiance which massaged the mind in preparation for a feast of art.

From the reception desk in the liquid lobby, several smartly dressed hosts stood smiling enthusiastically while handing out flutes of champagne and leading groups of guests into large elevators, which were decorated with black and gold zodiac symbols.

The Labirinto gallery earned its name due to its Labyrinth style design. It comprised of a series of corridors, the walls of which were lined with framed works, canvases and shelves upon which various sculptures and carvings were exhibited. Spotlights cleverly positioned in tiny recesses in both the floors and ceilings provided the perfect lighting for the displays, while the marble effect of the polished plaster walls created a subtle background. Finally, the distressed oak floors gave texture to the clinical milk white decor.

When guests finally navigated their way to the centre of the gallery, they found themselves in a large open plan exhibition hall. The entire hall was covered with artwork, but positioned in the centre of the room, was a huge canvas painting which extended up from the floor and continued into the buyer's lounge above, through a circular hole in the gallery ceiling. The detailed depiction of heaven painted upon this giant canvas would not have looked so out of place, had it not been for the dark nature of the collection which surrounded it.

Burgundy had already established galleries in Rome, Paris and London. However, it was while he was in London overseeing an auction at his Mayfair gallery, that he came across the work of an up and coming British artist by the name of Blackwell.

Blackwell's controversial collection entitled 'the poisoned apple' was a graphic and disturbing vision of New York, a decaying city in moral turmoil. It captured Burgundy's imagination, and he proceeded to purchase every piece of Blackwell's work while the young artist was still virtually unheard of. Eighteen months later, and Blackwell was the name on everyone's lips, with Burgundy himself looking set to increase his wealth considerably when the collection went under the hammer.

By 2100 hours, the main hall was filled with guests and the "clink" of champagne flutes as people toasted the poisoned apple collection, suggesting that Blackwell's work was every bit as impressive as the critics had suspected.

However, many members of the press in attendance were not quite so content. To them, the artist and his work were an afterthought. They had come for their first real glimpse of the man behind the empire, Mr Burgundy. But after three hours of waiting impatiently for his grand entrance, it became apparent that he would not be making an appearance.

Amidst all of the revelry, nobody noticed a rather shabby looking man, making his way through the crowds, occasionally pausing to observe the artwork. He wore a long sleeve sweater which clung to his torso and hinted at a well sculptured physique. His tight-fitting pale wash denim jeans were torn at the knees, and his white high-top trainers were covered with paint. His horn-rimmed black spectacles and stubbly beard gave a masculine edge to features which may otherwise be considered too pretty for a man.

The young man stopped to pluck a flute of Veuve Clicquot from the tray of a passing waiter, before scanning the room in search of anyone who may prove to be entertaining company. His gaze fell upon two women who were stood admiring a canvas in the far-left hand corner of the hall. From their puzzled expressions, they appeared to be confused as to the message that Blackwell was trying to convey.

The young man tilted his head back and drained the contents of his flute in one gulp, before strolling over to position himself within earshot of the women.

The taller of the two women stood just over six feet in her heels. She had a slender frame, and her excellent posture was that of a dancer, or perhaps a gymnast. Her long strawberry blonde hair complemented her fresh youthful features. She looked more cute than beautiful, like a young woman who was yet to grow into her looks.

Her companion was an entirely different creature. She was a tempestuous looking brunette with a full yet firm body, and she had the air of a woman who was fully aware of her own sexual potency. She wore a tight black dress with a zipper which ran from her buxom cleavage down to the hem, just above her knees. From behind, the dress dipped so low that it showed off almost every inch of her rippling back. With her heels accentuating her toned thighs and well-defined calf muscles, she stood, hands on hips inspecting the painting, before finally speaking.

"I just don't get it, Jasmine," said the frustrated brunette. Jasmine, who had not taken her eyes off the picture for almost two minutes, suddenly turned to face her friend, with the triumphant grin of someone who had just solved a difficult puzzle. She was about to speak, when the young man stepped in between them, interrupting their conversation.

"This piece conveys a very disturbing message about society's obsession with murder," he said, stroking his chin pensively while looking at the painting. The two women froze, unsure whether to be amused or offended by his intrusion. "Murder is the new sex," he continued. "It's the new cocaine. The new rock and roll. Murder is man's new addiction."

"You must be Blackwell," said Jasmine, smiling as she offered her hand to shake his. However, the brunette was not quite so welcoming, and stood looking him up and down suspiciously.

"He can't be Blackwell," she said. "I'm no expert, but I know a British accent when I hear one, and this guy definitely ain't British." She was about to turn on her heels and insist that Jasmine follow her to the ladies room to avoid him. However, as her eyes met with his for the first time, she noticed his striking features. He was well built and extremely attractive, and she could not help but wonder whether the intrusion would prove to be more of an opportunity than a nuisance.

She smiled at the young man before poking him in the chest playfully. "So, who are you, and what makes you think we need your help figuring out what the artist is trying to say?"

"My name is Day, and you need my help because you're not here for the art," he replied jovially. "You are journalists and you came here in the hope of meeting Mr Burgundy. I am an artist and I am also his most trusted friend and advisor, so I would be happy to help you. I'll gladly give you enough facts to piece together a story and all I ask in return is that you let me to talk you through this incredible collection."

This was an offer they could not refuse from a handsome young man with an unusual name, who claimed to know Mr Burgundy. They had already accepted the fact that he was not going to make an appearance, and they had only decided to stay for the free champagne. Now their chance encounter with his close friend had opened up a new window of opportunity. Perhaps there was a story to be salvaged after all.

"I am Miss Lenora Desouza," said the bold brunette. "But you can just call me Lenora."

"I know your names because it was me who invited you here," he replied confidently. "You work for 'My Style' magazine. I know this because it's one of Burgundy's favourites."

The two women could only laugh at the sheer irony of the situation. They had been plotting deviously ever since they received their invitations for the opening night. They had spent countless hours and an extortionate sum of money on suggestively low-cut designer dresses, extravagant hair styling and make-up, all with the sole intention of catching Burgundy's eye. But all the while, they had been hand-picked by the man himself right from the outset.

Day placed his long powerful arms around the waste of each of the women, with the confidence of a man whose physical advances were rarely ever rejected, and proceeded to stroll with them around the gallery, giving his own interpretation of each of Blackwell's pieces.

The women soon warmed to Day's effortless charm. He spoke with the eloquence and knowledge of a well-educated man, but did not take himself too seriously. He infused his informative commentary with wit and the occasional touch of innuendo. He pandered to their egos, commenting on their stylish choice of outfits, which complemented their very different, yet both very appealing body types. He made sure that their flutes were never empty, and as the evening flowed effortlessly into night, he remained totally engaging.

It was not long before both Jasmine and Lenora were flirting shamelessly with the young artist. Neither their notebooks nor their Dictaphones had left their bags when Lenora acknowledged that they would soon be too tipsy to collect any information of value from Day, and decided it was time to throw in a few questions about Burgundy.

"So, tell me Day, is Burgundy really a billionaire?" said Lenora inquisitively.

"I could not possibly discuss the man's true wealth," said Day, searching for a response that would answer her question, without the vulgarity of actual facts and figures. "Let's just say that he is a man with the ability to spot an artist's fuse before it is lit, so he is always at an advantage when that artist's career finally takes off."

"I see," said Jasmine, who was pleased with herself for deciphering Day's cryptic response. "What you are saying is that Burgundy made his money by discovering artists just like Blackwell and investing in their work, before they became big?"

"That's how it was in the beginning," replied Day. "But when a man becomes so well respected in this industry that his very endorsement can ignite the popularity of the next big artist, then he no longer needs to anticipate when that fuse is about to be lit, because he has the power to light it himself!"

"That's true," said Lenora, recalling a conversation she had just days ago with her editor. "This is a big money industry. I've heard that some artists become so famous that their paintings sell at auction for over a hundred million dollars each. It's insane!"

"Insane, but true," replied Day. "When an artist's popularity reaches its peak, their work can become almost priceless, accessible only to a few incredibly wealthy people."

Their eyes glazed over in amazement as Day spoke. They had heard the rumours of Burgundy's rise to power, but now the full extent of his success had become clear to them. The collection they had been admiring may one day hold a value in excess of a billion dollars and it was all owned by Burgundy, who had already discovered several other critically acclaimed artists before Blackwell. What they did not know was that Burgundy himself was once an artist.

Damian Burgundy was not born rich, but by his teens he had considerable wealth at his disposal, as the result of his father's professional accomplishments. But it was his mother who had first noticed his aptitude for painting. Like most young mothers who are fortunate enough to discover a hidden gift in their beloved child, she sought to nurture and develop his ability during his formative years.

The family's influence was used to secure him a place at the city's foremost school of artistic excellence. However, despite his talent, he failed to capture the imagination of his tutors. According to them, his work lacked originality.

Therefore, at the age of 18, and with more than enough money to fund his quest for creative inspiration, he took off on a trans-Atlantic adventure. He toured many of the major cities across Europe, but he felt most at home when he finally reached Italy. Rome, with its aesthetic beauty became his second home, and of all the city's historic monuments, the paintings and sculptures that lined the vast halls of the Vatican changed his perception of art forever.

Renaissance artists like Michael Angelo, and Da Vinci had created a legacy in their lifetimes that would last for all eternity, and Damian was seduced by the idea of a name that would transcend time. It did not matter to him whether he was loved or loathed. He would be happy with either adoration or notoriety, just as long as he was remembered when centuries had passed and all but the most exceptional of his era had long been buried and forgotten.

When a mind becomes so bent on a purpose that it can visualise nothing else but the accomplishment of that goal, the universe has no choice but to respond, and so it was that fate brought Damian to the home of the one person who had both the power and the knowledge to grant him everything that his heart desired.

Damian had responded to an advertisement in a well-known publication for a young and ambitious trainee buyer to accompany a wealthy collector by the name of Lucian Ferone on a buyer's tour across Europe. Lucian was an experienced art collector, but he liked to work with a second pair of eyes. After several conversations, he seemed taken with the young and ambitious Damian, who flew out to meet him at one of his residences in London.

Lucian took him under his wing, teaching him everything he knew about art, and the fickle, ever shifting industry that had formed around it. In the two years that followed, they became very close, forming a relationship bond that would surpass that which Damian had held with his own father. But it was not until they returned to Italy that Damian learned the true extent of his mentor's wealth and power. Lucian's personal collection of art alone valued in excess of seven billion dollars, and his multi-million-dollar estate in Tuscany, was just one of many lavish residences he owned worldwide.

Damian was astonished by what Lucian taught him. He spoke of the world and all its wonders with the depth and detail of a man who had seen and done everything that life has to offer, and Damian was inspired and motivated by his success. How had the man acquired such riches? Could his accomplishments be replicated? Damian was determined to have his questions answered, and one night, Lucian told him everything, in great detail.

Lucian was a man with many extreme ideas about life and man's true potential. One night while the two men were sat talking in his private study, he saw the flames of ambition burning brightly in Damian's eyes, and finally decided to enlighten his young apprentice. By the following morning, Damian's induction into Lucian's world was complete, and by the time he left the Tuscan estate the following month and returned to Rome, he had been re-born. He was now man of fierce vision and intense purpose, who possessed the secret that a select few rich and powerful men hold close to their chest. It was a secret that Lucian had described as "the most beautiful and liberating truth about this life…and the next!"

Just as Lucian had advised, Damian abandoned his family name and replaced it with the name 'Burgundy', in the belief that if he was to become a powerful and noted figure in the art world, his name would have to be both distinctive and memorable.

Little more than a decade after he left American soil in pursuit of his true calling, Damian Burgundy had returned as the billionaire owner of a string of art galleries around the world, and a well-respected authority on the subject of art.

Jasmine and Lenora were both enthralled, as Day spoke of Burgundy's rise to power with captivating enthusiasm. Lenora had peppered him with questions, while Jasmine jotted down notes in short-hand, smiling contently to herself as he fed them gems of information about the enigmatic mogul. He skimmed over the details of the time spent with Lucian, but the two young journalists were still left thoroughly satisfied with what he had told to them.

"It's time to treat you two gorgeous ladies to a feast of the senses," said Day, pointing in the direction of an elevator at the far end of the room. Two heavily built men stood either side, occasionally letting those who produced a small golden ticket pass through its doors.

"Are we going up to the buyer's lounge," asked Jasmine excitedly. This was an unexpected treat and although both women had been dying to ask whether a visit to the upper floor was on the cards, neither had wanted to spoil such a good evening by risking rejection.

"I hope we are," said Lenora. She was clearly attracted to Day, and was now trying to score points by feigning interest in the large canvas that disappeared through the ceiling above them. "Because I'd really love to see the rest of that painting."

Day stood between the two women and placed an arm around their waists once again, pulling them both in close so they could feel his firm body against theirs. His tactile nature was an alluring quality, and they both reciprocated positively. While Jasmine reached across his body and stroked his chest with the comfortable familiarity of a girlfriend or lover, Lenora leaned in close as though she was about to kiss him, manoeuvring sideways at the last minute to take a sniff of his neck.

"You smell delicious," said Lenora, deliberately stroking her lips across his check as she pulled away. "What is it?"

"If I told you...I would have to kill you," said Day smirking deviously.

They stepped into the elevator laughing, and Day pressed the little gold button for the 35th floor. As the doors closed, he turned to face Jasmine full on. "Now it's my turn!" he said, placing one hand firmly on her shoulder before leaning in so close that she could feel his breath on the side of her neck.

Her whole body froze and she blushed uncontrollably as he released her from his grip and stood looking into her eyes.

"A very full-bodied floral fragrance," said Day, tapping his lip with his forefinger and gazing up towards the ceiling in deep thought. "Viktor and Rolf, am I right?"

Before Jasmine could respond Lenora interrupted. "Do me now," she said, grabbing him by the arm and forcing him to turn around so that he was now facing her. Day gently caressed her face with his left hand. He bent his head down towards hers before slowly and suggestively running his nose from the ridge of her collar bone, all the way up her neck to her right ear.

"An elegant yet powerful scent that compliments your bold personality," he said, pausing for a moment as though he was trawling through his memory banks to recall the name. "Definitely a Dior fragrance."

As both women stood open mouthed, unable to comprehend how he could possibly have guessed both perfumes correctly, the elevator doors pinged open, and their gaze fell upon the magnificent spectacle of the buyer's lounge.

In a city which boasts a broad selection of swanky drinking establishments, this was without question the most sophisticated and ambient lounge that they had ever visited. They walked out of the elevator, and were immediately hit by a wave of refreshing cool air, that instantly re-invigorated them. Their slow blinking, low browed semi-intoxicated eyes were now wide and alert once more.

"It feels like a sudden rush of adrenaline doesn't it?" said Day excitedly. "It's a trick that Burgundy learned from the casinos in Las Vegas. They filter pure oxygen through the air conditioning to keep gamblers at the tables for longer. People go all night out there and wonder why they never feel tired or hung over."

"It's amazing," said Lenora as she stared around the room. "This has to be the sexiest bar I've ever been in."

The room had been meticulously designed to the very last detail to relax the mind and arouse the senses. Ambient lighting was provided by thousands of tiny white bulbs embedded in the black velvet-lined walls. They simultaneously dimmed to near darkness every thirty seconds, before slowly illuminating once again, like a perfectly starlit night sky.

The only window to the outside world was through the glass wall behind the bar, which gave stunning views of Manhattan by night. The bar itself was a thick granite surface, beneath which was a row of fridges, stocked with nothing but bottles of premium champagne. Across the back wall were shelves lined with various bottles of quality vodka, whisky, cognac and gin.

The floor of the lounge was a polished burnt oak which contrasted perfectly with the rich red dyed alligator-skin seating booths and the exquisite ebony tables. On a raised platform in the corner of the room, was a grand piano. Although it stood vacant, both Jasmine and Lenora imagined that it would add the perfect tone to an evening when an accomplished player was sat stroking its keys. However tonight, the beautifully soft and balanced vocals of Bebel Gilberto oozed from the sound system, setting the perfect mood.

In the centre of the room, the canvas that had started in the gallery continued up through the floor of the buyer's lounge, and disappeared once again through another hole in the ceiling above. Yet this section of the painting was a vivid depiction of bodies burning in hellfire, and while the two women stood observing the piece, Day swiftly ushered them towards a booth marked reserved. As the group sat down, a tall sharp-suited man approached the table.

"Ladies, allow me to introduce my good friend Quarter," said Day. Quarter must have stood no less than six feet and five inches tall. Through his perfectly cut suit, you could see the curves of a well-formed chest and bulging arms. He was in tremendous physical condition, but his features were very unusual. His skin was as smooth as a child's and had the rich coffee tone of someone who hailed from the island of Mauritius or the Seychelles. However, while his full lips and nose were unmistakably Caribbean, his hair was long, dark and perfectly straight. From his appearance, neither Jasmine nor Lenora could place his origin.

"Quarter?" said Lenora inquisitively. "That's an unusual name. What does it mean?"

Quarter laughed heartily and looked at Day, rolling his eyes as though it was a question he was tired of answering. "You had better ask Day, it was him who gave me that name."

His accent was strange, and once again left both women guessing. Day waved over a waiter and requested a bottle of Armand de Brignac, and some table candles, before addressing the two women.

"This handsome gentleman is called Tappi, but I call him Quarter on account of the fact that his mother is half Antiguan and half Filipino, and his father is a mix of Dutch and Cherokee Indian. Besides English he speaks Spanish, French, Italian and Cantonese and may just be the most interesting and well-travelled man I have ever met."

"I also speak Japanese," said Quarter, smiling in appreciation of Day's words of praise.

"How could I forget," said Day. "Quarter here is a man of unparalleled linguistic ability. A truly cunning linguist!"

They all laughed at Day's cheeky play on words, and as the waiter arrived with the distinctive Gold bottle and three flutes, Quarter wished them a good evening, before leaving them to enjoy their drinks.

"He sounds like an incredible guy," said Jasmine, searching in the dim light for her notepad to jot down more details.

"I imagine Quarter is pretty valuable to a man like Damian Burgundy," said Lenora. "Burgundy's business interests would no doubt take him to every corner of the globe, and a man who speaks several languages with such a diverse cultural heritage would surely be a major asset to him."

"You have no idea," replied Day. "Quarter is not only a fantastic interpreter, but he is also Damian's personal fitness trainer, chauffeur, and he's an accomplished chef. Damian never goes anywhere without him."

"And what about his woman?" said Lenora. "Surely a man like Damian Burgundy must have an incredible woman on his arm."

This was the one subject that Day had avoided, and he had done so deliberately.

"I'm afraid Burgundy's quest for love has been a tragic tale," said Day dismissively. "He's still waiting to find his Cinderella."

"I don't understand," said Lenora. "How could a man with so much to offer not find a woman to love him?"

"They call it the rich man's curse," said Day. The pain of Burgundy's ironic misfortune was now written across his face, as though he too shared the same burden. "You see, when you have everything, you crave a woman who will love you for the man you are inside, and not the power and wealth you possess. But now that he is a Billionaire, women only ever see him for what he has, and not who he is."

While Day spoke, Lenora had begun to fantasise about being the woman who might finally tame the billionaire bachelor, but it suddenly struck her that she had no idea what he looked like.

"I don't mean to sound shallow," said Lenora, "but I have to ask, is he good looking?" She turned to face Day and looked him up and down just as she had done when they first met in the gallery. "I mean if he looks like you, then he definitely ticks all the boxes!"

Day removed his glasses and placed them on the table. He ran his fingers through his hair and looked at Lenora with a cold intensity that made her feel uneasy. Realising that she was uncomfortable, he immediately softened.

"It's been said that he's not only incredibly handsome, but also very charismatic," he replied. "The kind of man who creates his own red carpet every time he walks into a room. So much so that he prefers to dress down and slide into the background to preserve his anonymity. He chooses to remain faceless because he believes that the strength of his brand is in the name and not the image, and until now, his face has successfully evaded the grasp of the media. But I am pretty certain Lenora that you would find him irresistible."

Both women sat in shocked silence. It was as if a glaringly obvious truth had just been revealed. While Jasmine slowly placed her glass on the table and began to shake her head in disbelief, Lenora, who was now trembling with a mixture of excitement and trepidation turned to Day and asked the question he had been waiting for all evening.

"Day isn't your real name is it?" she said in a low whisper. Day paused and looked down at the rim of his flute, before raising it to his lips and draining the contents. Without looking up at either woman, he reached for the gold bottle once more, tilting his glass so that it was almost horizontal while he refilled it. He raised his glass as though he was about to make a toast, and stared into Lenora's eyes.

"Day is short for Damian." he replied. "I am Damian Burgundy, and it has been my pleasure entertaining you both this evening."

Lenora and Jasmine sat staring back at him in stunned amazement. They were left speechless by the sudden realisation that the person they had taken for a friend and aid to one of the wealthiest entrepreneurs in America, was in fact the man himself.

"I apologise for the deception," said Damian, as he proceeded to fill their flutes with more Champagne. "But it was important that I got to know the real you, before revealing the real me."

Both women appreciated the sincerity of his apology. They could only imagine what it must be like to know that your world was about to be turned upside down. Anonymity had been his shield for so long, but on home soil, the press would not rest until they had made a circus of his life. Would the brand he had worked so hard to build survive the storm? Or would his name and his beloved art be thrust into the mainstream, and diluted by tabloid headlines, obsessed paparazzi and kiss and tell smear campaigns. In the so-called 'land of the free', a man like Damian Burgundy would soon become a slave to his own success. Perhaps tonight's little charade was his final farewell to life outside the spotlight.

"We will accept your apology on one condition," said Lenora, smiling playfully and winking at Jasmine. "You have to take us up to your penthouse apartment. We want to see how a billionaire lives."

Damian rose from the booth and proceeded to help his two guests to their feet.

"Ladies, your night is about to get a lot more interesting. Please follow me back to the elevator."

Chapter 6
Jabula

As the heavy doors of the elevator opened onto the 36th floor, Damian stepped into the darkness of his private apartment, followed by his two inebriated guests. Both Lenora and Jasmine became uneasy as the doors closed behind them, plunging the room into a pitch-black abyss.

"I'm afraid of the dark Damian," said Jasmine, clutching his arm and shaking nervously. "Please turn the lights on!"

"Is it really the darkness you're afraid of Jasmine?" said Damian. "Or is it the fear of what monsters might be revealed when the lights go on?"

Damian was content to let his guests remain on the edge of terror for longer than they would have wished. The charming and playful gentleman, who had been such an excellent host for most of the evening, was now displaying an evil streak. Like a child plucking the legs from a helpless spider, he was toying with their emotions and feeding off their anxiety like a fiend with a sick fetish. In just a few moments, either Lenora or Jasmine would give in to their fear, and a shrill shriek of despair would echo around the room.

Jasmine was about to break the tense silence, when Damian's deep voice cut through the darkness.

"Lennox…lights please!" Suddenly, one row of lights beamed down from above their heads, followed by row after row, all flickering to life one after the other like a wave of illumination racing across the ceiling before finally crashing against the shore of two large circular windows at the far end of the room.

The apartment was a spectacle of style and individuality unlike anything that either woman had ever seen before. Damian had fused ultra-modern with vintage decorative features in a manner that might have seemed unusual in the mind's eye, yet came together perfectly in reality.

Covering the entire floor were large high gloss black tiles, with thousands of tiny speckles of light glistening beneath the surface. Jasmine stared down in amazement. Were they real diamonds set within the tiles?

"Yes, they are real diamonds," said Damian, proudly preempting the question that was about to leave her lips. "I had the tiles custom made. The diamonds were a lavish afterthought, but I'm sure that you'll agree, the result is pretty stunning."

The huge open-plan room was bursting with detail. There was a large medieval-style distressed oak dining table in the centre, lined with eight high-backed chairs. Each chair was covered with the hide of some exotic beast. Zebra, Tiger, Leopard, Alligator, a jet-black fur which might have been a panther or bear. Just beyond the dining table was a rich brown leather sofa unlike any they had ever seen. It was a perfect unbroken circle, and anyone wishing to recline on it would have had to hurdle onto their seat. On the ceiling above the sofa was a circular track, on which a large slim-line television screen was mounted. Damian explained that the screen was wired to sensors in the 'doughnut' sofa as he called it. As soon as guests took a seat, the screen would automatically navigate its way around the track so as to provide optimal visibility.

In the far-right hand corner of the room, on a raised area just in front of one of the circular windows, was a red felted pool table, and to the far left there was a chaise longue. Was this where Damian sat on a hot summer afternoon, gazing out of the window at the skyline in search of creative inspiration? Jasmine pondered the chair's use as her eyes patrolled the distinctively Parisian detail of its baby blue crest patterned fabric, and gold painted wooden framework.

There was only one doorway in the centre of the room, no doubt leading to a bedroom and bathroom. Perhaps there were more reception rooms beyond the wood-grain door thought Jasmine as she strolled across the room.

As Jasmine's imagination ran away with her, Lenora turned back towards the main entrance. In their haste to explore the apartment, they had both walked straight past the final piece of the grand canvas that had first caught their eye down in the main gallery.

It rose through a perfectly cut hole in the floor and extended the entire height of the room. The artist's strokes finally came to an end where the canvas met the ceiling between two rows of lights, which shone down on the piece, highlighting its vivid colours and disturbingly graphic detail.

The third instalment of Blackwell's dramatic painting was a scene of decadent debauchery. In the centre of the piece was a banquet table upon which men and women were engaging in sexual acts. A woman poured wine over her naked body while a man, clutching his genitalia, buried his head in her groin. Gold coins spilled from several large sacks that were dotted around the room, and the table was piled high with food, some of which had fallen onto the floor, and was being trampled under-foot, or lapped up by yapping mongrels with blood red eyes. A deformed man with a hunched back stood in the corner of the painting playing a violin, while an overweight man in ladies lingerie stood laughing as he observed the chaos that was unfolding in front of him. He held a large bone in one hand and the blood of whatever creature he was devouring ran down the sides of his mouth as he chomped on its flesh. From behind a large red curtain draped in the background, several small faces could be seen peering in, their young eyes wide with horror as they observed a scene that was far too explicit for the innocence of youth.

Sat in the middle of the table was an extremely handsome man in a well-tailored red suit. He was pouring tea from an ornate silver pot into a china cup. Lenora felt a chill sweep over her body as she stared into the eyes of the man in the centre of the painting. It was as though he was smirking at her. All at once, she knew exactly who the man in the painting was supposed to be.

"Is that the devil?" said Lenora, looking to Damian for clarification. "I'm confused. So far, we've seen heaven and hell. So, what does this scary painting represent?"

As Jasmine strolled over to see what had captured Lenora's attention, she winced as she caught sight of the painting's hideous detail. However, Damian simply stood admiring the piece with a look of deep satisfaction.

"This piece is called 'the devil's tea party'," he replied. "You see, there is a particular group of people who believe that hell is in fact a place where the souls of those neither righteous enough to pass through heaven's gates, nor wicked enough for a seat at the devil's table are sent to be punished for their failure to commit to either extreme. The exceptionally evil are not sent to hell. They are sent to Jabula, the third realm of the afterlife. Upon their arrival, Satan, Lucifer or whatever you choose to call him, holds a grand banquet to welcome his new guests."

Sensing that his guests were becoming unsettled, Damian chose to resurrect the light-hearted mood that had preceded their discussion on the painting.

"Lennox, dim the lights please," he said, addressing his invisible servant who responded instantly by reducing the brilliant bright lighting to a more relaxed and ambient shade.

"Lennox, it's a little chilly up here," continued Damian. As the words left his mouth, the wooden splints in an open fire that was set in an exposed brick wall on the right-hand side of the room suddenly came to life, and a blanket of heat floated over to where the three of them were standing.

On either side of the fireplace, set in the immaculately plastered walls were four giant circular wood-grain doors, around nine feet in diameter with nothing but a small brass plaque on each. The plaque on the two right hand doors read 'tattoo parlour' and 'mannequin' while the two left hand doors read 'bar', and 'toys'.

"Lennox, let the libations loose!" as Damian shouted the command, the circular door marked 'bar' revolved to reveal a perfectly well stocked cocktail bar. The small marble counter was equipped with two cocktail shakers and several glasses, while the refrigerator below was filled with mixers, ice and three bottles of Bollinger champagne. The finest bourbon, vodka, gin, dark rum and scotch were sat in optics, ready to be relieved of their precious liquor.

Lenora and Jasmine watched as the room came to life under the instruction of their masterful host. They had heard about these amazing gadgets but this was the first time they had seen such technology in action, and it was a truly thrilling experience.

"Lennox?" said Jasmine, eager to know why he had chosen such an unusual name for his invisible electronic servant.

"Lennox was the name of my first dog," replied Damien. "He was a great companion and very loyal. When I was a boy, he would wait on me hand and foot, fetching anything I asked for. So what name could possibly be more fitting for my remote-control butler?"

Damian walked over to the bar and began filling three glasses with ice. He was a huge fan of cocktails. Full of colour, variety and rich flavours, he had always found that they were the best way to set the tempo and loosen inhibitions when entertaining women.

During the course of the evening his agenda had changed. He had hand-picked My Style magazine on account of their reputation for unbiased and honest journalism. Jasmine's work in particular had captured his attention, and his interest in her had been purely professional. However, it was not Lenora's work that had caught his eye. While browsing through the profiles of several journalists on a popular social network, he had come across images of Lenora that had appealed to his carnal senses.

She had a classic shape that most men craved, but only a real man could master. Her body brimmed at her full yet firm bust then flowed inwards down towards her tight, tapered torso before swelling once more at the borders of her thighs. From behind, her exaggerated posterior screamed sexual satisfaction to Damian. He was convinced that other women would feel threatened by her. They would curse her, while venomously berating their husbands and boyfriends for gazing longingly in her direction. She was accustomed to male attention, but only the most dominant alpha males would ever be given the opportunity to try and tame her in the bedroom. Damian was attracted to women like Lenora, as they presented him with a true challenge.

However, as the night had progressed, his fantasy of a tough pursuit had swiftly faded. With both her words and gestures, Lenora had made it clear that she desired him. He had hoped for a challenge, but the ease with which he had penetrated the layers of her defence disappointed him. Therefore, he had decided that Lenora alone would no longer be enough to satisfy his appetite. He would only be content if Jasmine also served herself up for him to devour. He wanted to sleep with both women, and now he was opening up his armoury of seductive tricks.

"Tell me, Jasmine," he said softly. "What's your favourite flavour?"

Guessing that he was alluding to cocktails, she decided to play it safe and give him little margin for error. "I like pineapple," she replied, "and dark rum too. But I can't stand Gin."

Damian grinned playfully, before turning back to the bar. He began tipping various bottles and cartons into a mixer, as the women watched with curious excitement. Jasmine, was eager to see what he had selected for her, and walked up behind him so that she was close enough to peer over his shoulder.

"A quarter ounce of coconut rum," explained Damian, "mixed with half an ounce of peach schnapps, half an ounce of grenadine syrup and pineapple juice with orange juice combined, for the lady with the sweet tooth."

"Wow, you know that by heart?" enquired Jasmine.

"Of course," boasted Damian. "A truly great host should always have dozens of cocktails in his armoury. This one is called 'heat of the moment'," said Damian suggestively, "because you never know where nights like tonight might take you."

Jasmine blushed at Damian's description. Was he hinting that he found her attractive? Lenora clearly had him in her crosshairs, and Jasmine began to wonder whether her friend would become overly competitive, if he persisted with his flirtation.

Suddenly, Jasmine's champagne induced confidence began to fade. She felt hot and flustered and needed a moment to gather her senses before her blushes betrayed her.

"I can't wait to taste it," she said, flicking her hair to one side. "But I think I need to visit the little girl's room to freshen up first."

"Second door on your right," said Damian, pointing at the door on the opposite side of the room. Jasmine departed without hesitation, bounding through the large door and into a wide hallway. She paused momentarily, contemplating a detour to see what secrets lay hidden behind the remaining doors. However, guessing that the apartment would probably be full of clever little surveillance devices, she thought better of it and headed straight to the restroom.

As she opened the door, a light automatically beamed to life, revealing a restroom unlike any she had ever seen. The floors, walls and ceiling were decorated with currencies from around the world, all encased behind a thick glass veneer. On the floor were pennies, nickels, dimes and other small change, then bank notes in low denominations covered the lower walls. By the time her eyes reached head level, she was looking at notes of considerable value, and when she looked up at the ceiling above, she could see rows and rows of hundred-dollar bills, enough to cover the rent on her own apartment for several years.

The toilet bowl and wash basin were both cast from precious metal, silver she guessed. The pan lid was pure gold, rich in colour and lined with rubies, emeralds, diamonds and sapphires. Jasmine could barely bring herself to be seated, but she had no choice but to slip down her underwear and set herself down on the cold ornate throne. As she did so, she noticed a small sign on the back of the door which read "I have not flushed in weeks!"

When a confused Jasmine returned to the lounge minutes later, Damian had opened up one of the large round windows, and he and Lenora had already retreated to the balcony. Jasmine stepped out onto the stunning multi-coloured mosaic tiled image of a ram's skull, which lined the balcony floor.

"Here, Jasmine, you simply gotta try this," said Lenora, staggering towards her, and thrusting the glass into her hand. "I've tasted yours already and it's out of this world."

Jasmine took a long deep sip of her cocktail. It was both sweet and refreshing and she had to admit, Damian had made a great choice.

"Mine is called a devil's tea party," said Lenora swaying unsteadily on her feet, "just like that naughty painting in there."

"Nearly," said Damian playfully. "It's actually called a 'devil's delight'. It's a mix of brandy, vodka, Grand Marnier, orange liqueur, lemonade and a squeeze of fresh lime."

Buoyed once again by the free-flowing alcohol, Jasmine began to feel more relaxed. "Tell me, Damian," she said, smiling so as not to cause offence, "but I have to ask what the hell you were thinking when you designed that lavatory?"

Damian let out a huge roar of laughter. He had been waiting for someone to finally see his masterpiece, and now he was only too happy to explain in detail.

"I owe my inspiration to Quarter," he replied. "When he saw my plans for this apartment he told me that I had so much money it was coming out of my ass! He warned me never to flush my toilet because I would lose a small fortune. That restroom showcases both my creativity and my childish sense of humour!"

Damian instructed Lennox to play some mellow music through the outdoor speakers, and heat the terrace to avoid a chill from the late evening breeze.

"I must say, Damian, you had me fooled," said Jasmine. "I mean with your unassuming appearance, I never saw you coming."

"Oh, I guessed he had money," said Lenora, contradicting her younger and less observant friend. "Remember we work for one of the city's leading style and fashion publications, so I know an Audemars Piguet when I see one."

She pointed at the watch on his wrist. It was a prestige piece of considerable value, and the mark of a well-oiled individual who had the budget for the finer things in life.

"Well spotted," replied Damian. "I have to confess to my love affair with the complex movements of hand-crafted Swiss timepieces. Just last month I flew to Geneva to collect a Patek Philippe Tourbillon, which set me back over a million dollars."

Both women looked stunned. They simply could not fathom how anyone could spend so much money on a simple accessory. However, when he revealed the potential long-term value of this fine wrist watch, it soon became clear to Jasmine and Lenora that he was a man who selected his acquisitions wisely. From timepieces, to classic cars, art, antiquities and real estate, Damian Burgundy was a man whose wealth was increasing with every day that passed.

"Life is a lottery," said Damian. His matter of fact tone did not match his bizarre behaviour. He casually began removing his sweater as he continued his speech. "You have to play the game to stand any chance of winning, but to win, you need to believe the odds are stacked in your favour. It's called the 'law of attraction'. When you are passionate enough about your goals and you believe with all your heart that you can achieve them, the Universe has a strange way of making your dreams come true."

His words floated through the air, escaping the consciousness of both Jasmine and Lenora as they stood, puzzled yet captivated by the sight of their host undressing in front of them. Neither woman dared to speak. Their desire to see his naked flesh outweighed their need for him to explain his actions, and the sight of his rippling, toned, tattoo covered torso had caused a throbbing sexual desire to erupt within them.

It was as though his body was calved from stone. He glowed like some mythical Greek God. His arms, chest, and back were covered with the tattooed images of angels and cherubs dancing in flight among the clouds. There were phrases in calligraphic script, detailed portraits and the now familiar ram's head on his right shoulder. Across the top of his back, the phrase 'light from darkness' was written in bold, black writing, and just beneath it, a small inconspicuous inverted red cross, blended into the collage of images. He truly was a living, breathing work of art, and while neither woman was particularly fond of tattoos on men, there was something sexually alluring about the sight of his body.

"I suggest you take off your clothes," said Damian, as he began unbuckling his belt and removing his jeans.

"Why would we want to do that?" asked Jasmine. Her heart was now beating hard and fast in the thrill of the moment. The suspense was almost too much to bear.

"Because that dress you're wearing doesn't look cheap," he replied, "it would be a shame if it got wet."

Before Jasmine had time to respond, Damian ordered Lennox to show them the tub. There was a brief moment of silence, followed by a loud thud as the floor of the terrace parted in the centre, and slowly opened to reveal a bubbling, steaming sub-floor Jacuzzi.

Lenora clapped her hands with excitement. She seized the opportunity to show off her curves, and immediately kicked off her heels and began wriggling out of her dress. Damian was not shocked to see that she had not been wearing underwear as she stood in all her glory, waiting for the retractable floor to grind to a halt, before stepping down beneath the warm blanket of frothy white bubbles.

"Come on in it's lovely," she said, waving a hand at her younger, less brazen partner in crime. Damian, who had undressed down to a pair of white underwear that bore a symbol resembling a royal seal, also slipped into the water. They both looked up at Jasmine, waiting to see whether she would finally let go of her inhibitions and give in to the moment.

Without saying a word, she stepped out of her shoes. Her eyes were locked on Damian's, as she slowly slid her way out of her dress to reveal a finely embroidered black lace brazier, and a matching pair of French knickers. As she climbed down into the water to join them, she touched Damian's shoulder with her slender, perfectly polished finger tips. He was no poker player, but he guessed that this was her tell. He sensed that both women desired him, and it was time to lure them into the darkest recesses of his mind, to a place where fantasy and lust knew no limits.

"Tell me, ladies," said Damian, shuffling himself into a comfortable position between them. "How would you describe your emotions right now, as you sit in a heated Jacuzzi, on the roof of a mid-town penthouse apartment, sipping cocktails with a billionaire?"

"I can't really explain it," said Lenora. "Have you ever been somewhere having the time of your life and had an almost-out-of-body experience?"

"Yes," said Jasmine. "I can relate to that." She was glowing with excitement as she spoke, as though Lenora had just taken the words from her mouth. "It's a strange feeling somewhere between euphoria and déjà vu. You almost have to stop, take it all in and ask yourself, am I really here?"

"I couldn't have put it better myself," said Damian. Although it was not unusual for someone in her profession to be so eloquent, Jasmine's conversational skill impressed him.

"What if you could bottle this feeling and make it last a lifetime?" he continued. "What if you could wake up each day and take a sip of happiness and fulfilment? What if I told you I had discovered the formula for such a precious elixir?"

Lenora and Jasmine sat motionless, totally mesmerized by the man and his metaphors. True happiness was a thing craved by most, but achieved by only a few. Damian knew the secret and was about to reveal all, and they were both determined to hear every last detail.

"The secret," he continued, "is not to play by the rules. Rules are restrictions imposed by people who have lots of money, to prevent those who don't from getting any."

Damian's voice dimmed to a whisper. He put an arm around each woman, pulling them so close, that they could feel his hot, sweet breath on their faces as he spoke.

"In my world there are no rules. Nothing is taboo, and there is no limit to success or pleasure." Damian looked each of them in the eyes, engaging them intensely as he continued his enthralling sermon. "Tell me ladies, what do you truly desire at this very moment?"

It was all too much for Lenora. Overwhelmed by the comfortable warmth of his embrace and the seductive tone of his voice, she finally gave in to temptation. She slowly slid her hand up and across his chest, up to his neck and then around the back of his head. Gripping a handful of his hair, her eyes finally met with his in a look of fiery intensity. He submitted to her command, and as she pulled his head down towards hers, their lips touched and their soft tongues danced the tango of a tender kiss. As Damian grabbed her hips and pulled her body in close to his, Lenora let out a gentle moan of satisfaction. As their kiss became more intense, she parted her legs and wrapped them around him.

Suddenly Damian withdrew his head from Lenora's. Her eyes were still shut as she swayed in the gentle current of the small pool. He turned to Jasmine to study her expression. Her mouth was open and her eyes were wide with anticipation. Was she ready to embrace the moment as he had suggested moments earlier? He was not about to let the tempo fade. He took her by the hand and led her towards him. She offered no resistance and glided through the water until all three bodies met as one. He softly placed a hand on the face of each woman, and began kissing them both alternately.

For Damian, this was an inevitable outcome, but for his guests, it was the realisation of their wildest fantasies. Their collective energy had reached boiling point. Both women lapped at his neck like ravenous vampires, pressing their groins into his body and running their hands all over his powerful arms and back. In turn, Damian slipped a hand inside Jasmine's knickers and began gently stroking her.

"Yes, Damian," she whispered, panting and shaking as she fought to control the waves of ecstasy that flowed from the tip of her toes, through her entire body and peaked at the crown of her head.

Lenora, eager not to miss out on her share of his attention, took Damian's other hand and placed it between her legs. She was clearly the more demanding of the two women. While Jasmine would be easier to please, he guessed that Lenora would require the more authoritative attentions of a dominant lover to reach her sexual peak.

He slipped two fingers deep inside Lenora, observing her reactions for a sign that he had indeed located her spot. She threw her body back and forth in time with the motion of his hand, and let out a long, loud moan of gratitude. Damian was a control freak, a manipulator who had now taken command of the mind and body of both women like a powerful puppeteer.

They slowly proceeded to the lounge where he brought them to the brink of orgasm time after time, but on each occasion, he withdrew his touch before the precious moment could be reached. However, neither woman complained. They had never encountered such a sensual and sexually confident man, and they trusted in his ability to deliver satisfaction in abundance, and enjoyed the way he teased them and prolonged their pleasure.

Finally, Damian led them to his bedroom. Jasmine clung to him as they made their way down the hallway, while Lenora, purring like a cat, playfully slinked her way into the room on all fours behind them.

He threw Jasmine's wet body down onto his bed, a large four poster lined with red silk sheets. Gripping her by both ankles, he licked his way from her calf, past her knee, right up to her inner thigh. Then he paused, savouring the moment like a predator taking one last look at his prey, before devouring her. Unable to resist any longer, Jasmine gripped his head with both hands and forced his mouth between her legs. Her body bucked in his grasp as his tongue massaged her throbbing flower.

Lenora threw herself down on the bed next to them and began stroking herself while she watched. Damian released Jasmine from his masterful grip and turned to Lenora. With one hand he whipped her onto her front before grabbing her hips and sliding deep inside her. "Yes!" she yelled, between gasps of pleasure. "Yes, Damian, yes!"

As Jasmine began to retreat, like a snake slithering away from a flame, he reached over and steadied her with one hand. Gripping Lenora by her hair, he slowly lowered her head towards Jasmine's open legs. Damian was not surprised that Lenora offered little resistance. However, Jasmine seemed apprehensive, and stiffened as Lenora's hot breath teased her groin.

"Let go," he whispered reassuringly. "Let go, and embrace freedom."

She obeyed his command and parted her legs to receive her friend's soft red lips. As Lenora's tongue probed with increasing intensity, and Damian's deep powerful thrusts gathered momentum, they descended deeper and deeper into his dark cavern of lust.

As the licentious ballet continued, the inevitability of an electrifying climax bore down on them like a perfectly wrapped gift, waiting to be opened, desperate to be appreciated. With every stroke, every whisper, every breath, they pulled each other closer to a blissful orgasm. Who would be the first to let their body play host to the cool, quivering demon of delight?

Ironically it was Jasmine who finally let go. Her body tightened, and her coarse wail of pleasure set off a chain reaction. Lenora swiftly followed, gritting her teeth and lifting her head to stare back at Damian, who in turn rode her to the point of explosion.

Still breathing heavily, Lenora and Jasmine lay back on his red sheets, like two bodies floating in a sea of blood. Every last drop of innocence had been drained from them, their souls forever tainted by sinful indulgence. They had been re-born into Damian's world, and he was their master. After tonight, everything else would seem ordinary and unappealing. They would never again settle for anything less than excess. He would see them on the path to the top of their profession and beyond, starting with his first exclusive interview and his endorsement of their worth as journalists to anyone who mattered within their industry. This would be his gift to both women, for fulfilling his fantasies for the evening.

Damian rose and immediately disappeared back into the lounge, only to return minutes later, carrying two fresh cocktails. Both women sat up to drain their glasses in silence, before reclining once again. As he lay down in the centre of his bed, they draped themselves over him, stroking his chest and kissing him affectionately before drifting to sleep.

However, it was not the usual slumber brought on by the relentless consumption of alcohol and strenuous physical exertion. This was an unnaturally deep sleep, induced by the powerful sedative that Damian had slipped into their last drink. He did not mean to inflict any harm upon his guests, only to ensure that they did not wake until well after dawn's first light. When they awoke, he would be there, lying between them as he was now, as though he had never left them.

He climbed out of bed, through to his living room and over to the circular door marked 'mannequin'.

"Lennox…show me the demon!"

The circular door revolved to reveal a tall and sinister mannequin. It was dressed in a well-fitted pinstripe suit with matching waistcoat, pocket watch, white shirt and purple tie. But on its face was a gas mask, with two large circular glass eyes, which stared back at him like some life-sized insect. The mask looked old and worn, like an antique from a long-forgotten war.

Damian removed the mask to reveal a lifeless version of himself. The dummy was originally crafted in his image, both for the benefit of his tailor and for his own vain amusement. Piece by piece, he removed each item of clothing from the mannequin, before dressing himself in the attire of his inanimate doppelganger.

Dressed in the pinstripe suit, Damian left the room and marched with purpose back towards the elevator. He punched three digits into the keypad and the heavy doors closed behind him as the elevator began its descent. Approximately ninety seconds later, the doors re-opened onto the sub-floor car park to which only he had access.

Damian's welted leather soles clapped on the concrete as he strolled towards the far end of the car park, to where a solitary black van was parked directly in front of two steel doors.

He walked to the rear of the van and punched a six-digit code into a keypad on the wall just to the left of the doors. A green light flashed, and the words 'access granted' appeared on a small screen just above the keypad. Damian took a deep breath and glanced down at the palms of his hands with a look of deep contemplation. A brief moment of doubt soon passed, washed away by an expression of steely determination. He placed a pair of black leather gloves on his hands, and pulled the ghostly gas mask over his face, before opening the doors and striding through into a scene of the most sickening horror.

Behind six inches of soundproof toughened glass, the dark unknown was about to become a colourful nightmare. With the flick of a switch, the room beyond the glass was illuminated, revealing the naked bodies of six women. They were not bound with any chains or shackles. Instead, they moved freely in the rudimentary make-shift prison within which they had been held captive. The ceiling, walls and floor were lined with reflective aluminium panels. The reflections cast by the walls were warped and distorted in places, where they had been pounded out of shape by fists and feet. There was a single white leather cushioned table in the centre of the room, a small service hatch in the ceiling through which food and water would occasionally be lowered, and one toilet bowl, wash basin and paper towel dispenser in the corner of the room. There was no door, no window, and until the arrival of their captor, no light.

None of these women had any idea why they had been abducted. They had screamed, they had cried, they had fumbled frantically in the dark and discovered the few hidden conveniences that the room had to offer. After days of weeping and whispering in the darkness, they had become familiar with each other's voices, and shared stories of the last moments before their capture. Some had been trapped there for what seemed like weeks, others for days. But all shared one common recollection. The same handsome and mysterious young man had charmed them all, just before the inexplicable loss of consciousness that had immediately preceded their arrival in this hell hole.

They also knew that while there were currently six of them, there was one amongst them who had been held captive longer than anyone else. She was the one who never spoke, and rarely moved from her spot in the corner of the room. She simply sat, clutching her knees, rocking backwards and forwards and occasionally muttering something in a tongue that nobody else could make sense of. Who was she? How long had she been there? Her presence, coupled with her inability to answer these questions made the ordeal of the other five women even more terrifying.

They had died inside a thousand times, as the thoughts and images of what gruesome fate might possibly await them filled their heads. As the lights beamed down on them for the first time since entering the room, their eyes struggled to re-acquaint themselves with the luxury of sight. As each woman slowly squinted their way back to vision, the tall and imposing figure on the other side of the glass gradually came into focus. His villainous mask hid any sign of emotion, but his presence immediately filled them with a sense of dread, for this masked man was surely the architect of their terrible predicament.

From where he stood Damian could hear nothing, but he could see everything. The five able women all charged up to the sound proof glass, beating at it with their fists, their mouths stretched wide in desperate and grotesque silent screams. Some slid to the floor hopelessly, and others pleaded with their eyes to be freed. As one woman placed her hands together in prayer, she looked up at Damian. Was he smiling behind the mask, at the sight of their fear and distress?

Only the silent woman in the corner failed to respond when the lights went on. She remained seated, rocking back and forth with her head slumped down and her long dark hair covering her face.

Suddenly, Damian reached out and pressed a button on the wall and as he did so, gas began to pour into the room. The women panicked once more, coughing and choking as they fought desperately for oxygen, but it was no use. One by one they fell to the ground. After a minute, small holes in the ceiling began to suck the gas back out of the room. As the women drifted out of consciousness, the last image they saw was the glass window opening and the menacing masked man in the pinstripe suit, walking towards them.

Chapter 7
The Beast with Two Backs

The perfect serial killer is a dark and twisted genius. He is extremely calculated, and seldom acts on impulse. He occasionally takes risks, but rarely fails to cover his tracks. He is a showman. A master of his craft, he is meticulous in his preparation and methodical in his execution. Above all he is a merciless hunter. He stalks his prey in shadow, and strikes when they least expect it. Fortunately for the citizens of New York, the mind of the perfect cop is not too dissimilar.

As he pounded the concrete on his customary late evening jog around Central Park, Jake pondered this strange irony. He had spent so much time inside the mind of homicidal maniacs that as he walked the streets by day and night, all he saw was potential victims, naïve men and women who were oblivious to their vulnerability as they unwittingly offered themselves on a plate.

Jake frowned as a passing female jogger winked at him suggestively. Why was she so confident that he was not a threat to her? She was followed swiftly by a lady wearing a pair of large headphones. As their paths crossed, he could clearly make out the artist and the track. He was also a fan of 80's classics, but Eurythmics would be her undoing if anyone chose to attack her from behind, because she would never hear them approaching.

One hundred yards on, a woman with heaving breasts and no sports bra bounced past him, chest first. As Jake's eyes followed her, he noticed that her shorts rode up excessively, exposing the bottom half of her appetising backside. *Suitable attire for a hooker trying to stay trim between turning tricks*, he thought, *but an easy target for a sexual deviant or murderous fiend.*

The well-built man that ran past moments later may not have seemed unusual to the untrained eye. However, on a warm summer evening, a sweater with the hood pulled tight over his head, and a pair of sunglasses seemed more like a disguise than running attire to Jake. Was this man pursuing the three women who had just run past seconds earlier? With the light fading fast, and plenty of bushes and secluded spots, the park was the perfect hunting ground for a would-be felon.

Acting on instinct, Jake turned swiftly and began running behind the man. This may just be another innocent jogger, but Jake didn't care. Deep down, he enjoyed the thrill of the chase.

Following his suspension, he had not taken Miss Monroe's advice and left New York on vacation. Instead he had chosen to remain in the city, and he had spent weeks doing nothing but reading books to sharpen his mind, eating a balanced diet and exercising.

The hooded man in front of him glanced back, and as he noticed Jake on his tail, he picked up his pace. Jake responded by opening up his stride. This guy clearly had no idea who he was up against. Jake would run hard and fast all night if he had to. He would not stop until he knew that the three women were safe from harm.

An hour later, having finally run the potential predator out of the park, Jake returned to his apartment. As he entered, he heard the unfamiliar bleep of the answering machine. Besides a few calls from Abrahams to re-assure him that everything was running smoothly without him, and a couple of messages from Miss Monroe to enquire about his wellbeing, he had not heard from anyone.

However, in the few hours since he had left his apartment, he had received no less than twelve answer-phone messages. He knew instantly that something was wrong, and ran over to the coffee table to grab his cell phone. The call log confirmed his suspicions. Abrahams had been trying to call him on both lines. Jake rang the Captain's office number, and waited for the all too familiar baritone voice to respond.

"Christ, Cannon, where the hell have you been?" Abrahams' tone was unsettling.

"Sorry, Cap," replied Jake, "I was out jogging. What's up?"

Abrahams did not answer. There was a deathly silence on the other end of the line. It was as though the Captain was piecing together sentences in his head, trying to decide how best to break the news to Jake.

"Well you've clearly not heard the news," said Abrahams. "Turn on CWC right now, and then call me back in five."

Jake heard Abrahams' phone slam down. As the line went dead, he envisaged the foam gathering at the corners of his moustached mouth as it often did when the Captain was caught in the eye of a storm. Whatever had happened, it was big. But why had he not just brought Jake up to speed? Perhaps he was unsure as to whether he was ready to return to duty. By leaving him to watch events unfold on the nightly news, Abrahams was giving him the chance to make the decision of his own accord.

Jake pointed the remote control at his television and the screen burst to life, revealing the familiar face of news reporter Belinda Bryce. She was standing outside a derelict building somewhere in Manhattan. Behind her, the entrance to a crime scene had already been cordoned off, and the press, emergency services and police were pacing backwards and forwards, addressing members of the public and assembling equipment. As Jake's eyes zoomed in on the scene, Belinda began to speak.

"I'm here at what used to be the 'Repro Man' printing company on the corner of 55 and 9th Avenue, where officers responding to an anonymous call have discovered the bodies of two women in their mid-twenties on the sixth floor of these abandoned offices. Earlier this evening in a brief statement to the press, Police Chief Edward Castilian re-assured New Yorkers that the NYPD are already on the hunt for clues, and urged anyone who might have any information as to who may have carried out these horrific murders to come forward

immediately. While the full details of what has been discovered inside have not yet been released, it is clear that this was an extremely brutal double murder of a ceremonial nature, sparking fresh fears that a new killer may be loose in the city, just a few short weeks after Sebastian Bronson known as the 'Hangman' was captured by..."

Jake switched off his television and sat staring at his cell phone for several minutes, before finally calling Abrahams and receiving a short yet detailed brief. The call ended with the confirmation that Jake was to return to work immediately. He was not to proceed to Police Plaza and collect his gun and badge. His orders were to go straight to the crime scene where Detective Gibbs and the forensic team were waiting to talk him through the harrowing details. They were under strict instructions not to tamper with the bodies until Jake had given the site his full assessment.

Jake had longed for this moment for weeks, but now that he'd finally received the call, he began to question himself. Was it too soon? Was he ready to go back to work?

Suddenly the emotions of the Hangman case came flooding back to him. The desperation he felt in the hours leading up to the discovery of those children. Their faces as they knelt bound and gagged, awaiting death. Jake's breathing grew heavier and his hands began to shake.

"Stay cool, Jake, stay cool!" He pleaded with himself, searching his mind for fortitude. Even just the illusion of courage would suffice. He took a deep breath to steady his nerves. Somewhere out there, a new killer had made his first roll of the dice. The game had begun, and it was down to Jake to make sure that the NYPD did not lose control of the board.

Jake did not waste time. He showered, changed into one of his many tailored suits, and was at the scene within the hour.

It all looked so familiar to him. The flashing lights under the blanket of darkness and the hubbub of the crowds of spectators who had gathered outside in the hope of seeing something awful. The tense yet efficiently alert news crews wrestling for a stronghold close to the strand of yellow tape, which marked the end of the line for anyone besides the unfortunate few who had the job of observing whatever nightmare lay beyond it.

Jake entered the building and climbed six flights to where the forensic team were patiently assembling their equipment, ready to dissect the scene once he had departed. He was greeted by Detective Gibbs, a short, surly bulldog of a man. The colour had drained from his face, and his glassy wide-eyed expression told Jake that whatever he had seen inside, had shaken him to the core.

"Thank God you're here, Cannon," said Gibbs, dabbing his mouth with a handkerchief between sentences, and handing Jake a pair of rubber gloves "I...*we* are all glad to have you back."

Jake had never been one to court compliments, and waved his hand in a gesture that suggested praise was not necessary.

"What are we up against here?" said Jake, in his usual business-like tone.

"It's like nothing I've ever seen before!" replied Gibbs. "The best way to describe it is like some sort of..." he paused and held his hand over his mouth, desperately trying not to vomit. Gibbs was no lily-livered murder scene debutant, so Jake could only imagine what had unsettled him. What evil had been unleashed inside?

"Better you just take a look for yourself, Cannon," said Gibbs, ushering him into the large open-plan office.

The entire room was dark, dusty and bare, except for several metal pillars erected strategically around a square platform in the centre of the room. High intensity lamps were fixed to the top of each pillar, and the shafts of light that they beamed down created a huge spotlight for the mound of flesh that was laying on the platform.

As Jake walked towards the light, every gory detail of the shocking picture that the killer had created fell into focus. The platform was in fact a large canvas. Usually an artist would apply paint to such a surface, but this canvas was stained with the blood of the two naked women who were lying upon it.

Their limbs had been violently shattered and twisted so as to create a hideously unnatural image. He had seen such contortions before, in books detailing the characteristics of a person in the final stages of demonic possession. But this was not the work of any supernatural entity.

Jake began to circle the canvas and noticed that their stomachs had been sliced open. The entrails of both women had been pulled from their bodies and had been twisted, tied and sewn together. From the putrid stench of rotting human flesh, Jake guessed that the women must have been lying dead for several days.

"Their 'you-know-what's' have been sewn together at the labia," said Gibbs, choking into his handkerchief as he struggled once more to avoid being sick. Jake placed a toothpick in his mouth. It was a customary ritual whenever he inspected a crime scene. Then he placed a glove on each hand before lifting the thigh of one of the women. Sure enough, the rough stitching around was clearly visible. Why had they been slaughtered and displayed in such a bizarre manner?

Jake began creating a profile of the killer in his head. Was this the work a jealous ex-boyfriend? Had he discovered that his beloved partner was having an affair with another woman, and exacted brutal vengeance? Jake swiftly eliminated the notion that this was a vendetta killing. This had not been a frenzied attack, nor was it the work of a man or indeed a woman motivated by rage. This was a carefully orchestrated act of precision.

Jake looked up at the light pillars and then back down at the blood-soaked canvas. It was not the standard lighting used by the forensics team. This lighting belonged to the killer. He was proud of the spectacle he had created and wanted his audience to marvel at his ghastly work of art.

Jake's face was a picture of concentration as he circumnavigated the bodies, taking mental snapshots from every angle. These were attractive women. Not the type to be lured from safety by the stereotypical pervert in a trench coat, or at least not without a struggle he thought. However, their wrists and ankles had not been bound. Besides the heavy bruising around their broken limbs, there were no visible signs of an aggressive abduction. It would have taken some charm to lure these women to an abandoned office of their own free will. This was either the work of a beguiling wolf in sheep's clothing, or someone who knew how to administer a strong sedative.

"Ain't you gonna take notes," said Gibbs inquisitively, assuming that the details of the crime scene would be too complex for him to memorise. He shuffled around in his pocket for his scruffy notepad and handed it to Jake.

"I don't do notes," replied Jake dismissively. He did not accept the pad or even raise his eyes to look at Gibbs. He simply pointed to his forehead as he stared down at the two corpses. "My mind is the only place I keep notes," he said.

Suddenly Jake noticed it. It was small and feint, but his eyes had not deceived him. On the back of the left hand of one of the women, carefully etched with a very fine blade was the number 666. Her hand was tightly clenched into a fist, and he could see that she was clutching something. He knelt down and slowly prized the hand open. Inside was a moist, brown, grassy clump of weed.

"What the fuck is that?" said Gibbs, looking down over Jake's shoulder at his discovery.

"Tobacco," replied Jake. "Did you notice that the killer had carved three sixes on the back of the victim's hand?"

"The mark of the beast," said Gibbs. "That's some satanic shit, right?"

"Here is wisdom," replied Jake, closing his eyes as he recalled the biblical quote. "Let him who has understanding calculate the number of the beast, for the number is that of a man; and his number is six hundred and sixty-six."

Despite being well read on the subject, Jake had never been one to embrace religious extremes. The beast, the devil, Satan. Whatever name he was given, Jake did not subscribe to the notion that some supremely evil being would soon return, to plunge the world into eternal darkness. There were many who believed that the reign of the antichrist was imminent, and others who believed that he was already walking among us, controlling the economy, the media, the world!

"The tobacco is a clever play on the words 'two' and 'back' I think," muttered Jake, gazing down at the bodies once more. "It's a famous literary term…the beast with two backs."

Jake was certain that his assumption was correct. The corpses had been intertwined and positioned as if the two women were engaged in a sick sexual act. The sewing together of their internal sexual organs and their labia symbolised the complete merging of two bodies, coming together as one in a moment of passion. This was the imagery invoked by Shakespeare when he first coined the phrase.

"Okay, Gibbs, tell forensics to wrap this up," said Jake, retreating back towards the doorway. "I have everything I need."

Jake left the crime scene and returned to headquarters, where he was greeted with unexpected warmth by his colleagues. When he walked into the dusty office, the entire room fell silent. Then one by one, everyone rose to their feet and began to applaud the man who had finally brought the Hangman to his knees.

"Welcome back, Jake!" Alice Flynn, an analyst with a soft spot for the broody detective, threw her arms around him. As she did so, others followed suit, offering handshakes and hugs while displaying their gratitude to the man who had always been somewhat of an enigma within the department.

Jake was lost for words. He had been misunderstood, misquoted, and sometimes even despised. But now it was as though they really were glad to have him back. He was not used to empathy from his colleagues, and he knew just whom he had to thank for championing his cause. Felicity Monroe had obviously been busy while he was away, spreading word of his selfless deeds.

The imposing figure of Abrahams suddenly came thundering into the room, saving Jake from the awkwardness of reciprocating the amity with which he had been welcomed. Without saying a word, he gave Jake a brief but firm handshake. Abrahams knew the stoic young detective all too well. Jake would always favour a swift nod and a shake of the hand over a show of affection.

"I am sure that you all share my gratitude to Detective Cannon for the excellent work he's done in the line of duty!" shouted Abrahams, making sure that the whole floor received his sermon loud and clear. "But now we need him more than ever. As you are all aware, the discovery of two bodies tonight has sparked another manhunt. So, all of us here, and in every damn precinct in this city are gonna have to work together to get rapid results. Lengthy investigations cost lives, and we don't want another Hangman situation. It's our new killer's first outing, but I can see more blood on the horizon. So, I want facts and figures and I want them fast. I want names on our two Jane Doe's, I want addresses, background information and close friends and family members brought in for interviews. I want forensic intelligence collected swiftly. I want details cross referenced with every known felon in the system."

He turned to Jake, and ushering him to come forward to where he was standing, addressing the crowd of officers from his imaginary pulpit. "Cannon is going to play point on this investigation," continued Abrahams. "Work with him people, give him everything he needs to build a profile of this psycho. I want you to turn every pocket of this city inside out until this asshole drops out!"

The Captain was never one to mince his words and now more than ever he meant business. As the crowd of officers was dismissed, he called Jake into his office for a debriefing.

As both men sat down, the Captain picked up Jake's badge and tossed it to him, before reaching into his desk and pulling out his Glock 17 sidearm and handed it to his top detective.

"Welcome back, Cannon!" he said with unquestionable sincerity. "Now tell me, did you get anything solid from the crime scene?" He was used to Jake's unorthodox style, so he was not surprised when he did not reach for any notes, and immediately launched into a detailed recollection.

"This will make the hair stand up on the back of your neck, Captain," said Jake, setting the mood for the harrowing facts that were about to follow. "We have two women killed in a ceremonial fashion, but this one is all message and no clear motive. We have not reached serial status yet, but I'm sure that we will."

"Go on, Cannon, I'm all ears." Abrahams leaned forward in his seat. He knew Jake was smart and he trusted his judgement. He knew that whatever he was about to say would be worth listening to.

"Art!" continued Jake. "The scene was meticulously prepared. The bodies were presented on canvas, and he used his own lighting for dramatic effect. He wanted us to see his work in its best light, Captain. I think that our man is an artist."

Jake continued to explain the cryptic demonic references and the sickening lengths the killer had gone to in order to create his 'beast with two backs'.

"I think he's all about the imagery," said Jake confidently. "Our killer wants us to see something. He wants us to understand the meaning behind his art. That message is still unclear, so I think he'll kill again and again until we all see his point."

Abrahams scratched his head. His frustration was evident and there was little Jake could do to re-assure him that this case would not become a messy bloodbath with an epic death toll.

"As I was saying, Captain, I am sure he will kill again," continued Jake. "While I can't say when and how, what I can say is that if his ego is half as inflated as I think it is, he will want to increase the scale of his work. Think about it, Cap, that lighting was his. I'm also pretty sure he did not lure those women to an abandoned office, or drag them there by force. There was no sign that they were aggressively restrained, so I believe these women were sedated. If so, he would have had to transport both women and his equipment from somewhere else. Somewhere not too far from the scene."

"He would need a vehicle large enough to bring all of his equipment to the site," replied Abrahams. He was starting to see the picture Jake was painting for him, but he was still a little confused as to his logic. "There are hundreds of high sided vehicles in the city by day and night. He would hardly stand out, Cannon."

"You're right, but to set up a scene like this he would need to do so without interruption," replied Jake. "He would need abandoned buildings with little or no security, and travelling with such a risky cargo he wouldn't want to be driving too far. So, my guess is that he has some sort of stronghold close by."

"Of course!" yelled Abrahams triumphantly. A high sided van parked near one of the few empty and unpatrolled commercial units in the heart of Manhattan would be more than co-incidence, and Jake's assumptions regarding the proximity of a possible stronghold, gave them a chance of narrowing down the radius of his next attack.

Jake's perceptive investigative skill had put the fire back in the Captain's belly, and put the homicide team back on the offensive. Abrahams thanked him for his sterling work before heading back into the department, to bring the rest of his team up to speed.

Jake returned to his desk and made a call to forensics. He wanted to see the blood toxicology reports on both victims as soon as possible, to confirm his suspicion that they had been sedated. While he waited on hold, Felicity Monroe's business card caught his eye. He had been looking for an excuse to see her again, and who better to help him piece together a psychological profile than an expert in the field.

He decided that he would invite her for coffee. She would be more than happy to help, and this collaborative effort might work in his favour. The Captain had not yet tried to assign anyone to work alongside him. He knew Jake would resist for as long as possible, but if the case progressed and more bodies were discovered, Jake's lack of a partner would soon become a problem, and the subject of discussion as it had been so many times in the past.

Jake rose from his seat and strolled back through the office. He was about to leave, when he noticed something. Alice Flynn was standing in front of the coffee machine picking loose change from her purse. Tucked under her arm was the latest issue of My Style magazine. Although it was folded in half, Jake could still make out the image on the front cover.

He followed Alice back to her desk, and as he approached, she threw the magazine down on her table so that the face on the front was in full view. Jake stood statuesque, frozen in a state of disbelief.

"Are you okay, Jake?" asked Alice. "You look like you've seen a ghost?"

Jake pinched the skin between the bridge of his nose and his brows and ran his tongue around his mouth, desperately searching for moisture. A million questions raced around his mind. There was far too much to be explained.

"Do you know who this guy is, Alice?" he asked, trying his best to sound relaxed. He was conscious that his erratic behaviour would soon rouse her suspicion.

Her eyes lit up immediately. "Of course, I do!" she replied enthusiastically. "He's that totally gorgeous billionaire art guy who just opened the new gallery right here in Manhattan."

"That's great," replied Jake. Her animated expression reassured him that she would focus her efforts on carrying out the task that he was about to set for her. "I need to speak with him, so I want you to try and make contact."

Alice was overjoyed at the prospect of meeting Damian Burgundy. "Do you want me to contact his people and ask if Mr Burgundy can come here to meet you?"

Jake gave a wry smile. "That's exactly what I want you to do," he replied. "I want you to speak to his associates and tell them that Detective Jake Cannon would very much like to talk to Mr Burgundy, about a very important police matter."

Chapter 8
Mr Red

Celebrity summer nuptials in New York were always big news, and the wedding of 'Wild Child' rock 'n' roll front man Tommy Riley and Francesca Goldberg was no exception. Goldberg had become one of the world's leading brands in the hotelier and hospitalities industry, and Francesca was the sole heir to the family's considerable fortune.

"I want to see the name Goldberg hit the Forbes list of the top ten most grandiose weddings of all time!" This was the brief given by Francesca's father, Larz Goldberg. His ego was almost as big as his bank balance, and with only one daughter, he was determined to make the most of the opportunity to flaunt his cash. Fortunately for Larz, the planners and co-ordinators exceeded all expectations, and delivered a lavish reception of unparalleled extravagance.

The New York 'Rotundra' was an iconic cylindrical high-rise building, and the Goldberg's flagship hotel. The Maxi Lounge, located on the top floor of the hotel proved to be the ideal location for the grand event. The lounge was adorned with the usual cliché decorative touches. Huge ice sculptures, floral and candle arrangements and crystal chandeliers were not original features for a celebrity wedding. However, it was the wedding favours that left guests speechless.

On entering the lounge, they were greeted with champagne, caviar and personalised top handles and keep all bags from a well-known French designer; each filled with a unique set of gifts including diamond encrusted wrist watches, exquisite fragrances and other fine accessories. For pals and acquaintances there were flight tickets to Dubai, the Mahali Mzuri, Puerto Los Cabos and Necker Island. For those fortunate enough to be a seated at the bride and groom's table,

Larz had gone to even more frivolous extremes. Inside their gift bags were keys to customised Italian supercars.

A room full of a-list celebrities from the world of sport, music and cinema would normally have descended into a snake pit of fork-tongued slander, assassinating each other under their breath for their hair, make-up or tailoring failures. However, the Goldberg's generosity had left everyone in high spirits, and set a warm and vibrant tone for the rest of the evening.

With speeches out of the way, the groom and his band treated guests to a live performance as they enjoyed their one thousand dollar-per-head silver service meal. Only a performance by an iconic legend whose music transcended genres and spanned four decades could ever match up to the occasion. But once again, expectations were exceeded as a nameless artist formerly known by a royal title, took to the stage to indulge a stunned audience with a rare display of his musical genius.

By 2200 hours that night, the dining tables had been cleared, to make way for roulette, poker and craps tables. In the centre of the room, the lights had dimmed and the DJ had the crowd bubbling with the electrifying energy of a Nevada nightclub. Goldberg had successfully brought the unmistakable vibe of his spiritual home, Las Vegas, to the metropolis of New York.

Every woman in attendance had brought out their Academy Award-winning wardrobe for the event. Men looked on with lustful gazes, as beguiling females slinked and cavorted their way around the room like a carnival parade of tanned flesh and fine fabric. Whether they were single or with their husbands and partners, they had all gone to an immeasurable effort to look their best, in the hope of catching the eye of New York's most eligible bachelor, Damian Burgundy.

However, the guest of honour was nowhere to be seen. He had apparently shunned the ceremony, sparking fresh rumours that despite the very open and candid magazine article that had unveiled him to the world, he had already returned to his reclusive ways.

Burgundy's absence had upset one guest in particular. Gabrielle Franco was the latest young Hollywood starlet to captivate the media. The critics had warmed to her performance as a young Elizabeth Taylor, in her first outing as a leading lady. The biopic had cleaned up at Cannes and was tipped to launch Franco's career into orbit. It had also captured the attention of Burgundy, who was reported to have suggested that Franco had re-ignited his childhood crush on the late and undeniably great Elizabeth Taylor.

As Gabrielle stood at the bar casually drinking and joking with friends, she could do little to mask her disappointment.

"All the cash I blew on this cute little number, he'd better show up!" said Gabrielle. She did indeed look divine in a strapless chiffon gown, with a slit that ran down her left thigh, exposing one of her long and perfectly toned legs. "We should have tried to get a table with the Nicks boys," she continued. "Free drinks all night!"

As the group laughed and chattered, a tall man carrying a silver tray walked up and stood at the bar beside them. He wore a fitted claret suit, black patent leather apron tie shoes and a black shirt with glittered black tie. Gabrielle would have assumed that he was just another well-dressed guest had it not been for the unusual masks worn by him and several other men seen patrolling the venue, taking orders and serving drinks. The mask was a faceless jet-black stocking, speckled with glitter and diamante, which covered his face and disappeared under the collar of his shirt. Although she could not see his face, there was something about this man's demeanour that caught her attention, and she immediately broke away from the group and turned in his direction.

"I'm gonna call you Mr Red," said Gabrielle, punching him on the arm as though they already shared an affectionate familiarity. "I've seen your buddies Mr Green, Mr Gold and Mr Silver wandering around, but I've been here all night and this is the first time I've seen you."

"I'm more of a behind the scenes kind of guy," he replied. His voice was muffled from beneath the mask, and Gabrielle moved in closer so that she could hear him above the noise of the party.

"Well I'm Gabi," she continued. "I love your outfit by the way. It's creepy as hell, but I find the whole mystery-man-behind-the-mask thing very sexy."

Mr Red simply nodded his head in gratitude. "The suit is Oswald Boateng, a London designer who I happen to love," he said, placing his silver tray on the counter and leaning up against the bar. "As for the mask," he continued, "that's just a little something I threw together last minute for dramatic effect. It makes the waiters stand out don't you think? The groom loved the idea. It appealed to his darker side!"

Gabrielle's friends had now gathered around him, eager to see who had captured her attention. As he spoke, the group listened, totally entranced. They touched his suit, stroked his sparkling faceless visage, and one by one, their body language began to suggest that they were falling for his charm.

With the mask, there was no story behind his eyes and no hint as to his emotion or the sincerity of his words. Yet, Gabrielle could not help but marvel at how fascinating he was. His energy was incredible. It radiated from him, drawing them in like a magnet.

Mr Burgundy had been forgotten, eclipsed by Mr Red. How could a man without a face be so devilishly attractive? Beneath the mask, he might have lacked everything Gabrielle believed to be desirable in a man. Did his appearance matter? Could she settle for a man of limited means, if his company and conversation made her truly happy? As the questions mounted, she could no longer contain her curiosity. She had to see his face.

"Well Mr Red, you are beginning to sound like Mr Perfect!" She cupped his face with both hands, hoping that touch would achieve what sight could not, and help her determine what he looked like. The face seemed firm and symmetrical, but was it handsome? Gabrielle conceded that she simply could not invest any more time in this man unless he removed the mask.

"Call me shallow, but I have to see the face beneath that mask," she said assertively.

Without hesitation, he removed the stocking to reveal the face of an incredibly good-looking man. He was more than handsome; he was beautiful thought Gabrielle. His hair had been freshly trimmed in a short, almost military style. He was clean shaven, very well groomed and his piercing dark eyes stared back at her, immediately setting her nerves on edge.

One by one, guests around the room turned and caught sight of him. As the music scratched to a halt, a chorus of whispers and gasps of amazement became audible.

"Pleased to meet you, Gabi," he said, patting his hair and flashing his ice white teeth as he smiled at her. "By the way, this suit is not red—it's burgundy!"

It was as though someone had just pressed the pause button, sending the entire room into a trance. All eyes were fixed firmly on Damian. Finally, the DJ cut through the painfully awkward silence. "Ladies and Gentlemen, I am pleased to welcome the guest of honour, the magnificent Mr Burgundy!"

Every camera in the room began to flash. The paparazzi could barely believe their good fortune at being granted access to cover the reception, and now the late arrival of Burgundy was the icing on the cake.

Gabrielle did not have to say a word to her entourage. They made their excuses and swiftly removed themselves from the scene, so that their friend could make her move on the young billionaire.

"Wow!" she said, still staring at him in awe. "You certainly know how to make an entrance."

"Oh, you haven't seen anything yet!" exclaimed Damian.

In an unusual display of recklessness, he climbed onto a stool and leapt up onto the bar, where he could be seen by everyone, and scanned the room until he caught sight of Tommy Riley and his beautiful new bride.

"Ladies and gentlemen," he shouted. "Tonight, the drinks are on me, and I won't let anyone leave until the bar is dry."

As guests began to clap and cheer he signalled to the bar staff. "Start popping every bottle of champagne you have," he said. "Line the bar with flutes and start handing them out, I want to see it raining corks in here!"

As he spoke, everyone behind the bar began emptying the fridges of gold bottles. They hurriedly filled glasses and passed them out to guests, while the remaining masked men darted around tables handing out flutes until everyone in the room was ready to join in Burgundy's toast. Burgundy bent down, picked up a half-full bottle from the bar, and began to speak once more.

"I am sure you'll agree that Francesca is looking flawless in Galliano this evening," said Damian. "For those of you who are sticklers for detail like myself; the gown weighs over 50lbs. It has a 15-foot train, over 300 yards of white Duchess Satin, 1500 pearls, 8.8 carats of green diamonds and a 5-carat white diamond. I know this because I co-designed it, but I won't tell you what it costs, because if Goldberg's accountant is here, he will have a heart attack!"

Larz Goldberg beamed with pride, as Burgundy continued his toast and the room was filled with laughter and applause. This was the response he had craved when planning the ostentatious reception, and Burgundy had delivered the kudos he desired on a silver platter. He would most certainly repay him with the contract to provide the artwork for his hotel chain. The lucrative deal that Burgundy had aggressively pursued for several months was most certainly the reason behind his show of generosity and praise, but as a fellow businessman of considerable worth, such tactics were not foreign to Goldberg. If anything, he respected the balls of the young man, whose meteoric rise looked set to eclipse his own success.

"Now, Tommy, may be one of the few true rockers in here right now," continued Damian. "But tonight, we're all gonna party like rock stars!"

As Damian urged everyone to raise their glasses, the venue erupted and the DJ spun back into action with a Wild Child classic. He stepped down from his makeshift podium, and re-joined Gabrielle.

"I have never seen anyone grab a party by the balls like that before," she said, holding her sides as she laughed. "You're not what I expected. Why have you stayed out of the limelight for so many years, when you shine like a star when the spotlight is on you?"

Damian laughed at her compliment. This must have been the question on everyone's lips he thought. Yet the answer was simple. Like most artists, he was a perfectionist. From his tattoos, to his business ventures and his bulging bank balance, Damian had always seen himself as a work-of-art in progress. He had surrounded himself with mystique and avoided returning to New York until now, because he felt that he had only just reached the pinnacle of his potential. He knew that once he was back in his homeland, it would be virtually impossible to remain an enigma to the media, so the only thing left for him to do, was unveil himself to the world.

It all made perfect sense to Gabrielle, and as he explained his life to her in thrilling detail, she found herself falling deeper and deeper under his spell.

"I'm glad you liked the mask," he said. "The magazine article was released within forty-eight hours of the interview, but it seems like my world has already been turned upside down. I used to thrive on drawing people in with just a smile and my sense of humour, but now everywhere I go, my face attracts attention. But tonight, I proved once again that people are intrigued by the unknown. The mask gave me back my anonymity. It gave me a sense of mystery. I was here for hours and nobody looked at me twice, until I spoke to you. The greatest trick the devil ever pulled…"

"The Usual Suspects!" shouted Gabrielle. She was impressed by his reference to a true cinema classic. Damian was showing his appreciation of her profession and she was warming to him even more as a result. He had her right where he wanted her, caught firmly in his web. The press had been correct in their assumptions. Gabrielle was indeed his target, and for one night only, he intended to make her his leading lady.

However, the beautiful young actress was not the only thing he craved. Like a full-moon to a werewolf, the intensity of the evening had awoken the monster lurking within him. He had a thirst for blood, and tonight was the perfect time to kill again. He would continue to charm Gabrielle, and hundreds of witnesses would see them leave arm in arm. Once she had satisfied his lust, he would drug her before slipping away to select his next victim from the women he held captive. The next morning, Gabrielle would awaken from her slumber. She would assume that her heavy head was owed to the consumption of too much champagne and remind herself of her limits. Then she would leave his apartment wearing tonight's dress and beaming with satisfaction. Like Lenora and Jasmine before her, Gabrielle would be the source of great pleasure, and also the perfect alibi.

As the party raged on around them, Damian kept the drink flowing to maintain the tempo of their conversation, whilst the feisty young actress became increasingly more tactile. They traded sexual innuendo and their eye contact became prolonged and more lustful.

Now the demon inside Damian had truly awoken, and as they spoke, he struggled to suppress his violent urges. He began to visualise all of the many ways in which he would love to kill her. He imagined breaking the stem of a flute and plunging it deep into her chest. There would be screams of horror as she fell back against the bar, clutching her breast, with her eyes fixed on him in an expression of disbelief. Then he imagined lifting a bottle of champagne and pouring it over her head. As both blood and bubbles ran down her body, he pictured himself placing his glass on her abdomen, and catching some of the frothy pink cocktail of blood and alcohol before guzzling it down, while the crowds of distressed guests looked on.

It was time to leave! Damian had never struggled to contain his blood lust before, but now his desire to kill was growing dangerously intense. He needed to get back into character. His craving for sex and blood would soon be satisfied.

"Have you ever played secret kisses?" asked Damian.

"Secret kisses?" replied Gabrielle. "Now that does sound like fun, but what are the rules?"

Damian leant in close. The sexual tension between them was intoxicating and as their bodies came together he could feel her heart thumping in her chest. He placed one hand on her cheek and brought his lips to her ear, whispering the details of his crude game so that only she could hear.

"Well, Gabi, the rules are that you have to point to a place on your body, and wherever you point, is exactly where I have to kiss!"

"Anywhere on my body?" replied Gabrielle, no longer concerned with subtlety. It was now abundantly clear what they both wanted.

"Absolutely anywhere!" confirmed Damian, "the naughtier the better."

They stood occupying each other's personal space, consuming each other's energy. In their minds eye they were already touching. Clothes were being peeled back to expose smooth, moist skin. Damian's hands were gently exploring the rippling waves and soft valleys of her ripe young body. Her tongue was already navigating its way across his lips, probing for an opening.

As they stood in silence enjoying the deliciously seductive fantasy, their audience looked on over shoulders and through slanted gazes, trying not to get caught staring at the hot young couple. The chemistry between them was obvious. In those few moments, they had already created tomorrow's tabloid headlines.

Gabrielle was the first to break. She placed a leg either side of Damian's thigh, pushing her groin into his body so that he could feel the force of her intent.

"Take me home right now, Mr Burgundy!"

Damian did not say a word. He simply placed a hand under her elbow and swung her around so that she was facing the exit, and together they strolled out of the lounge. No ceremony, no goodbyes, just a swift departure. They made their way to the lobby, trapped like goldfish on display in the huge glass elevator.

Upon exiting the building, they were met by Quarter. He was dressed in a pristine black and grey chauffeurs' outfit. He smiled at Damian as they walked through the revolving doors.

"Home, sir?" said Quarter as he ushered them into the rear of a gun metal grey and silver Maybach.

"Yes indeed!" said Damian, pausing to assist Gabrielle into the car before sliding in behind her. As the vehicle pulled away from the entrance of the Rotundra, Damian picked up a small remote and pointed it at the privacy partition between them and the driver. The transparent glass misted immediately, and they were suddenly sat alone, in a butter-soft leather lap of luxury.

"I cannot wait to get you out of that dress," said Damian, gently running a finger over her collar bone before placing one hand on her cheek and pulling her face towards his.

Gabrielle's response surprised him. She flicked a slender leg over his so that she was straddling his lap, facing him. She placed one hand on his chest, forcing him back into his seat. Whipping her hair away from her face with a glance of her head, she began kissing him with the confidence of a woman more experienced than her years, and Damian could tell that she knew exactly how to satisfy a man.

"I'll warn you," she said, biting his bottom lip between sentences. "I am an animal in the bedroom."

"Excellent," replied Damian. "We'll be the perfect match, because I am an absolute beast!"

Back at his apartment, Gabrielle did not disappoint him. Despite her innocent appearance, the young actress proved to be quite the vixen. Hours passed before she finally tired, and after one of Damian's potent goodnight cocktails, she drifted into a deep sleep.

Had it not been for his vile plan, Damian may have succumbed to exhaustion and fallen asleep beside her. But he was in no mood for rest. Buoyed by the adrenaline of his savage addiction, he soon found himself face to face with his mannequin. After relieving it of the suit and mask that had become the regalia of his murderous alter-ego, he headed to the elevator and to his underground killing room.

Damian punched the code into the keypad and entered the small observation room, before putting on his mask and gloves and flicking on the light. As he did so, the naked figures of his prisoners who lay slumped and scattered about the room, shuffled to life.

Some of them were already awake, overcome by a fear-induced insomnia. Through tearful whispers, many of the women had bonded in the darkness, whilst others had huddled together for comfort and wept themselves into a torrid sleep. There were no sweet dreams. In the pitch-black prison room, their unknown fate only provoked the most vivid nightmares.

As their eyes adjusted to the light once more, each woman glanced around the room. Although two women had clearly been taken, the groups' number had increased considerably since the masked man had last appeared behind the glass. Now the women looked around anxiously, putting faces to names and tallying up how many were among their ranks. There were nine in total, and the five new prisoners stared in shock at the man who some of the original captives had described as 'the monster in the mask'.

The last time he appeared, he had not spoken. He had simply stood watching them until the gas had filled the room and left them all unconscious. So, they were taken by surprise when he flicked a microphone switch on the wall so that he could be heard through the glass, and then twisted a small black device fitted over the mouth of his gas mask, and began to speak.

"Listen to me carefully, your life depends on it. We are going to play a game of chance, at the end of which, one of you will die." The mask distorted his voice into a menacingly deep tone. He sounded unnatural. More like an ogre than a man.

There was a huge commotion, as panic-stricken women ran up to the window, hammering against it with their fists and begging to be released. Some were angry, threatening and cursing their masked captor in brave defiance, while others wailed in self-pity.

There was only one of them who showed no emotion. The silent woman in the corner did not scream, shout or protest. She said nothing at all, and simply sat rocking back and forth with her face hidden behind long strands of matted brown hair.

"In a moment, a deck of cards will drop down through the hatch above your heads," continued Damian, instantly silencing the commotion. "I want you to open the pack and place it on the table. Then I want each of you to pick a card from the pack, walk up to the glass and show me the card you have selected. Whoever picks the card which matches the one I have in my pocket, will die by this blade."

Damian raised his left hand, which had been held behind his back, to reveal a large knife. It was rusting in places and the wooden handle was stained with blood, but even from a distance, they could see that the blade looked razor sharp.

"I hope you rot in hell you fucking creep!" yelled one woman. Another walked right up to the glass and clasped her hands together and closed her eyes in prayer.

"Oh God help us," she cried. "Lord God please spare us all!"

Damian's head rocked back as he roared with laughter. He was taking great delight in their suffering. He brandished the blade, holding it up to the face of the woman who was still stood with her eyes closed just a few inches away, behind the toughened glass.

"Your God can't save you now," he said. "But my God is the Lord of all evil. He hungers for flesh and thirsts for blood, and tonight I will honour him with a worthy sacrifice."

As he reached over and pressed a button on a small panel to his right, the ceiling hatch opened and the deck of cards dropped down onto the floor.

Nobody wanted to touch the pack. The cards were a symbol of doom for one of the group, and there was not one among them who wished to initiate the masked monster's game of death.

"Never!" yelled one woman. "We won't play your sick game!"

Damian stopped laughing. He raised his arm, pointing the blade directly at the woman who had spoken out in defiance.

"Play the game and you may live, but defy me and I will disembowel every last one of you with this blade! You have just one minute to decide your fate."

There was a moment of panic as the severity of his words sank in, before one of the women walked over to the pack and removed the cards from their box. Everyone watched in muted suspense as she placed the deck face down on the padded table. Then she swiped the top card and walked nervously up to the window. She pressed the face of the card against the glass, gritting her teeth and wincing as she awaited his response. Surely from an entire deck she could not have selected the one card that would seal her fate.

Damian did not prolong her agony. He shook his head and waved her away from the window, before gesturing to the rest of the group to follow suit. One by one they plucked cards from the deck, and each was met with a shake of the head. Finally, when the first eight women had all pulled a card, they turned to the woman in the corner.

She did not move. It was as though she was oblivious to the ordeal of the other captives. They had all stumbled across her in the pitch-black room and had been met with the same lack of response when they had tried to communicate with her. She had displayed all of the characteristics of insanity, but now it was a matter of life or death, and nobody sympathised with her.

"What about her?" yelled one woman. She did not want to see the odds of survival slashed because one of them refused to participate.

"Not her!" yelled Damian. He gave no explanation as to why the woman in the corner was excluded. He simply ordered the remaining eight women to continue picking from the ever-decreasing pack.

The game rolled on until everyone had picked three cards each and they were into the fourth round. The tension mounted with each draw. Then a frail woman, who had stood scratching a rash above her navel, stepped forward and selected a card. She walked up to the glass, her hand shaking violently as she held it up for Damian to see. The woman squinted, pressing her eyelids shut so tight that her whole face turned red.

Damian did not shake his head. Instead, he reached into his right pocket and pulled out a playing card. He held it up so that everyone could see the intricate detail of the queen of hearts. As the woman holding the card opened her eyes, the rest of the group let out a gasp of relief mixed with pity. She had not looked at her own card before showing it to Damian, but it was obvious that she too held the queen of hearts.

The woman did not cry. She did not shout or yell and she did not beg to be spared. In that moment, she felt a surprising and overwhelming sense of relief, because despite the fact that death was imminent, her harrowing ordeal was about to come to an end.

While others around her pleaded with Damian not to take her life, she remained silent. As the gas began to pour into the room, robbing them of their senses, she simply smiled back at him. In that moment, she was ready to die.

*****

It was almost noon the following day, when Gabrielle finally woke. As she observed her unfamiliar surroundings, the events of the night before came flooding back to her. She looked over to where Damian had fallen asleep beside her, but he was nowhere to be seen.

Her head throbbed under the weight of an unusually heavy hangover. She could not understand it. Champagne was her poison of choice and besides the cocktail which Damian had made for her before she fell asleep, she had not mixed her drinks.

Rubbing her forehead and rising unsteadily to her feet, she walked out of the room, through the hall and into the living area where she found Damian. He was wearing nothing but a small pair of running shorts. His tanned, tattooed body was circling a mannequin in the corner of the room. As Gabrielle approached, she noticed that the mannequin had been made in his image. However, he was now defacing it. He had begun smearing red and black paint about its face and body.

"This is my latest piece," said Damian. He did not raise his head to acknowledge her as he continued his frenzied painting. "I'm going to call it 'the demonising'," he continued. "It represents a man's struggle to save his own soul, as it slowly slips into darkness and evil."

"Wow!" said Gabrielle, impressed by his creative genius. She had read that the collector had started his career as an artist, and she found it incredibly attractive to watch him at work. "You're a talented little devil, aren't you?"

Damian's head did not shift from his beloved mannequin, but his eyes momentarily flashed in her direction. "You have no idea," he said smirking. His smile was laced with the devious treachery of a cunning fox.

Their conversation was disturbed by the loud ding of the elevator. Quarter had called Jake's cell before Gabrielle had awoken, to ensure that it was appropriate to enter the apartment. He came bounding into the room and placed a note in Damian's hand.

"The lady who called said she's been trying to reach you for days," said Quarter. "She said it was urgent and that I had to make sure you got this right away."

Damian read the note and smiled. "I'm sorry Gabi but it looks like I'm going to have to leave you," he said candidly. "I've been asked to meet with the police to help with an important investigation."

Chapter 9
Heartless

The 'beast with two backs' double murder had been sensationalised by the press, sparking public paranoia. The unknown menace had already earned himself the name 'Ladykiller', and the NYPD was coming under increasing pressure to throw a net over this case and bring him to justice before he struck again.

Jake had arranged a mid-morning meeting with Felicity at the Brown Bean Café. The quirky coffee house had become known as the 'Blue Bean', on account of its close proximity to Police Plaza. It was a popular meeting place for officers passing the baton between shifts, and detectives working over the details of their latest case. Felicity had relished the chance to get closer to Jake, and help him piece together a profile of the killer, and in recent days, the coffee shop had become their regular meeting place.

The information that had come to light about the first two victims had already given Jake a powerful insight into the Ladykiller's world. There were striking similarities between the women, both of whom had enjoyed an extremely privileged upbringing. Their social habits and daily routines had earned them a reputation as 'Socialites', a title given to women who moved in very wealthy circles and used their looks to attach themselves to rich and powerful men.

It did not take long for Jake to realise that women like these presented an excellent target for the Ladykiller. With no employment to speak of, they were able to drop everything at a moment's notice to accompany their high-flying suitors to exotic locations around the world. Vanishing acts had become such a common occurrence, that their friends and family members had shown little concern when the two women had disappeared without a trace.

The killer had been hunting in the rich man's game reserve, and found himself the perfect prey. However, in doing so he had showed Jake his hand. Even as a man who had inherited a small fortune as the son of a sporting legend, Jake had hit a brick wall when he tried to penetrate the affluent Socialite circle and ask questions. Entry to the big league could not be bought, it was by invitation only. So, the Ladykiller had to be on the inside. He had to be one of them.

"It all makes perfect sense to me," said Felicity, adding weight to Jake's theory. "Artistic creativity with a flair for literature and a taste for the eccentric, fits the profile of a well-educated and wealthy man. But what really has me convinced that this guy has money, is the way he seems to trivialise murder." She paused to sip her iced chai tea latte through a plastic straw before continuing.

"I'm not saying that every man with money is a homicidal maniac of course, but it's as though he kills to entertain others and amuse himself at the same time. It's as if he thinks he's above the law, and this mentality is something I've seen before, with super rich guys who believe they can buy their way out of any situation."

Jake was impressed beyond words. He could not have hoped for a better partner to brainstorm with. Felicity shared his vision and his intuition, which was something he could not say for many of the detectives in his department. As he prepared to delve deeper into her thoughts, they were interrupted by a loud commotion.

All around the café, officers slowly clambered to their feet, clutching their radios as news of a serious crime hit the airwaves. One by one, each officer turned to stare at Jake, and he could tell by their expression that there had been another murder.

"It's him," said Jake. "It's the Ladykiller!"

Felicity wanted to offer words of encouragement, but as she looked across the table, she could see nothing but frustration in his eyes. A fresh crime scene would provide more clues to the killer's identity, but Jake could not disguise his disappointment at allowing another victim to die.

"I guess this means goodbye for now," said Jake. As he rose from his seat and prepared to leave, Felicity grabbed hold of his hand. She had acted on impulse, trying to stall for time while she worked out how she was going to ensure that they met again soon.

"How about we continue this meeting at my place?" Jake did not speak, he simply stared back at her giving no clue as to whether he would accept or decline the offer.

Felicity's face turned bright red. There was no hiding her embarrassment. She immediately regretted her spontaneous invitation and was about to retract it, when an officer came over and interrupted them.

"I think you should hear this," said the officer, handing Jake his radio.

The radio message indicated that a body had been found. The victim was a Caucasian female, brown hair, approximately late twenties, identity still unknown. She had been discovered in a deserted abattoir.

Jake handed back the radio and thanked Felicity for her time, before making a swift exit. He left her licking the wounds of rejection, but despite the obvious chemistry between them, he was determined not to break his own rules and let their relationship become personal. He stormed out of the Blue Bean and headed to his car, and within minutes he was on his way to the crime scene, in the heart of the stylish and fashionable area known as the Meat Packing District.

The district had become a centre for leisure, art and fashion. The streets were awash with high quality restaurants, designer shopping boutiques, luxury hotels and art galleries.

However, the area was once a hub of industrial activity, and its name stemmed from the hundreds of slaughterhouses that used to line its streets.

The Baxter Meat Company was one of the oldest slaughterhouses in the district, and unfortunately it was the latest casualty of the worst recession in modern times. The disused building was also the canvas of choice for the Ladykiller's latest work of art.

As Jake arrived, he could see a small group of officers congregating outside the building. He could tell that they had been inside. Their faces looked as grey as the shabby walls of the morbid meat factory.

He walked straight past the haggle of police without saying a word, and on towards a dishevelled-looking street sweeper who was sitting on a wall just a few yards away. The man was shaking and staring down at his feet, trying to avoid eye contact with anyone. Jake could tell by his demeanour that this was the man who had made the gruesome discovery.

"How are you buddy?" said Jake, attempting to build a rapport, and set the man at ease. "I'm Jake. Can I get your name?"

The timid young man did not look up. He mumbled his name under his breath, vigorously rubbing his hands on his pocket cloth, as though he was trying to remove the skin from his palms.

"Wa...Walter Walker, sir." As he replied, his lips began to tremble and a single tear ran down his cheek.

"Well, Walter, it's a brave thing you did, calling the cops. I've seen guys walk away from scenes like that, afraid of the responsibility of raising the alarm. That girl's family will be really grateful to you for what you did here today. But I'm gonna need you to help me out a little by telling me what you saw."

Walter's expression changed immediately. He wiped the tears from his face and looked up at Jake, buoyed by his words of praise, and empowered by the sense of purpose that had been bestowed upon him.

"Well it was the right thing to do, ya know," replied Walter. "I walk up and down dees alleys with my cart on the regular, I know em like the back o' my hand man. So, I juss knew suttin' was up when I seen how dat side door was juss swingin'. It was wide open. Buildin' been empty fo' weeks now, so I figures somebody done broke in. Don't know what made me wanna look inside. Juss curious I guess."

"Well that was real courageous of you, Walter," said Jake, flattering him in the hope that he would provide more detail. "Did you happen to see anyone enter or leave the factory?"

Walter looked down at the cobbled pavement, trying to recollect the passage of events that took place less than an hour before. "Nah, man, I didn't see nobody 'part from dat dead girl in there. Soon as I seen what I saw, I juss ran out. I was gonna call 911, then I seen dat officer over there and told him everythin'. Right after dat y'all juss started showin' up. Dat's it, man, I can't tell you nuttin' else."

Walter was still traumatised and a little confused, but Jake believed him. He was sure that the killer had long gone by the time Walter had stumbled across the body on his cleaning rounds.

The alley that ran down the side of the slaughterhouse was a filthy hive of activity by night. Bums with their blankets and cardboard boxes wrestled for a place to sleep. Dealers ducked out of the streetlight to make a swift transaction, and hookers unbuckled belts and shuffled down pants to give oral pleasure, in exchange for a few bucks.

As Jake dipped under the yellow tape and walked down the alley towards the service entrance, the rotten stench of the night before still hung in the air, a reminder that even this fabulous district had its dark spots.

Inside the abattoir it was cold and damp. The white tiled walls and rubber lined floors were stained with the blood of the thousands of animals that had been slaughtered and processed in the large ground floor warehouse. Conveyor belts and huge steel appliances stood inanimate, no longer churning over at the hands of the workers for whom this place had been home for eight hours a day, five days a week. How did they cope with the stench? Jake gagged as the pungent odour of dead animal flesh filled his nostrils.

There was no sign of life on the factory floor, but to the rear of the room, smoke billowed through sheets of transparent plastic that hung in the doorway, obscuring the view of what lay beyond. The frosty mist suggested that the freezer fans had been activated. Jake guessed that the doorway led to the chill room, where carcasses were once hung and preserved.

As he walked cautiously towards the entrance, the whirling hum of the fans grew louder and the chill became sharper. He whipped back the strips of plastic and as he walked through the icy fog he could see six large shapes dangling from meat hooks in the centre of the room. The report had said one woman had been found, and Walter had only referred to one victim, so who or what were the other shapes strung up next to her?

Jake's confusion was short lived. When he was just a few feet away, he saw that the five shapes hanging next to the victim were lambs. They had been skinned and bled before being brought to the site, hinting once again that the Ladykiller must have used a large vehicle to transport his victims, along with numerous props, to the scene of his heinous crime. As he stared at their faces, their big black eyes looked like marbles against their flayed pink flesh.

Five lambs hung next to a sixth body, the Ladykiller's third victim. He had officially reached serial killer status and this murder looked even more vicious than his first. The large pool of blood on the concrete floor directly beneath her body suggested that she had been killed at the scene. She had been hung from her back, with the hook entering her body just below her right shoulder blade. It would no doubt have pierced a lung, causing her excruciating pain. She would have choked on her own blood, while also being subjected to the killer's torturous attentions.

There were splatters of moist, fresh blood on both the ground and on the wall over thirty feet away from the body, suggesting that the killer had repeatedly stabbed and hacked at her with incredible force. The body was an unrecognisable wreck of lacerations and open wounds. It appeared that she had been torn apart with an extremely sharp blade and the main focus of the killer's attention had been her rib cage, which now hung in tattered strands around a gaping hole that was once her left breast. As Jake looked closer, he could see that the cavity in her chest was empty. Her heart had been torn from her body, and was nowhere to be seen.

For a moment he questioned whether or not this was the work of the Ladykiller. The first double murder was inventive and original. Had it not been for the obvious downside of fatality, it could have been considered the work of an artistic genius.

However, this looked more like the crazy frenzied attack of a mad man. It lacked the finesse that Jake had been expecting. Was he mistaken? Was this just another impulsive vengeance killing by a one-off amateur? His questions were swiftly answered when he spotted the Ladykiller's hallmark, a red and enflamed area on the victim's left hand, on which the number 666 had been etched.

Jake could almost taste the evil in the air. He flinched suddenly, turning sharply to see if someone had joined him, but there was nobody there. What was this silent eerie energy that had crept into the room? Had the Grim Reaper finally arrived to claim his prize?

Jake searched his pocket for his toothpick. The small splinter of wood was his way of reconnecting with reality, and recovering his focus. He placed it on his tongue, and rolled it around his mouth, then he pulled a pair of rubber gloves out of his pocket and placed one on each of his hands, before gripping the dead woman's left arm. As he did so, he noticed a small card stuck to her hand. He plucked it from her palm and held it up to the light. It was a playing card, the queen of hearts, stained with blood. His thoughts raced as he tried to piece together the relevance of the card, but unlike the tobacco at the first crime scene, no clever wordplay sprang to mind.

Realising that he had not yet inspected the victims face, Jake lifted back her hair. He expected to see more carnage, but was surprised to see that her face had been left untouched. He could not help but notice that she bore a startling resemblance to the first two victims, convincing him that this was definitely the work of the Ladykiller.

Tall, attractive brunettes ranging from late twenties to mid-thirties seemed to be his prey of choice. But why such a contrast between the two killings, and what the hell had he done with this poor woman's heart?

Jake glanced around again, and noticed a large stainless-steel walk-in freezer in the far corner of the room. He paced over to the door, released the locking leaver and pulled it open before walking inside.

As the frosty mist cleared, he could see that the freezer was completely empty besides a small steel table. In the centre of the table, pale and speckled with frost, was a lump of frozen flesh. It was the victim's heart. Placed next to the heart was a hand-written note.

Jake walked gingerly towards the table, until he was close enough to read what was written on the small scrap of paper.

"Her heart was as cold as ice, and I was willing to sacrifice."

"Of course!" said Jake out loud. Lambs, goats and rams were all animal associated with blood sacrifices.

The five lambs were a clue as to the nature of this killing. It was a sacrificial murder, but a sacrifice in whose honour? Had all three women been killed as a blood offering to the devil?

That would make sense, thought Jake. The demonic symbolism on the left hand of the victims and the shameless disregard for the sanctity of human life could well be the hallmarks of devil worship.

There were still so many questions left to answer, but the Ladykiller had left a treasure trove of new clues for Jake, and he intended to put every last detail under the microscope.

Back at the station, Jake delivered his findings to the team in an emergency briefing. As he spoke, the faces of a handful of clueless detectives stared back at him, occasionally pitching in with ideas of little merit. Jake tried hard to conceal his arrogance, but both his tone and demeanour suggested that he did not deem them worthy of contributing to a serious case, involving such a complex and intelligent killer. They were just talking heads. Nodding, blinking and gabbling, but offering nothing of true value.

Jake did not need forensics to confirm a time of death to know that the victim had not been dead long. The area of the Meat Packing District where the slaughterhouse was located would have been way too chaotic on a Saturday night to pass through inconspicuously in a high sided vehicle, so the killing must have taken place when the streets were clearing just before dawn. So, Jake suggested that a team of officers take to the streets surrounding the Baxter building and question anyone who would have been working in the early hours, who may have seen a van parked up or cruising the area. It would be several hours until the woman's dental records would confirm her identity, so another team was tasked with trying to obtain this information ahead of the autopsy report.

The Real Time Crime division had been called down to take notes in the hope that they may be able to pull down useful information from their vast criminal database that may help with the investigation. These intelligence analysts lived on the eighth floor, and anyone who wished to call upon their expertise normally made the trip up to their department. The fact that Abrahams had pulled them into the meeting proved that he meant business. Jake had a lot of faith in the Real Time team, and he was quick to provide them with any intelligence that might put them on the right track.

As the briefing continued behind closed doors, a smartly dressed man made his way up Park Row before walking through the large double doors of Police Headquarters. He glanced around the lobby at the dozens of uniformed officers darting off in all directions. They were all part of the big blue machine. Yet they were blissfully unaware that the city's most wanted killer was now stood in their midst.

Damian strolled over to the main desk and was greeted by the bubbly receptionist.

"Hello, sir, can I help you?" she said, smiling politely.

"Yes, you can, Penny," replied Damian, reading the name badge on her breast. "I'm here to see Jake Cannon. Can you let him know I'm here?"

"I can try," replied Penny, blushing under the pressure of Damian's intense gaze as she dialled up to the homicide department. "Who shall I say is here to meet him, sir?"

Damian could not help but smile. His face was all over every news stand in the city, yet nobody in the lobby, including the young receptionist appeared to recognise him. He could not resist the opportunity to let the cat loose amongst the pigeons, and set the tongues wagging among Jake's colleagues.

"Tell him Damian is here to see him...Damian Cannon."

Chapter 10
The Pandorium

Damian and Jake walked side by side through the pristine white halls of the Labirinto Gallery, reunited for the first time in over a decade. It felt like only yesterday that they had been young boys, blessed with talent and opportunity. Yet circumstance, like a cruel fairy-tale curse, had stolen their innocence and condemned them both to grief and mental anguish.

Shortly after the unexpected death of their father, Elsie Cannon had turned to drugs and alcohol to help dull the pain of losing her husband. It was not long before her will to recover subsided and she disappeared late one night, leaving her teenage sons to fend for themselves, without a goodbye or a farewell embrace.

Jake had been inconsolable. He had loved his father, but he idolised his mother and could not understand why she had abandoned them. Within a year he had dropped out of music school and spent months on the streets of New York, desperately trying to find her. He left no stone unturned as he searched every filthy, depraved and corrupt corner of the city.

Before long, the cruel and unforgiving world that he had been sheltered from as a child became his own. The privileged life he left behind no longer had substance and meaning. He never found his mother, but what he did find on those streets was a sense of true purpose. At the age of twenty, he joined the force and immediately began to show signs that he would be an exceptionally gifted officer. With a gun and a badge, he became justice personified, determined to right everything that he felt was wrong with his beloved New York.

Damian in contrast had felt only bitterness and anger when the family had collapsed. Jake had always been the apple of his mother's eye, and his father's treasured first-born son who could do no wrong. Damian on the other hand, had always seen himself as the unwanted outsider.

As Damian held a thousand grudges imprisoned behind pursed lips, his eyes told Jake everything that he needed to know about the resentment and rage burning within his heart. Damian had neither forgiven, nor forgotten, and now Jake began to weaken under the weight of his own guilt. As the two men stood locked in a tense and ugly silence, Jake felt an overwhelming urge to apologise.

"I'm sorry, Damian," he said, floundering as he searched for the words that would convey his sincerity. "For years I've acted as if you didn't exist. I didn't try to find you or contact you. In fact, when I joined the homicide team I convinced myself that I was protecting you by keeping my distance. But the truth is that we were never close, and that was my fault. I pushed you away Damian and I can only imagine how alone that made you feel. I can't turn back the clock. All I can do is tell you how sorry I am, and hope that you can forgive me."

Damian's head turned slowly, as he shifted his gaze from a framed exhibit to face his brother. He felt no love for him and forgiveness was not in his nature. His heart had become a cold and unforgiving wasteland where such emotions as love and compassion simply did not exist.

"Save your apologies for the families of those dead girls, Jake," replied Damian spitefully. "After all, the investigation is why you've contacted me isn't it? I'm guessing you've painted a picture of the killer in your head, and you want to call upon my expertise to help you put the finishing touches to the image you have created. Am I right?"

"You're absolutely right," said Jake. "I want to crack this case so bad it keeps me awake at night. But that's not why I asked to meet you." He turned to look at some of the priceless works of art that Damian had collected from around the world. He had built an empire, and Jake felt a genuine sense of pride for his brother's achievements. "Look at all of this," he continued. "Look at what you've created. I read that article in My Style magazine and I was amazed by all of the things you've done. Whether you choose to believe it or not, I am proud of you."

Jake held out an open palm, hoping that he would reciprocate with a handshake. However, Damian ignored the outstretched hand and gave a wry smirk.

"I've waited a long time to hear those words from you, brother," said Damian, faking sincerity in order to lure Jake into a false sense of security. "For years, I delayed my return to New York because I have always felt the need to impress you. I watched you from afar, progressing through the ranks as a cop on these tough streets. You've achieved so much in your career that I simply could not return until I was certain that you would look at me and see someone who was worthy of your praise."

Damian could see that his cunning attempts to attack his brother's ego were working. Jake liked to be in control, and the idea that someone had been keeping an eye on him from a distance did not sit well with him.

"With all my power and connections, I was able to track your progress from vice to homicide," continued Damian, gunning for a reaction. "Then there was that mess with your old partner, what was his name…Gant?"

Jake did not respond. He simply looked at Damian with a steely glare. If he lost his temper, he would not get the answers he so desperately needed, so he could not take the bait. He had to remain calm.

"Yeah that was a real bad time for you," continued Damian. "Then, of course, there was the letter from mom two years later, to say that she only had weeks to live! The news of her passing broke my heart, but I know how close you two were. It must have destroyed you!"

Damian knew that Jake was close to breaking point, but as much as he enjoyed toying with him, he was determined to find out if Jake was close to uncovering the truth. In order to do so, Damian would have to conceal his burning hatred under the illusion of forgiveness, and convince Jake that he really did want to help.

Without warning, Damian grabbed hold of Jake and locked him into a tight embrace. As the two men hugged for the first time since their youth, a wave of mixed emotions washed over Jake. He felt more like a child being re-assured by the comforting arms of a father, than a man being reunited with his younger brother.

"We can't let the past come between us any longer," said Damian, leading him through the Labyrinth and towards the central exhibition hall. "Come brother, there are lots of things you must see, and even more we must discuss if I'm going to help you catch this sick son of a bitch!"

The two men continued on through the maze, and while Damian listened intently, Jake broke everything down. From his observations at both crime scenes, to his theories on the killer's wealth and social circles. Jake gave Damian every last detail, in the hope that it would enable him to shed some light on the killer's methods and motives.

When they reached the heart of the gallery, Jake briefly cast an eye over the haunting poisoned apple collection, before focussing his gaze on the large heavenly canvas in the centre of the room.

"The pearly gates?" he said quizzically. "It seems a little out of place in Blackwell's dark collection."

"This is not part of the poisoned apple collection," replied Damian. "This is the first of a trio of paintings depicting the three dimensions of the afterlife. heaven, hell…and Jabula."

"Jabula?" said Jake. Perhaps this was just another name for purgatory? Although Jake decided not to show his ignorance by raising the question, Damian still proceeded to shed light on the subject.

"There is a small group of people who have a very rare system of beliefs concerning the afterlife," said Damian. "They believe that while the righteous ascend to heaven, hell is in fact a middle ground. Jabula, the third realm, is reserved only for those wicked enough to earn a place at the devil's table. In Jabula there is no punishment. Only reward for sinful deeds!"

Jake was not a man of any defined faith, but Damian had touched on a point of great interest. Perhaps the connection between art and religion ran deeper than Jake had ever considered. The 666 on the left hand of the victims was still a mystery, and he now hoped that his brother could help him crack the code behind the Ladykiller's biblical references.

"Do you see the worlds of art and religion crossing over often?" said Jake, urging him to provide yet more detail.

"Crossing over?" said Damian. He laughed, pointing around the room. "Art and religion are one in the same. Look around you, Jake. People put on their best attire and come here to give thanks and praise to their idols. Some will even put their hands in their pockets and fill my collection box as they try to buy their way into paradise. The gallery is their church, and I am their priest. Can I get an amen?"

Jake laughed, but perhaps Damian's analogy was not far from the truth. Maybe there was a crossover between the two worlds. Perhaps the killer also believed in the existence of Jabula, and the sacrificial murders were his bid for an invitation to dine with the devil. Just moments ago, such ideas had seemed too far-fetched to Jake, but now it dawned on him that these radical concepts did not have to be true, for someone as sick and twisted as the Ladykiller to embrace them.

As Damian showed him the remainder of the collection, Jake began to understand the true power of art. With a paintbrush, colours and a canvas, an artist could communicate the most powerful message, without uttering a single word. But while Blackwell's message about the decaying city was clear, the Ladykiller's message was still obscured by shadow.

"I'm convinced that our man is an artist," said Jake. "But I just can't figure out exactly what he's trying to tell us with his graphic murders."

"The hardest question to answer is always the most important," replied Damian. "You still have no idea 'why' he is he killing these women. What is it he wants you to see? What is he so desperate for you to understand?"

Damian was right yet again thought Jake. In order to capture the killer, he needed to understand him. What made him tick, what inspired him and what had driven him to commit murder?

"I've played around with so many ideas," said Jake. "The only possibility I'm left with is that he's some sort of sexual deviant. The long brown hair and the tall slender figure is a running theme. The similarity between all three victims tells me that he definitely has a 'type', so I think he selects his women based on physical desire. Something about the way they look draws him in. Perhaps he's some sort of sadomasochist."

Damian could feel his face tightening into a grimace. He simply could not understand how such an intelligent and resourceful detective had come to the conclusion that the Ladykiller was little more than a pervert. To Damian, each murder he committed was a masterpiece in its own right, inspired by circumstance and intended to deliver a meaningful message. The very suggestion that he had been motivated by sexual deviance offended him deeply.

Now it was Damian's turn to try and keep his cool. His eyes were like two dazzling red flames as he fought the urge to explode into a torrent of abuse. He would have to demonstrate just how weak his brother's theory was, and he decided that he would do so by opening Jake's eyes to the tantalizing truth about the so-called pleasure principle.

"Come with me, big brother!" said Damian, taking his cell phone from his pocket to call Quarter and instruct him to ready the car for their departure.

They set off back through the labyrinth and took the elevator down to the ground floor. By the time they reached the liquid lobby, Quarter was already waiting to see them out of the building and into the shimmering Maybach.

"Where are we going?" asked Jake inquisitively.

Damian smiled with fiendish amusement, like a child who was about to open a gift that was meant for someone else.

"I am taking you to the Pandorium," he replied, laughing to himself as he imagined Jake's reaction at what he was about to experience. "I have to admit, I'm excited for you, Jake!"

As the car pulled up at the entrance minutes later, Jake began to feel uneasy. The Pandorium was an exclusive gentleman's club, with less than fifty members. The reason for the small number of patrons was simple. Of the few people who could afford the astronomical membership fee, even fewer had the stomach for what went on inside. While Jake had no idea what to expect, the anticipation alone put him on edge. He imagined Abraham's raised eyebrow and stern expression as he explained that a lead in the case had brought him to a glorified strip club for the super-rich, in the middle of the afternoon.

"Settle down, Cannon," he muttered himself as he got out of the car behind Damian. "This is work, and you've seen and done a hell of a lot worse in the line of duty!"

From the outside, the building looked small and unassuming. The entrance was sandwiched between a fancy cocktail bar and an oyster restaurant. There was no name above the red door, only a big brass knocker which had been crafted to look like the head of a wolf. Damian grabbed the knocker and pounded it against the wolf's jaw, and as the door opened with a loud creak, Jake recognised the security guard immediately.

Mike Travis, was a former line backer for the New York Jets. He was destined for greatness until two serious knee ligament injuries put him out of the game. When Jake caught him with two hookers and two ounces of cocaine in the back of his jeep in broad daylight back in his days as a vice detective, Travis made front page news. He lost his job in the commentary box and now it appeared he was making a living standing in doorways looking mean.

As soon as Travis caught sight of Jake, his row of gold teeth crept out from behind a pair of dry lips, as he grinned with satisfaction. The Pandorium was a private venue and he could deny entry to anyone who was not welcome inside at his discretion. If Jake was there on official police business,

Travis would insist on seeing a warrant and do everything he could to make it difficult for him to enter, and Jake knew it.

"Welcome to the Pandorium, sir," said Travis, greeting Damian with the courtesy expected of staff addressing a member. "May I see your membership card?"

"Of course," replied Damian. He pulled a small metal plaque no larger than a business card from his pocket, and Jake noticed that there was no writing or numbering on it. It was blank save for an embossed wolf insignia which matched the knocker on the front door. Travis examined the plaque and waved him inside. As Jake went to follow behind him, Travis held out one of his thick arms, stopping him dead in his tracks.

"Members only, Mr Cannon," said Travis. "So, unless you have a membership card, I'm gonna have to refuse you entry." His tongue lashed out from between his teeth and lapped at the ridiculous gold grill, which he no doubt wore to add even more menace to his large frame. He was clearly enjoying the fact that the balance of power had swung in his favour. However, before Jake had time to respond, Damian stepped in to impose his authority.

"You must be new here," said Damian, frowning at Travis with evident distaste. "My name is Mr Burgundy and I hold a premium membership. Mr Cannon is my guest, and he will be joining me today."

Travis' demeanour changed instantly. He may not have met Damian before, but the mention of the name Burgundy filled him with dread. He bowed his head in shame, afraid to look Damian in the eyes and trembling as he spoke. "Please accept my apology, Mr Burgundy, I had no idea! Step inside, gentlemen, I am very sorry if I've caused either of you any offence." He welcomed them both inside, closing the door behind them.

"Well I'll be damned," said Jake, laughing at the ease with which Damian had made Travis change his tune. "When you told him your name, it put the fear of God in him."

"Not God, Jake," replied Damian. "God could not afford premium membership!"

The two men laughed as they made their way down the long narrow flight of stairs and into a large hexagonal shaped room, where they were greeted by an exotic looking woman. She was naked apart from a pair of gold heels and several patches of glitter which covered her breasts and groin. Her jet-black hair was braided into one long ponytail which ran down her spine and ended just above the dimples in the small of her back. Even in the dim light, Jake could see that there was not a single blemish on her dark skin. She could not have been more than twenty-five, but she carried herself with the powerful confidence of a woman more senior in years.

"Hello, gentlemen, my name is Onyx, and I would like to welcome you to the Pandorium." As she spoke, Jake's eyes were fixed on the watery gloss of her plump pink lips. The apprehension he had felt moments earlier had vanished. Even the Ladykiller case had momentarily slipped from his mind. He was totally caught in the moment, mesmerised by the beauty and elegance of the host.

Onyx pointed to a number of doorways, obscured by red silk curtains. "There are six doors, and every one leads to pleasure in abundance," she explained. "A tantalising feast to satisfy your appetites lies beyond each curtain, so simply choose your path and embark on a journey through the depths of your wildest fantasy."

Damian did not hesitate. He removed his jacket and handed it to Onyx before walking over to the second doorway, with the demeanour of a man who knew exactly what was in store.

"May I take yours too, sir?" She smiled at Jake as she offered to relieve him of his jacket, but he refused politely. Although the temperature was rising in the unusual subterranean club, Jake did not wish to cause alarm by revealing the gun which he had holstered to his chest.

Onyx's perfectly round buttocks swayed rhythmically as she turned on her heels and walked over to the second doorway and whipped back the curtain, before ushering them both into the narrow passageway.

Suddenly, the mood became notably more sensual. The lighting was tinted with a subtle rainbow of neon illumination and on both flanks of the passageway, women lay bathing in roll-top baths covered in bubbles and rose petals, suggestively caressing their silk smooth bodies as they swayed seductively to the trippy down-tempo melodies that hummed through the sound system.

As Jake passed one of the baths, a petite woman reached out and gently stroked his face. "Would you like to rub me down?" she said in a sultry tone. She pulled a sponge from beneath the water and squeezed it dry before handing it to Jake. He stood speechless, looking her up and down as she rose up from beneath the bubbles to face him, jutting out her chest so that her pert breasts were directly in his line of vision.

Jake would happily have given her a sponge bath. For the first time in as long as he could recall, he was not thinking or acting like a cop. This was Jake Cannon the human being, submitting to curiosity.

"You are welcome to indulge her," said Damian, who had walked into the room at the end of the hall and then returned to see what had caused Jake to stop short. "However, I promise you that what is waiting in the next room will eclipse whatever Mai Ling here has in mind for you."

Jake followed Damian through the door and into total darkness. As Jake's eyes adjusted to the lack of light, he was almost able to see the layout, although the dimensions of the room remained a mystery.

Just a few feet from the entrance, he could just about make out a series of small steps leading down to a sunken seating area which consisted of a large round black leather sofa, with a glass table nestled in the centre. A solitary candle sat on the table, providing a subtle hint of light.

"There are six fantasy chambers here," said Damian, his eyes glowing with excitement against the dark setting. "This is my favourite chamber. It's called 'the ring of fire', and in a few minutes, you'll see why."

Jake followed him cautiously down the steps and as they fell into the soft leather sofa, Damian explained that the design of the seating area in his own apartment had been inspired by the chamber's circular theme.

Without warning a burst of flame shot up behind Damian, and traced its way around the perimeter of the sunken area until an entire ring of flame approximately six inches high flickered and burned around them. "Impressive, isn't it," said Damian, studying Jake's expression.

Jake did not respond. He was too busy absorbing his strange new surroundings and soaking up the ambiance.

Damian waved his hand in the air and a figure emerged from the dense darkness behind him. She stepped over the ring of fire, in a pair of red heels. She bowed her head towards Damian who was seated directly beneath where her slender and completely naked body was now stood, and handed them a small leather backed book containing a selection of drinks.

"I'm in the mood for something bitter sweet," said Damian playfully. "I'll have three shots of your premium Vodka with fresh watermelon, and Jake will have a...Hendricks and tonic with a slice of cucumber."

Jake had not taken a drink for many years. He believed that anything which killed brain cells and tampered with his judgement could not be a good thing. Dangerous women with no strings attached had always been his one and only vice, and while he was prepared to convince himself that this visit to the Pandorium was all in the interest of the investigation, his will power would not falter where alcohol was concerned.

"Just the tonic for me please," replied Jake, overruling his brother's request. However, Damian was not about to take no for an answer. Tempting him off the wagon would be noted as another victory in his mission to corrupt Jake, and lure him down the path to self-destruction.

"Like fuck he will!" yelled Damian assertively. "He will have exactly what I requested."

She nodded her head obediently and then stepped back into the darkness from which she had emerged, while Damian continued his attempt to break down Jake's resolve.

"Have faith in me, Jake. By the time we leave this place, you will have made significant inroads towards a greater

142

understanding of your killer, this I promise you. But you have to trust me. You have to let go and slip into his world, and that includes breaking some of your precious rules."

Jake reluctantly bowed his head in agreement. He agreed to submit to Damian's agenda in the mistaken belief that it would help him crack the case. He still had no idea how this would end, or exactly what Damian was trying to prove, and now he had unwittingly placed his faith in a villain who sought to derail him.

The two men sat sipping drinks and chatting for almost half an hour, before Damian decided that it was time to reveal the chamber's true treasures. Without warning, he leaned forward and blew out the candle on the table. Within seconds, the ring of fire was also extinguished, plunging them into darkness once more.

"What's happening?" whispered Jake, feeling confused and slightly uneasy.

"Relax, brother," replied Damian. "You are about to find out."

From somewhere in the shadows, the faint "pitrang" of a guitar rose steadily until it was met by a low "thump" of bass. Then came the hissing "tusk" of a snare and finally, the repetitive "tock" of wood on hollow wood. Moments later, the rhythmic marriage was consummated by a soothing, yet almost masculine female vocal. Jake knew the song well. It had often been a source of comfort in dark times, when only thoughts of Angels would erase the faces of dead victims from his mind, as he sat alone on his moonlit mezzanine.

Suddenly, the chamber came to life as light beamed out from the florescent strips which framed six triangular alcoves set in the walls of the circular room. Sitting inside each alcove was a woman dressed in a hooded mink gown, which provided a vivid contrast with the ice white leather which lined the interior of their snug triangular nook.

Damian watched Jake closely. Would he embrace the moment and submit to his desire? He had no idea which way Jake would turn, but he could not wait any longer to find out.

"Choose a girl," said Damian. "I have arranged a private show. Each of these six women has a unique skill that they would love to share with you. All you have to do is pick one."

Jake was beyond the point of restraint. He was genuinely intrigued and accepted the offer without hesitation. He stared long and hard at each woman in turn, but they all wore hoods which hid their faces, so it would have to be left to chance.

"I choose her," said Jake, pointing at the woman sat directly opposite him. The florescent white light surrounding her turned red and she stepped out of the alcove and strutted over to the edge of the sunken seating area. The woman slipped the heavy mink gown off her shoulders, allowing it to drop down to her feet and reveal her exquisite bronze body. She was completely naked besides a pair of black leather stilettos with long gold heels and small gold toe caps. A thin gold chain with an emerald pendant hung from her hips and dangled just below her navel.

Her thick black hair was cut into a perfectly straight fringe which ran low across her forehead, hiding the mystery of her gaze as she looked down at her feet. Jake's heart beat quickened as his eyes traced a straight line from her chin, down her firm breasts which curved up to a point before sloping back towards her toned midriff, and then down towards her perfectly groomed paradise portal. Her labia hung invitingly above a heart shaped void between the two fleshy borders of her inner thighs.

As she lifted her head to look at Jake, her green eyes sparkled in the darkness with a brilliant clarity that matched the jewel in her navel pendant. She was one of the most perfect creatures he had ever laid eyes on.

"My name is Sheeba, and I welcome you to the ring of fire chamber." She stepped down to where they were seated, before taking Jake by the hand and leading him back up the steps towards a small hidden doorway between two of the triangular alcoves.

Jake followed Sheeba into an intimate little lounge lit with a red filter that reminded him of a photographer's darkroom. She gently pushed him onto a blood red sofa, before stepping back towards the rear wall upon which a large projector screen was mounted.

"Relax," she said, licking her cherry lips suggestively as she dropped down to her knees, and prowled on all fours like a panther through the thick black fur of the rug that covered the entire lounge floor.

Jake prided himself on being able to gage someone's origins from their accent and features, but there was something unusual about Sheeba. The unmistakable twang to her speech suggested that she was Latina, but the hint of Caribbean in her features and disposition had him convinced that she was from somewhere close to the islands, in the Northern tip of South America. Could she be Venezuelan?

Before he had time to pose the question, Sheeba clicked her fingers and a light beamed out from somewhere above his head onto the screen, projecting a black and white recording of two women cavorting on a four-poster bed. The women were both blindfolded, and moaned with satisfaction as they kissed and stroked each other's bodies with a fiery passion that Jake found incredibly arousing. Sheeba turned to face him. Her hypnotic green eyes totally engaged him, as she slowly parted her thighs, revealing the pearly conch of moist flesh between her legs.

Sheeba began gently rubbing her middle and index fingers over and around her button while Jake watched, barely blinking, completely mesmerised. She stroked harder and faster, casting a shadow over the projector as the two women in the background ran their hands over each other. Jake could hardly control the urge to reach out and touch her. He could feel the temptation coursing through his veins.

His vision became slightly blurred and as he looked back at the screen, the features of one of the women on the bed had changed. Her hair was dark and tied in a bob, and her face looked familiar to him. It was Felicity! He looked down at Sheeba, and once again it was Felicity's face staring back at him, smiling as she writhed and moaned with pleasure.

Jake sat bolt upright and rubbed his eyes before looking back once more at Sheeba and the screen behind her. The illusion had faded, and Felicity had vanished. Was it the liquor that had sent his mind and body into shock after years of abstinence?

At that same moment, Sheeba licked one finger before running it down her body and sliding it inside herself. One after the other, she continued to slip more fingers in and out. Then to Jake's amazement, she folded her thumb across her palm and slid her whole hand inside. She winced as she held both pleasure and pain in the balance for a few seconds, before clenching her hand into a paw, sending her pelvis bolting forward as her entire fist vanished down to her wrist.

Jake watched open mouthed as Sheeba writhed about on the rug, shrieking in a pitch that turned his stomach. Her groans sounded more like discomfort than ecstasy, and the expression on her face flitted back and forth between smiles of joyous rapture and the sickening grimace of agony.

He looked away, torn between feelings of deep desire and utter distaste towards Sheeba's explicit act. Part of him, the part he knew best, wanted to leave the Pandorium and never return. But there was also another part of him, lurking deep within his subconscious that wanted to ravage her like some savage sexual beast.

As Jake turned back to look at Sheeba once more, her legs began to spasm violently. Her screaming, lip quivering climax was perfectly synchronised with that of the two women on screen above her.

Sheeba slid her sopping hand free from its fleshy vice, and began to lick each finger in turn.

"Come and play," she said, giggling and still dazed from the effects of her powerful orgasm. "You can do whatever you want to me, I am all yours!"

She beckoned him to come closer, but Jake was in no mood to participate. The graphic intensity of the private show had disturbed him. He liked sexually confident and adventurous women, but Sheeba had gone too far.

Without saying a word, he leapt from his seat and stormed out of the room, and back into the chamber where his brother was waiting.

"How was she?" said Damian smirking in anticipation of intimate details.

"What the fuck was that all about, Damian?" said Jake, draining the contents of his glass, and pointing back towards the private lounge. "Is this some sort of sick joke? If so, I ain't laughing. I want to know why you brought me here!"

Damian's mouth curled into a smile. While it was always his intention to push the limits of taste and tolerance, he now sensed something else in Jake's demeanour. The detective was coming apart at the seams.

"I brought you here to prove my point," replied Damian calmly. He leaned forward and grasped Jake's hands firmly in his own, eager for him to absorb every last word. "Out there in the real world, women use sex to get ahead. But down here, we've simply re-set the balance of power. Only the most divine women are invited to join the Pandorium and for the right price, there is absolutely nothing they will not do to satisfy a man's deepest, darkest desires."

"I'm a cop!" yelled Jake. "You've compromised me by bringing me here."

"How?" said Damian. "No money changed hands between you and this woman, and what happens behind closed doors between two consulting adults is their business, am I not right?"

Jake fell back into the seat as the truth struck him with an incredible force. Damian was right. It would have been unacceptable in the eyes of his superiors, but he had not committed any crime. Furthermore, Damian has also proved his point regarding the Ladykiller. He was no sadomasochist. In places like the Pandorium, any fantasy could be satisfied for the right price, so if the killer had money as Jake suspected, he would not need to kidnap and kill women for sexual gratification.

Jake felt foolish. The killer was indeed a complex individual who would not fit into any of the conventional pigeon holes that he had tried to place him in. To catch him, Jake would have to dig deeper, and be far smarter, but there was something clouding his judgement and holding him back.

He had no idea what it was, but there was only one person who could help him overcome this hurdle. He would have to meet with Felicity, and empty his head of old demons, in the hope that she could help him regain his focus.

"I'm sorry, brother, I don't know why I reacted that way," said Jake apologising for his outburst. "Today you showed me a world with no boundaries where money can transform men into Gods. It's a secret world that exists here within the city I thought I knew, right under our noses, so close but yet totally out of reach to every day guys like me."

There was genuine excitement in his voice. The experience had left Jake shocked, but also invigorated. He was alive with the thrill of the Pandorium, bitten by what Damian's mentor Lucian Ferone had once referred to as the 'Serpent of Darkness'. It would not be long until he craved more exposure, and Damian was only too happy to give it to him.

As they left the club and walked out onto the busy sidewalk, Damian stepped into the Maybach, and gestured for Jake to join him.

"Thanks for the offer," said Jake. "But I need to clear my head before heading back to see the Captain, so I think I'll take the subway."

"No problem, Jake," replied Damian, waving through the open window. "Let's meet again soon. I'll take you to dinner."

The car rolled off before Jake had time to respond. Damian was feeling very pleased with himself. He activated the privacy partition in the Maybach so that Quarter would not hear his conversation, and then reached for his cellular phone to call the one person who would be glad to hear how his evil plot was unfolding. Damian scrolled down to the letter "L" and when he came to the name Lucian, he pressed the call button.

Meanwhile, as he marched off in the direction of the subway, Jake also took his cell phone from his pocket and swiftly made a call. After only four rings, a recording urged him to leave a message after the beep.

"Hi Felicity its Jake…when can we meet up, I really need to talk to you!"

Chapter 11
Iron Cast Hero

Felicity walked back into her lounge where she had left Jake just moments earlier, to find him flicking through a hardback from her bookshelf.

"Do you ever stop behaving like a cop?" she said, laughing out loud as she handed him a mug of piping hot coffee. "I leave you alone for two minutes and you are already looking through my stuff. Are you trying to piece together my profile now Detective Cannon?"

There was a hint of affection in his eyes as he smiled back at her. Jake was one of the most serious men she had ever met, but on the rare occasions when he smiled, Felicity found him irresistibly charming. He made no attempt to disguise his actions, and continued looking through her personal possessions.

Over the last few days, Jake had made several attempts to contact her. He finally concluded that she was refusing to respond following the embarrassing rejection at the Blue Bean Café. So, he decided to call her from a payphone on route to her apartment to confirm that he was on his way, and he arrived only minutes later. Yet despite the lack of prior warning, her home was still immaculate.

There was a lot to be said for a woman's touch thought Jake. She had only moved in a month earlier, but Felicity had already managed to transform the small shoebox of an apartment into a comfortable nest of warmth and relaxation. From the moment he set foot inside, he had been swaddled by the soft pastel colours, gentle textures and fresh floral aroma that he associated with clean living.

"I'm sorry for disturbing you so late, Felicity," said Jake, shunning her invitation to take a seat. "I hope you don't mind me coming to see you at home like this, but I really need to run something by you."

He put his coffee down on the table and pulled a scrap of paper from his trouser pocket and unfolded it before handing it to her. Felicity put on her reading glasses and looked at it long and hard. It was a copy of the hand-written note found next to the heart of the Ladykiller's third victim.

"Well I'm no handwriting analyst," said Felicity "but I would say he was a lefty judging by the smudges on the page. I'm guessing he wanted you to know he was a lefty too, because most people who write with their left curl their hand over the top of the page so that they don't smudge the ink."

Jake paced back and forth between the open window at the front of her lounge and the rocking chair resting against the wall at the back of the room.

"Exactly!" he shouted. "That's the first thing I noticed. I've been reading about myths surrounding the left hand all evening. Some people say that it's a blessing, a sign of creative genius. But did you know that in some parts of the world it is considered to be a sign of demonic possession? I even read that in some cultures they tie their kid's left hand behind their back, and beat them until they learn to use their right!"

Felicity could see that Jake was not himself. He seemed anxious, and his constant pacing began to make her feel nervous. He had obviously spotted the clues left within the killer's note, and did not need her to substantiate his theory. There was clearly something else bothering him, and she sensed that his spontaneous visit was more than just a brainstorming session. It was a cry for help.

"Please sit down, Jake." Felicity pointed towards the rocking chair. The gentle rocking had always helped her to relax, and she hoped that Jake would also find it soothing. "I want you to be honest with me," she continued. "You're not here to discuss the case, are you? There's something else you want to talk about, right?"

Jake did as he was commanded and slowly eased himself into the seat. He had felt a connection with Felicity back when they had first met in her office all those weeks ago. She understood him, and he was certain that she would be able to help. He had made up his mind that it was time to share the nightmare that had haunted him for so many years, in the hope that she could finally help bury the guilt he had been harbouring for so long.

He closed his eyes and pushed his feet into the thick chocolate brown carpet, gently rocking himself back and forth as he began explaining how it all started many years ago.

Back in his early twenties when Jake was working vice, he received an unexpected call from Abrahams advising him that Bobby Gant, the man regarded as homicide's number one detective, had refused to partner up with anyone in the department. Instead, Gant had filed a transfer recommendation for Jake to join the homicide team, and work along-side him.

Gant was a decorated Gulf War hero, but when a series of injuries led to a medical discharge from military service, he chose to join the NYPD. The police proved to be a natural progression, and his intimidating physique coupled with a militant approach to detective work, soon earned him the title 'Big Bobby Gant'. He was respected by his peers, and feared by anyone on the wrong side of the law.

It was not long before Gant's talent caught the attention of the ambitious Captain Eddie Castilian. Castilian brought him to homicide to partner up with another outstanding young detective, Ron Abrahams. Their bond was instant, and in the years that followed the city began to feel like a safer place under the watchful eye of Gant and Abrahams.

When Castilian was finally promoted, it was Gant who was earmarked to succeed him in his role as the Captain. However, Gant believed that he belonged in the field and not behind a desk, and even the prospect of a significant hike in salary could not lure him off the streets. So, it was Abrahams who seized the opportunity to progress, and as Captain, his first major call was to follow the recommendation of his former partner, and poach the vice department's rising young star, Jake Cannon.

"How did that make you feel, when Gant requested you above everyone else?" said Felicity. She kicked off her shoes and lifted her feet onto the sofa, making herself comfortable as Jake continued his detailed recollection.

"I was on top of the world," said Jake, reflecting back on his emotions at that time. "I was doing everything I could to get noticed, and suddenly the Captain of homicide told me I was the chosen one. It changed me. I honestly started to believe that I could become the best detective on the force."

It was a happy period in Jake's life, and his mood lifted as his thoughts drifted back to his golden era. He was already an excellent detective but Gant wanted to make him better, and he knew just how to get the best out of him. Before embarking on a voyage of edification, Gant insisted that Jake must first 'unlearn' everything he had already learned as a detective. By cleansing his mind of useless ideas and ineffective practices, he would be free to reinvent himself as the very model of efficiency and logic.

Within twelve months, Jake had conditioned his body to function on only four hours sleep a night, so that he could devote more time to his work. He began reading in his spare time, and was encouraged to reacquaint himself with the piano for the first time since his youth. Gant also insisted that he spent countless hours travelling in the back of taxi cabs, until he knew every street and side alley of the New York grid like the back of his hand.

Jake quit smoking and drinking, and maintained a strict diet. Gant suggested that he plan his meals in advance, insisting that a man who never decided what to eat when he was hungry, never choose junk food over a healthy nutritious meal. He took Jake running with him several times a week, and in turn, Jake taught him the art of boxing.

"Gant used to call us the Iron Cast Heroes" said Jake, laughing with embarrassment. "Hearing myself say that now sounds so stupid, but Bobby used to collect comic books as a hobby, and he also sketched cartoons in his spare time. He came up with the idea that we were like some sort of comic strip duo on a crusade against crime. It sounds ridiculous now, but back then it seemed so real. It made us inseparable."

It didn't sound stupid to Felicity. During her therapy sessions, she had often suggested drawing strength from fiction and fantasy. She could see how an imaginary superhuman status could help cops like Jake cope with the horrors they witnessed on a daily basis.

She was under no illusion that the man sitting in front of her had been forged in the fire of Gant's vision of an elite partnership. He had poured every part of himself into Jake, and created a protégé who was every bit his equal. However, the relationship had gone far beyond mutual professional respect. At some point, the two men had developed an affinity which was more akin to that of a father and son, than a master and his apprentice. Had Gant become the paternal figure that Jake had longed for since the tragic loss of his father?

"He loved you didn't he, Jake?" said Felicity. She was eager for him to go into even more detail. "Was there anyone else in his life at the time? A woman perhaps?"

"A cop with a weakness is a cop who can be exploited," said Jake, reciting his mentor's mantra in a mechanical manner. "He encouraged me to seek satisfaction from women, but he always said that I should never allow myself to develop feelings for them. He would tell me that a wife or kid could be a distraction during an investigation or worse still, they could be used against cops like us."

Jake smirked to himself, as though he was considering some hidden irony in the statement he had just made.

Felicity was fascinated by Jake's account of his relationship with Gant. Being a good listener was an occupational requirement, but for the first time for as long as she could remember, she was genuinely interested. She knew that somewhere beneath Jake's coarse exterior was a man capable of tenderness. If she could somehow make him see that connecting with his emotions did not make him weak, then perhaps he would finally release his guilt and let go of the past.

"It sounds like a happy time for you Jake," said Felicity. "So, what changed?"

Jake's brow dipped into a frown, as he stared into the empty cup clasped tightly in his hands.

"Do you have anything stronger than coffee?" he said. It had not been long since he had fallen off the wagon, and he was already craving the numbing effects of alcohol.

Felicity did not question his request, and disappeared momentarily before re-appearing with a bottle of Bourbon and a bowl of ice. She poured a healthy measure into two tumblers and dropped three ice cubes into each, before handing one to Jake.

Jake tilted his head back and glugged down the entire contents of the glass, beating his chest like a Silverback and coughing as the drink scorched his throat. Many years ago, he had always taken his bourbon with a mixer, so he had underestimated the kick of the sweet-scented neat liquor.

"My mother always used to say, be careful what you wish for," said Jake, slowly settling himself back into the rocking chair. "Well she was right," he continued. "I had spent years sharpening my tools and I was desperate to put them to use, but it was peacetime. Murder rates were down and the term 'serial killer' was something old folks said to scare young children out of misbehaving. In the real world, they were all but extinct. So, part of me was glad when we got the call that day. I was finally going to put my new-found skills to the test, but nothing could have prepared me for what I saw one afternoon in November. The 'Boogie Man' was real, and he was on the loose in New York."

Felicity trembled as the cold chill of terror flowed through her body, like a ghost tip toeing silently across her grave. She knew at once who Jake was referring to. It was a story that had dominated the media for weeks. Back then, before the dozens of homicidal psychopaths that Jake had put behind bars, before the Hangman and before the Ladykiller, there was one man who had redefined the word 'fear' for an entire generation. His real name was Vladimir Volkoff, but he would forever be remembered as 'The Impaler'.

Vladimir Volkoff was the son of a ballerina from Moscow by the name of Katerina, who married an American folk singer when Vladimir was in his teens. Having re-located to America with his new family, Vladimir developed a love affair with photography, working freelance for several magazine publications.

However, his life was turned upside down in 2009, when his mother was embroiled in a huge scandal involving former Soviet nationals accused of secretly working as spies for the Kremlin while posing as repatriated American citizens. The world around Vladimir swiftly fell apart as his mother was hunted down by the C.I.A and subjected to a torturous programme of interrogation which eventually claimed her life. Overcome by grief, Vladimir became a bitter and twisted recluse. In 2011 he finally snapped under the strain of his rage and sought to exact bloody vengeance against the nation that had vilified his beloved mother.

The frightful memories all came flooding back as Jake recalled the sickening discovery of Vladimir's first victim, a woman in her mid-twenties who had endured days of pain and anguish at the hands of her killer. She had been subjected to a series of callous sexual attacks before she was finally murdered. She was found riddled with stab wounds and impaled on a huge iron stake. Scattered around the scene were dozens of photographs capturing her ordeal from the initial abduction, right through to her gruesome execution.

Jake had been praying for an opportunity to prove himself to Gant. However, Vladimir Volkoff proved to be a far more daunting adversary than he had ever hoped to encounter. As more victims emerged, Jake turned to Gant in the hope that the more experienced officer would guide him, but much to his dismay, Gant was fast becoming a fading shadow of his former self.

"Gant's fire was all but extinguished," said Jake. "I needed him to burn as bright as the sun, but he was more ash than flame. The great Bobby Gant was all burnt out."

Felicity puzzled over the metaphor. How could a detective as disciplined and as focussed as Bobby Gant suddenly fall apart at the height of such big case? Had the onset of old age and pending retirement finally taken its toll?

The truth was that Gant had begun to break his own rules. He had started drinking heavily, and often smelt of liquor when he arrived on the job. Jake soon noticed that his standards had started to slip, and when he followed Gant home late one night, he was shocked to discover that his drinking habit was not the only secret his partner had been hiding from him. Gant had developed a serious relationship with a cocktail waitress by the name of Marnie, whom he had met at a local bar. When Jake finally confronted him about the secret life he had created outside of work, Gant came clean and revealed that the pair had not only been seeing each other for months, but she was also carrying his child and had agreed to marry him.

"What a fool I was," said Jake, shaking his head. "A Goddamn detective and I couldn't see what was going on with my own partner."

"Don't be so tough on yourself, Jake," said Felicity, offering words of encouragement. "Sometimes the most difficult truth to uncover is the one right under your nose. Besides, I read your file Jake. You caught the Impaler and went on to set new standards within the department. You should be proud of what you've achieved right?"

She was not even close. There was no pride in Jake's expression, only guilt and regret. She knew the outcome of the investigation, but she knew nothing of the scandal that had almost torn the department apart in the final days of the Impaler case.

While Jake had been happy to accept his partner's relationship with Marnie, he could not accept Gant's excessive alcoholism. As his drinking got worse, it had a huge impact on the case. Finally, when a poor judgement call by the floundering Gant allowed the Impaler to slip through their fingers, Jake could no longer stand by and watch his partner and mentor destroy his reputation and put the investigation at risk. He filed a report against Gant, and while his partner was suspended from duty, Jake focussed his efforts of catching the killer alone.

Finally, a major break in the case came out of the blue, when Jake received an unexpected visit from Marnie. Vladimir had clearly discovered her romantic connection with one of the lead detectives in the investigation and had begun stalking her movements, determined to make her his next victim. Fortunately, Marnie had a very intuitive nature, and when she began to suspect that she was being followed, she brought her concerns to Jake. Gant's sloppy detective work had put her at risk, and although Marnie was eager to help in any way she could by acting as bait to lure the killer out of the shadows, Jake was not comfortable with the idea of putting her in harm's way, even if it meant catching the Impaler.

In the end, it was Abrahams who made the final judgement call. Knowing that Gant would never agree to Marnie's involvement in a snare operation, Abraham's insisted that he was kept in the dark. Although Jake felt uncomfortable about lying to his best friend and partner, he agreed to play his part in the grand deception, in the belief that her safety would be guaranteed, and the net would finally fall over Vladimir.

"I was wrong," said Jake, covering his head with his hands to hide his shame. "Vladimir was much smarter than we'd ever anticipated. He turned our whole operation on its head and then vanished without a trace. When the dust settled, we realised that Marnie was gone too. She had been taken by that monster."

"What was her last name, Jake?" Felicity did not have to wait for his answer. She had already put the final piece of the jigsaw puzzle in place. 'Marnie' had been short for Marianna and her last name was Cartwright. Felicity remembered her name from tabloid reports as being among the four women discovered at the site of the 'Brooklyn Bridge Massacre'. In one last brutal act, the Impaler had taken her life, before he was finally captured in an epic showdown with the brave young Detective Cannon.

"I was being hailed as a hero," said Jake. "But deep down, I felt like a villain. If details of the botched operation were ever leaked to the press, the damage to the NYPD would have been catastrophic. So, the whole scandal was swallowed up within the department. It was not the first time the force had rallied together to protect one of their own, and it won't be the last, but it just didn't feel right.

"As for Gant, he never recovered from the loss. He quit his job, and the last time I saw him he was living in some hell hole in Queens, trying to drink himself into an early grave. I tracked him down because all I wanted to do was to apologise for the way everything turned out, but he wouldn't listen. He just looked at me with a hatred in his eyes that has haunted me to this day. He held me and the Captain responsible for the murder of the woman he loved and his unborn son, and I've never stopped blaming myself ever since."

"It wasn't your fault Jake," said Felicity. Tears of compassion streamed from her eyes as she offered words of solace. "Marnie was Gant's light, but instead of treasuring her and keeping her safe, he lost sight of what was important. If he hadn't got himself suspended, then the Impaler would never have been able to get close to her and she'd still be alive."

Jake was touched by Felicity's attempts to comfort him in the wake of his shameful revelation. Perhaps she was right. Marnie had been a shining light in Gant's dark world, and given him a reason to finally hang up his gun and shield and look towards a bright new future. His only mistake was taking his eyes off the road before his journey as a cop was truly over. Jake was determined not to make the same mistake. He would remain focussed until the job was done, and the Ladykiller was safely behind bars.

However, as he sat watching Felicity wipe away her tears, he began to contemplate a life without darkness and death. She was like a soothing tonic that helped to ease his troubled mind, and besides Abrahams, she was the only person who truly understood him.

Felicity was overwhelmed with pity for Jake's predicament. She wanted to hold him in her arms, comfort him and tell him that everything was going to be alright. She had fallen for him, and now more than ever, she wanted to come clean and declare her feelings for him.

"I truly believe that you're the best detective in this city Jake," said Felicity, smiling at him as she wiped the tears from her face. "Do you remember the first day we met in my office? You analysed me in an instant and everything you said was true. So, I want you to do it again Jake. I want you to treat my apartment like a crime scene, and profile me."

Felicity knew exactly what she was doing. While this exercise would help restore his self-confidence, it would also help her to understand how Jake really felt about her.

She rose from her seat and picked up his empty glass, before walking off towards the kitchen. "Feel free to go wherever you like, my apartment is yours for the next five minutes."

With the exception of his beloved piano and the inside of a boxing ring, this was his field of excellence, and he was determined to rise to the challenge. Clearing his mind of everything but the task at hand, Jake glanced at his watch and then looked slowly around the room. Everything in the immaculate little lounge was perfectly neat and tidy. He had already cast an eye over her bookshelf, which was filled with a mixture of professional texts and lots of fictional novels. He began painting a picture in his head of a woman who loved to escape from the harsh reality of the world, and immerse herself in fantasy.

Jake leapt up out of the chair and marched over to a shelf which contained dozens of movies, most of which were black and white classics. He ran his finger along the cases until he reached one which looked far more weathered than the rest. He slid the box off the shelf and looked at the cover. It was an old James Cagney film which he knew well, and he could see from the battered box and the scratched disc inside, that it had been watched many times.

He placed the film back on the shelf, and walked out into the hallway. Straight ahead of him in the kitchen, he could hear Felicity humming along to a tune while she prepared their drinks. It was a moody and melancholic track by 'London Grammar'. Far from upbeat, their music invoked connotations of heartbreak and unrequited love. If a person's choice of music really did reflect their emotions, then this track provided him with a valuable insight into her present frame of mind.

He took another look at his watch. Five minutes was not a long time, and the bathroom would not yield much in the way of useful information. So, he chose to venture into her bedroom in search of more clues. He pulled the door open and a fat scruffy looking cat darted out and ran down the hallway into the lounge.

Like the rest of the apartment, Felicity's bedroom was spotless. She had a double bed besides which was a small nightstand and reading light. Beyond the bed on the far side of the room was a vanity table and a cushioned stool positioned in front of a mirror. There was an old-fashioned wardrobe made of carved oak stood against the wall to the left of the entrance, and one large wall mounted painting of the sun setting over a family of elephants stomping across the open planes of Africa.

Jake walked over to the bed and picked up a stuffed bear which was sat between two pillows. It was missing an eye and judging by the shabby coat, the bear had been her night time companion for many years. The room smelt like freshly picked strawberries, and the colour scheme of pink and biscuit cream made it feel more like a child's room than that of a grown woman.

Jake did not stop to consider whether he was crossing the boundaries of appropriate behaviour when he pulled open her drawers one by one, in search of anything that would help him piece together her profile. He paused as he opened her bottom drawer, laughing under his breath as he sifted through several pairs of extremely unattractive underwear until he finally found what he was looking for. Amidst a sea of boring beige knickers was a solitary black lace thong. "Bingo!" said Jake, stuffing it into his pocket before strolling into the kitchen where Felicity was still mixing cocktails.

"Wow, I'm impressed," said Felicity. "It's been barely four minutes so either you are as good as I think you are, or my apartment didn't reveal much."

Jake smiled confidently, as he took a seat at the bar and unbuttoned the collar of his shirt. Felicity sat down opposite him, and slid a tall glass of vodka and freshly squeezed orange juice across the table towards him. He took a mouthful of the deliciously tangy beverage before clearing his throat and launching into his detailed description.

"You are a dreamer," said Jake. His voice was soft and calm. He was back in control doing what he loved, uncovering a hidden truth. "By day you are Dr Monroe, courteous, dedicated and totally professional. You speak in linear terms and your brain works by the strict application of logic and reason. But here in this apartment, the walls of formality and restraint crumble, and you are free to drift into a world of fantasy. You sit in that rocking chair and escape into your own imagination. You lay in bed at night and dream of far-away places."

Felicity tried not to give much away, but her expression betrayed her. As Jake felt his way around the unknown borders of her character, he could tell that his description was already sounding alarmingly accurate.

"I'm guessing you come from a military family," continued Jake, committing himself to statements of fact which might have made him look foolish, had they not been accurate. But they were true, and she was eager to know what had given her away.

"That's pretty damn impressive, Detective Cannon," exclaimed Felicity. "How the hell did you figure that out?"

"Your regimental attention to detail," replied Jake. "Your books are all filed in alphabetical order, the quilt on your bed doesn't have a single crease in it, and there isn't a spot of dust in sight. I know you didn't serve in the military, but I'm guessing one of your parents did?"

She nodded in acknowledgement, confirming that he was right yet again. Her father had been an Officer in the Marine Corps and her mother had served as a nurse in the navy. They had met on a military tour and formed a bond that lasted a lifetime.

However, Jake had already guessed what Felicity could not bring herself to tell him. There was not a single photograph anywhere, which suggested to him that they were both dead. She was clearly fond of tradition and relics of her past, so photographs would have been a welcome feature in her home, had the memory of her parents' passing not been too painful for constant reminders.

"Your favourite movie is *Angels with Dirty Faces*," continued Jake, choosing to skip over the issue of her family, and onto a more pleasant subject.

"How are you doing this, Jake?" Felicity's eyes were wide with disbelief. "I adore that movie, I must have seen it a thousand times. How did you know?"

"It was clear from the case and the disk that you've watched that film more than any of the other's in your collection," replied Jake. "You might not know it, but that movie has had a profound effect on you, Felicity. You really felt something when you saw the way Cagney looked out for those street kids. I think you like to see the good in people, and you love the idea that there is someone out there, a true hero who is willing to do everything they can to protect the innocent and the vulnerable. That's why you chose to come and work for the NYPD, and it's probably why we have such a strong connection."

Everything he said made sense to her. By tracking down the Hangman and saving all of those children, Jake had won a place in her heart before she had even laid eyes on him.

"You've got me all worked out," said Felicity, trying to mask her overflowing emotion with smiles and comedy. "So, if I was a criminal, what crime would I have committed?"

As Jake stared deep into her eyes, Felicity felt a sexual tension that she had not experienced since their first meeting.

"Yours would be a crime of passion," he replied, reaching into his pocket. "Like me, you are a very passionate person, but you rarely let anyone get close. Our lifestyles are a defence mechanism. We have few friends and enjoy our own company. We throw ourselves into our work by day and return to our private space by night, convinced that we are happy in our solitude. But you have so much more to give Felicity, so much love and affection."

Jake clenched the black thong tight in his fist, contemplating whether or not he was bold enough to finish his analysis with one final stroke of intuitive genius.

"You are the last of the true romantics," he continued. "You will never give your heart, your soul, or your body to a man who has not earned both your respect and your love. One-night stands are totally out of the question."

He stood up, walked around the bar and stood next to Felicity. She could tell by the look on his face that he was about to do something mischievous.

"Tell me, Miss Monroe, why is it that you are rarely prepared for intimacy?"

Felicity did not break eye contact. Her pouting lips arched into a smile. "What makes you say that, Jake?"

Without hesitation, he pulled the thong from his pocket and threw it down on the table in front of her.

"My hunch is based on the fact that you only have one pair of sexy panties in your bottom drawer. The rest are all ugly as hell, so I'm guessing you don't misbehave too often!"

Felicity turned bright red and burst into laughter. This was a side of Jake she had longed to see. He was human after all, and his warm and playful side made her feel safe.

"You were doing so well," said Felicity, taking another gulp of her cocktail. "But I'm afraid you're wrong this time. I actually own two pairs of sexy panties."

She put down her glass and ran a finger over the back of his hand and along his forearm. Her tactile response was the first time they had ever made physical contact besides a courteous handshake, and Jake was instantly aroused by her soft touch.

"I put the other pair on right after you called to say you were coming over."

Jake stared into the ocean of her eyes as they enjoyed a rare moment of flirtation. The temptation was almost too much for him to handle. She had touched him, and he could not resist the urge to touch her back. Suddenly the image of Sheeba's body writhing on the thick fur rug back at the Pandorium flashed into his mind, and for a brief moment, he contemplated lifting Felicity onto the bar and tearing away at the layers of clothing until nothing but her ripe body and that second thong remained. But before he could act, she grabbed hold of him with both hands, and pulled his body towards hers. As she kissed him tenderly, he knew at once that his carnal aggression would not be well received. Felicity was the mellow breeze to his wild tempest, and in order to achieve true bliss for the first time, he would have to calm the storm brewing inside him.

Jake had always romped wildly with women, but as he stood holding her face in his hands and kissing her soft lips, he knew that he wanted to be gentle with Felicity. He would take his time caressing every inch of her, and then he would make love to her until she reached the thrilling peak of ecstasy.

"I feel like I'm at my best when I'm with you," said Jake. "You make me feel stronger than I've felt in a long time."

"I feel it too," said Felicity. Her eyes had glazed over with the warm glow of desire. "I don't want you to hold back Jake…I want the best of you."

She led him into her bedroom and dimmed the lights down low and turned on a small stereo beneath her bed. The hypnotic melody of Portishead's *Dummy* massaged them into a trance. Jake felt his legs become weak as he stood kissing the goose bumped curves of her body.

Neither Jake nor Felicity broke eye contact as they slowly undressed each other. The energy between them was electric. They had never felt so connected. It was as though their souls had fused, while their bodies swayed and merged in the pursuit of sensual satisfaction. Hours passed like minutes as they glided effortlessly from one heart pounding orgasm to the next until finally, locked in Jake's embrace, Felicity drifted into a deep sleep.

Jake lay perfectly still, reflecting on an eventful and emotionally charged few days. The abattoir, the unexpected re-union with Damian and the bizarre visit to the Pandorium had all been eclipsed by one night with the incredible Dr Monroe.

Felicity may have been the biggest mistake of his life, but she was a risk he was willing to take. His former partner had fallen foul of the effects of liquor and women, but unlike Gant, Jake was convinced that the same two vices may have helped him achieve clarity.

Then it hit him like a powerful epiphany of hope. After years of working as a cop, he had developed a poisonous affinity with homicide. Murder had become a dangerous addiction. Would he feel relief when the Ladykiller was captured, or would he just crave the next crime scene, like a vampire with an insatiable lust for fresh blood? He began to question whether *he* was the problem. Without its iron cast hero, would the city finally cease to spawn new villains?

As a detective, New York had taken the best of him, and perhaps it would soon be time for Jake to move on, before it claimed the rest of him. Felicity was his light, the shinning beacon of hope that would guide him out of the darkness. He would treasure her, he would learn from Gant's mistakes and protect her, and he would love her unconditionally.

He ran his fingers through her hair, and in the comfort of his thoughts, he fell asleep under the blue tint of a moonlit night sky.

Hours later, the sound of his cell phone startled Jake from his peaceful sleep. It was morning, and he squinted as the sun poured through the open blinds.

"Hello," said Jake, trying hard to sound awake and alert.

"Cannon!" bellowed Abrahams. "Get your ass down to the Orbit health club. It's the Ladykiller. He's killed again!"

Chapter 12
Witch Hunt

Just three days ago the body of the Ladykiller's third victim, thirty-one-year-old Alison Granger, was discovered in an abandoned abattoir formerly owned by the Baxter Meat Company, in the Manhattan meat-packing district. Granger, who was found by a member of the public, had been brutally slain in what can only be described as a ritualistic killing, sparking fears that the killer may be a member of some sort of cult. This morning I am here on the corner of Franklin and West Broadway, outside the building which until recently was home to the Orbit private health club, where an anonymous 911 call has led to the discovery of a fourth victim.

We do not yet have an identity, or any information as to exactly how she was killed, but we do know that the victim is definitely female, and probably in her twenties. Just moments ago, Captain Ron Abrahams was seen entering the building behind me along with Detective Jake Cannon, the officer responsible for the capture of Sebastian Bronson, also known as 'The Hangman', earlier this year. Abrahams refused to offer a statement on the progress of this investigation, fuelling concerns that the NYPD have neither the staff nor the resources to cope with the rising murder statistics. As police struggle to establish any suspects, the citizens of New York are left asking a familiar question. When will this nightmare end? This is Belinda Bryce reporting for CWC News, Manhattan, New York.

As Jake and Abrahams marched towards the heart of the Orbit building, their synchronised footsteps echoed loudly down the long hallway. They approached the glass doors leading to the central spa, and could already see the cameras flashing as the forensics team set up camp around the Ladykiller's latest piece.

"Hold up a minute, Cannon," said Abrahams, grabbing Jake by the arm and stopping him dead in his tracks. "Do you have any idea how that bitch Bryce knows so much about this case?"

Jake opened his palms to the sky and shook his head, confirming what Abrahams already knew. Jake had no idea who had talked to Belinda Bryce. He was far too experienced to leak vital information about the case that may find its way into the press and ultimately tip off the killer, unless that was the department's intention. Abrahams had made the decision to keep the investigation water tight, but somehow Bryce had obtained and broadcast more detail than he wished to reveal to the public.

"It's like I've always said, Cannon," continued Abrahams, "when you're standing in the eye of a shit storm, you keep your fucking mouth shut!"

Jake smirked at the imagery conjured up by another of Abrahams' classic one-liners.

"Of course, Captain," he replied. "Bryce is an attractive woman, and it would be just her style to open her legs to an inexperienced young cop just to get her story."

Ironically, it was Damian who had given the tenacious young reporter her juicy scoop. Jake had no idea that he had divulged vital details to the killer himself, when they had met at the Labirinto gallery. Damian had used this information to his advantage, and made several calls to Belinda Bryce. He claimed to be a member of NYPD homicide, operating off the grid and without the blessing of his superiors. He fed her just enough to stir up trouble within the department, and Bryce had taken the bait.

"I want you to find out who is responsible for spilling their guts to that reporter," said Abrahams. "But first things first, I need you to do what you do best, and take control of this crime scene!"

"Of course, Captain," replied Jake, fumbling in his pocket for a toothpick. He did not consider himself to be a superstitious man, but it was as though this small piece of wood was the key which unlocked his insight, intuition and intelligence. In truth, Jake's ability to see what other detectives could not was down to his rare and valuable capacity to capture the sight, sound and mood invoked by the aftermath of a serious crime. He often compared it to an out of body experience. It was as though he was hovering over the scene, watching it all unfold, writing and then re-writing the dark script in his mind, until the most logical and probable turn of events presented itself with clarity.

Jake had never visited the lavish Orbit club, and as they walked through the heavy glass doors, he was blown away by the palatial pool area, designed in the image of an ancient Roman bath. The pool was lined with stone pillars that stretched up to the curved ceiling, which was a decadent decorative feature of imitation Renaissance art. In the centre of the ceiling was a huge stained-glass window, through which the afternoon sun filtered beams of beautiful technicolour light down onto the water below. The pool area was the perfect backdrop for another of the Ladykiller's murderous masterpieces.

Officers and forensic experts who had been buzzing around the room like busy worker bees, suddenly ground to a halt and stood watching in awe of the legendary Detective Cannon. Abrahams leant against one of the pillars and observed with hawk-like intensity, while Jake slowly paced around the pool.

Jake walked over to the water's edge, and knelt down to get a closer look at victim number four. The woman was still completely submerged in water, tied to a wooden chair which appeared to have been drilled to the floor of the pool. She looked like a beautiful aquatic ghost. With her pale naked body and her long brown hair swaying in slow motion in the untroubled water, she was a haunting vision of serenity.

Jake did not have to wait for the toxicology report or the coroner's verdict. The absence of blood or any visible sign of trauma to her face and body confirmed his suspicions that she had died right there in the pool. But unlike his previous victims, the killer had not inflicted a deadly blow. He had simply opened the faucet and watched her fall apart with despair as she contemplated the inevitability of her imminent death. The cold soft kiss of nature's most powerful force would have danced about her feet, and then her ankles, before slowly and steadily rising to the fatal depth. As Jake stared down into the murky ripples of her turquoise grave, her unblinking eyes, still wide with terror, stared back at him. This may have looked like a clean kill, but her ordeal would have been no less terrifying than that of the Ladykiller's first three victims.

Suddenly, a camera flashed in the background, as a member of the forensic team began taking photographs of something smeared on the wall on the opposite side of the room. Jake snapped out of his post murder trance, and looked up. He noticed that something had been daubed on the white tiles in rich cherry red paint. It was a vertical line no more than six inches wide and roughly a metre in height. The single red column had not featured at any of the previous Ladykiller crime scenes, but as insignificant as it might appear at first glance, he was sure that the relevance of this symbol would soon become clear. On a much smaller scale, next to the bold red line was the familiar '666'. Jake considered it to be good fortune that the killer's 'mark of the beast' calling card had not been leaked to the press. The last thing he needed were copycat killers complicating the manhunt.

Jake looked around the room again, and spotted a man in a gym suit staring anxiously at the woman in the water.

"Are you Clarence, the club janitor?" Jake pointed at the man, who swiftly raised his hand in a gesture of affirmation, before walking over to join him.

When Abrahams had called him that morning with news of the latest murder, Jake had insisted that the person responsible for maintaining the pool was summoned to the scene without delay. However, despite assurances that his attendance was merely a formality that would greatly assist the investigation, Clarence was still extremely nervous.

"Correct me if I'm wrong, Clarence, but I'm guessing that this pool holds around twenty thousand gallons of water," said Jake, scratching his head as he made several swift calculations. "Does it have a pump filling system?"

"Yes, it does, sir," replied Clarence. "You turn it on at full power and it'll pump out 21.5 gallons of water a minute, non-stop until it's full to the brim."

Jake's eyebrow raised and the dark pits of his pupils dilated with excitement. The look on the brilliant detective's face was one that the Captain knew well. Jake had uncovered some startling fact that was about to launch them all into action. As Abrahams sprang from his perch against the pillar and darted towards him, Jake began shouting instructions to nearby officers.

"Baines and Mallory, I need you to secure a perimeter around the crowds outside the building!" yelled Jake. "The killer is close ladies and gentlemen. I think he's watching the drama unfold, so everybody outside gets checked, and nobody leaves until the Captain says so!"

As they sprang into motion in response to his command, Jake continued to delegate tasks. Time was of the essence, so nobody dared to ask questions. While officers rallied to the cause, Jake made sure that Clarence was escorted safely off the premises before turning to enlighten Abrahams as to what he had discovered.

"Are we certain that the anonymous 911 call came in at exactly 8:10 am this morning, Captain?" Jake asked.

"One hundred percent," confirmed Abrahams. "Gibbs took the call. The caller claimed he'd been sleeping rough outside the building. He snuck inside this morning when he noticed the door was open, and called it in from a payphone just outside when he found a body in the pool."

"That was no bum who made that call," replied Jake confidently. "It was the Ladykiller. I'm sure of it!"

Since establishing that the killer was targeting derelict commercial premises, several buildings including Orbit had been the subject of routine police patrols. Ironically, the luxury health club was considered a low risk site, and was only checked once a night. Jake figured that while the police had been watching the building, the killer had been watching them.

Jake had made a call to headquarters on his way to the crime scene and was informed that officers' Stokes and Parry had carried out their routine inspection of the Orbit in the early hours of the morning. They had left just before 1.15am, at which time the site was secure and the pool was most definitely empty.

"Let's assume the Ladykiller watched Stokes and Parry leave here around 1:15 am," said Jake. "Then he came in and started setting up straight away. At 21.5 gallons a minute, it would have taken seven hours to hit nine thousand gallons, which is the water level at which this girl's face would have been totally submerged."

Abrahams smiled triumphantly as Jake's explanation finally hit home. "So, what you're saying is that even if he started filling up this pool the minute Parry and Stokes left the building, she would not have drowned until say 8:15am this morning?"

"That's exactly what I'm saying, Captain," replied Jake. "I'm pretty damn sure this woman was still alive when that anonymous call came in at 8:10 am, so I'm guessing that the killer made that call, then stuck around a few minutes more to watch her die. So, we need to check the footage from any surveillance cameras near the building, just in case he's not as smart as we think. He might have left us a visual, and we definitely need to run checks on everyone stood behind the yellow tape outside. The sick bastard may well have stuck around to see our reaction to his handy work."

Jake and Abrahams left the forensic team to finish their analysis and ran back down the hall towards the entrance. Outside the building, order had swiftly descended into chaos, as a handful of uniformed police tried to marshal the crowds of onlookers. One officer was stood in front of them barking instructions into a loudspeaker, pleading for patience whilst other officers painstakingly noted down the details of each and every member of the public who had gathered to watch.

What expression would be written on the killer's face at that moment? Would it be a sardonic smile, a poorly disguised scowl of malicious intent or complete indifference? Jake scanned back and forth through the sea of spectators, processing every face in search of anyone who looked out of place.

Suddenly, an eager young officer sprinted over to Captain Abrahams and handed him a radio. Jake could not hear what was being said, but he could tell by the look on the Captain's face that it was not good news. After a brief exchange of words, Abrahams handed back the radio, and hurried over to where Jake was standing.

"The shit just hit the fan that's spinning directly above our heads, Cannon!" said Abrahams, looking over his shoulder to make sure that nobody else was in earshot. "A call just came in from 1st Precinct over on Ericsson Place. We've got another Jane Doe at Barollo's, and it sounds like the Ladykiller has messed her up real bad!"

Jake mopped a thin layer of sweat from his brow and shook his head at the realisation that they had been outsmarted once again. The whole charade that was unfolding outside the Orbit was nothing more than smoke and mirrors. The killer was a magician, and the seemingly tame drowning was his sleight of hand distraction that would keep them occupied while he slew his fifth victim just a short distance away, off the junction of Thomas Street and West Broadway, in yet another vacant building that until very recently had been home to a well-known Italian restaurant.

"I need you to leave quietly and head over to the restaurant," continued Abrahams. "I'll send a team of forensics and more men as soon as I can, but we can't let the press get a hold of this shit just yet. I'll buy you some time here Cannon. If it's a statement Bryce wants, then that's exactly what I'm about to give her."

Jake slipped away, leaving Abrahams to distract the news crews with the interview they desperately craved. He whipped the classic 911 through lights and traffic and arrived at Barollo's just a few minutes later.

The quiet location at 78 Thomas Street was almost deserted, no doubt due to the spectacle back at the pool. Outside of the restaurant there were no members of the press present, and no public audience. Just two very nervous officers standing guard, making sure that nobody went in or out of the building. As Jake turned the corner and approached the entrance, one of the officers made a frantic grab for the gun holstered at his hip.

"Stand easy, fellas," said Jake calmly, holding one hand in the air and brandishing his badge with the other. Both men smiled apologetically as the familiar face of Jake Cannon drew closer.

"I'm gonna head inside and take a look," said Jake. "I need you both to stay alert and keep the site secure until the rest of the team arrives. Can you do that for me?"

As the two officers shook their heads in acknowledgement, he could see the relief on their faces. They had been the first to respond to the radio alert, but what they had witnessed had left them both visibly shaken. They were more than happy to stand guard, if it meant they did not have to go back inside the restaurant.

Jake walked through the door and into the silence of the once-vibrant dining hall. He recalled the sweet aroma of Alfonso Barollo's famous Melanzane Parmigiana, but now the air carried nothing but the musty stench of abandonment.

Although the room was dark, the partially tilted venetian blinds let in just enough light for Jake to see two large streaks running across the centre of the dusty wooden floorboards. The marks had been made by shoes, a clear sign that the victim had been dragged across the restaurant and through the double doors which lead to the chef's kitchen.

Jake advanced cautiously, and as he drew closer he noticed a thick dark fluid smeared across the small circular windows in each of the swinging doors. He slipped a fresh toothpick between his lips and removed a pair of rubber gloves from his breast pocket. This was going to be a messy crime scene and he could not afford to leave any prints which might create unnecessary work for the forensic team.

As he reached the doorway, Jake finally realised that the dark substance covering the windows was blood. He was about to walk into a nightmare.

The doors creaked eerily as he pushed them open and walked inside. After just a few short paces, he stood frozen in disbelief as his eyes finally focused on the violent extremity of Ladykiller's latest and most grotesque murder. From the watery scarlet spray of the first cuts, to the free-flowing claret of the slow bleed, and then finally the dark rich clotted maroon of the internal organs, everywhere he looked there was nothing but a sea of red. The ceiling, walls, counters and floors were awash with blood.

The body of victim number five had been savagely dismembered, and her limbs and torn torso lay scattered across the sodden crimson canvas of the chef's main table. A selection of knives and cleavers which had been used to separate flesh from bone were lined up in a neat row, but one blade in particular caught Jake's attention. The victim's severed left-hand lay palm down on a wooden chopping board, and the calving knife that had been driven through the knuckles and into the wood had no doubt been used to etch the familiar series of three sixes across the back of her hand.

Jake scanned every corner of the kitchen. The woman had been decapitated, but her head was nowhere to be seen. Tomatoes, carrots, onions and other decaying vegetables had been tossed about the room, and he visualised the killer removing them from the refrigerator to make way for the final piece of his vile work of art. Jake tried his best to avoid the pools of blood which had settled on the tiled floor, as he walked over and heaved open the heavy door.

Inside the refrigerator was a single silver champagne bucket filled with ice. Nestled in the centre of the cubes was the head of a beautiful young woman.

"The sick fucking animal!" yelled Jake, turning away and biting into his forearm in an attempt to suppress his anger. Her wide-eyed expression coupled with the make-up that had been liberally applied to her face made her look more mannequin-like than human. The killer had been meticulous in his work as there was barely a trace of blood in or around the ice bucket. However, her head had been completely shaven.

Why had the killer removed the victim's hair? Jake struggled to make sense of this peculiar detail, but as he leaned in closer to inspect her scalp he noticed that although she had been sheared with an extremely sharp blade, a few fine flecks of hair still remained. Blonde hair!

"What if she wasn't a natural brunette?" said Jake to himself. Each of his previous victims had been brunette's, so by selecting a blonde, the killer had gone against his own trend. Or had he? What if she was not blonde when he had abducted her? Perhaps she had died her hair brown, a fact that may only have been revealed as her roots began to show, after days or maybe even weeks locked away in his private prison. It would have been too late to release his catch back into the wild, so instead the killer had chosen to cut off her hair and then her head as punishment for her deception.

Jake may have continued to pick apart the scene, had he not noticed the second symbol. Smeared on the back of one of the swinging doors were two blood red columns, each exactly the same as the single column he had seen back at the health club. The meaning of this marking had been a mystery back at the pool, but now it all began to make sense. Each column represented the number of victims he had clocked up in this latest killing spree. By deciphering the code behind the killer's symbolism, Jake had stumbled upon a significant truth. This was not merely a random sequence of murders. It was a witch hunt, cleverly orchestrated to mimic the work of a long forgotten serial murderer.

Jake recalled the details of a case he had studied dating back to the late 1970s, when a killer by the name of Randolf Kemp turned himself in after committing a series of murders in Manhattan.

An author by trade, Kemp had been vilified by the media after publishing a hugely controversial book entitled 'Three Ways to Kill a Witch'. The book chronicled the persecution and torture of women who had been accused of witchcraft in medieval Europe, and was banned shortly after its release due to the author's violent and discriminatory views towards women.

At the time, many people believed that the loss of his professional credibility caused the ostracised author to lose his mind. He embarked on a vicious killing spree, callously murdering three women who he later described as 'Westernised Witches'. His book had referred to public executions, in which women who had been accused of witchcraft were peppered with rotten vegetables and then, either tied to a chair and thrown into a river to drown, decapitated or burnt alive. Kemp had killed all three of his victims in line with his own text, and now Jake was convinced that the Ladykiller was paying homage to the author's work.

Jake was overcome by a deep sense of dread. Although he had uncovered a source of inspiration for the last two kills, it suddenly dawned on him that if there were indeed three ways to kill a witch, then somewhere not too far from Barollo's, the killer may be about to complete a bold trilogy of murders to mimic Kemp's Manhattan witch hunt.

Jake slipped out of his crime scene dream state. It had taken just a few seconds for him to figure out the possible location of the third kill. So far, the Ladykiller had followed Kemp's text to the very last detail. Therefore, he was likely use fire to burn his next victim alive. But like most perverse serial killers, Jake was certain that the Ladykiller would not be able to resist staying at the scene once the fire had been lit. He would want to stay and watch her pain and suffering. So, the kill room would need to be large enough for him to look on from a safe distance, whilst the smoke and flames folded into a fatal inferno.

Jake scrambled through his pockets in search of his cell phone. He was prepared to set the entire might of the NYPD in motion based on intuition alone. If he was wrong, then he would happily pay the consequences, but he was not willing to risk another life when the signs all pointed to a third murder.

"Talk to me, Cannon!" Abrahams answered the call within two rings, hoping that Jake would have something positive to report from the Barollo's crime scene. However, Jake did not have time to explain his discovery in great detail to the Captain. The only thing Abraham's needed to know was that a rapid response had to be co-ordinated.

"The Paragon Theatre!" yelled Jake. "Don't ask me how I know, Captain, just trust me on this. Send everyone you can over to the Federal Plaza on the corner of Leonard Street and Lafayette, I think there's a third murder about to go down there!"

The Paragon had stood abandoned since the turn of the year, when the huge shadow cast by Broadway finally forced the small independent theatre to close. As Jake raced towards the scene, he visualised the grid within which the day's events had taken place. He suspected that it was no coincidence that the Orbit, Barollo's and Paragon stood at almost equal distances apart, in the area known as the 'triangle below canal street' or 'Tribeca' for short.

The Tribeca was one of New York's most fashionable neighbourhoods, and had become a Mecca for many of the city's artistic fraternity. This was most definitely a deliberate detail in a plan devised by a murderous artist.

As Jake pulled up outside, he could already hear the high-pitched whirl and whoop of several police sirens in the distance. The helicopter would soon be overhead, throwing a visual net over the whole scene. If the Ladykiller was still inside, in just a few minutes he would have nowhere to hide. However, Jake could not wait for re-enforcements to arrive. The life of another young girl hung in the balance, and her chances of survival were deteriorating with every precious second that passed.

He sprinted up the steps, past the box office and on towards the front entrance. The killer would not have wanted to be seen walking into the building. He would have driven into the deserted rear car park and unloaded both his victim and his tools without fear of detection. This would also be his means of escape, but unfortunately for Jake, the drive to the rear of the building would have added minutes to his journey. Minutes which he could not afford to lose.

Jake kicked the lock clean off the door before yanking it open and stepping inside. In the distance, the high ceilings carried the faint echo of screams to where he was standing, confirming instantly that his hunch about the third murder had been correct. Somewhere in the heart of the building a woman was suffering, but she was still alive!

He gripped his weapon with both hands and raised it to eye level, controlling his breathing while staring through the sight and down the barrel. His arms remained steady as they guided his gun in every direction, in perfect alignment with his unblinking eye as it inspected each corner of the lobby.

There were two corridors either side of a central staircase, and the sign above the stairs read 'Main Hall'. Guided by the assumption that the Ladykiller would not settle for anything less than the main stage, Jake proceeded up the red carpeted steps to the first floor.

The doorway to the main auditorium stood at the end of a long corridor. As he made his way towards the entrance, his heart sank at the sound of another piercing scream. This was nothing like the scream he had heard when he first entered the building. It was the delirious shriek of someone in unimaginable pain. As the smell of burning wood hit his nostrils, Jake lowered his weapon and sprinted towards the entrance. For the woman on the other side of the door, death had become more than just a terrifying possibility. Death was upon her, taunting her as it licked her flesh with a tongue of red flame.

She would already have sustained grave injuries, but Jake was not going to give up on her. He burst through the door and thundered down several flights of steps which ran between endless rows of seats, towards the stage. Through billowing clouds of grey smoke and leaping flames, he could see the woman's naked body, wriggling and writhing wildly as she struggled to free herself. The fire had slowly slithered its way up through piles of wooden chairs that had been stacked around her, and was already scorching her lower body as it crept to within a few feet of the base of the heavy wooden pillar to which she had been bound.

Although there was no sign of the Ladykiller, Jake could not be certain that he had already left the building, but he would have to rely on the swiftly advancing blue cavalry to impede the killer's escape, while he focussed his efforts on a daring rescue.

Jake looked up at the ceiling. The sprinkler system hissed and whistled but there was no spray. It was clear that the killer had drained the system so that the fire could rage on with no interruption.

Without thinking, Jake thrust his hands into the bonfire and begun hurling the burning chairs aside, only to retreat in pain as the red-hot timber seared his skin. Suddenly the screaming stopped, and as Jake looked up he could see the woman's head and shoulders slump forward as she fell unconscious. His eyes danced around the hall, searching for anything that would help suppress the blaze, until he spotted a shiny canister hanging from the wall near the side of the stage.

Praying that it was still full, he ran over and ripped the extinguisher from the wall and darted back towards the girl. He sprayed the cool white foam in every direction, until there was nothing left of the fire but a few crackling embers, then he kicked and clambered his way through the charred rubble until he reached the pillar, before finally freeing her wrists and ankles and moving her away from the smoke and fumes.

Jake carried her heavy limp body out of the exit and placed her on the ground in a small dark passageway which was lined with dressing rooms. He pressed two fingers against her neck and placed his cheek against her open mouth, checking for any sign of life. He was relieved to discover that she had a pulse and was definitely still breathing, but she was not out of the woods yet. Her skin had been badly burned, and she needed urgent medical attention.

He looked down the hall at the fire exit door that was still swinging back and forth. Through the gap he could see the squad cars pulling into the rear car park, and back in the main hall, the footsteps of half a dozen officers could be heard scrambling down the steps towards him.

"Over here!" yelled Jake, coughing as his lungs tightened from the effects of the smoke he had inhaled. "We're over here in the hallway!"

As Special Weapons teams filtered into the passageway from the front and rear, Jake waved a hand in a gesture of submission.

"Lower your weapons guys, he's long gone!" He did not need to inspect the remainder of the building to know that the killer had made his escape shortly after the fire had been lit. When he had made a dash for the fire extinguisher Jake had noticed the paint from a third much shorter column streaming down the wall next to two complete columns which matched those he had seen at the two previous crime scenes. Upon hearing Jake's rapid approach, the Ladykiller had no doubt been forced leave his motif incomplete and exit the theatre before the final curtain.

Jake had saved a life, and prevented a bitter end to a truly dark day. Three murders committed by the same killer at three separate locations, would have been an unprecedented sequence of events for the city and its blundering police force. However, this fact was of little comfort to the frustrated detective. It could be days before the woman nestled in his arms regained consciousness and was well enough to be interviewed. By then it could be too late, and more innocent lives might be lost.

As the paramedics arrived to relieve him from his vigil, Jake rose to his feet and staggered towards the exit. He was exhausted and desperately in need of fresh air, but before he had the chance to catch his breath, his cell phone began to ring.

"Captain!" said Jake, assuming that it was Abrahams calling for a briefing on what had transpired.

"No not the Captain," said the voice on the other end of the line. "It's Damian. Did you miss me?"

Jake could never have known that he was being taunted by the very man responsible for the morning's murderous mayhem. He had spent the morning hunting his own brother, and now he was relieved to hear the sound of his voice. In their last meeting, Damian had asked him to try and uncover the killer's motive, and after the discoveries made at the last three crime scenes Jake was convinced that he had the answer.

"Sure, I've missed you," replied Jake, trying hard to hide the disappointment in his voice. "But not as much as I've missed that club you took me to!"

Damian roared with laughter. He knew full well where Jake was, and what a strain it must have been to disguise his frustration with a touch of arid humour.

"That's great," said Damian. "I just saw what went down at that Orbit place on the news this morning. I would love to help you find this asshole Jake, and I was kind of hoping you could meet me for dinner tomorrow night at 18 Red to discuss the investigation some more."

Jake did not have to give it a moment's thought. He had always wanted to eat at 18 Red, but the exclusive restaurant was always fully booked months in advance. For someone like Damian, such things as waiting lists never presented a problem. For Jake, it would be another opportunity to get a rare glimpse of society's elite at play, and also the perfect chance to pick his brother's brain again.

"Dinner would be great," replied Jake. "Just give me a time and I'll be there."

Chapter 13
18 Red

"Are you sure you're not tired of all this attention yet, Damian?" Jake raised his voice in order to be heard above the festival of sound outside the prestigious Club 18 Red. The camera flash frenzy had begun the minute the two brothers stepped out of the Maybach, and continued long after they walked through the glass fronted entrance doors, as a handful of paparazzi competed for the perfect picture of New York's golden boy.

Burgundy was most definitely flavour of the month, but while he was happy to put on a good show for the fanatical public, there was a deeper truth hidden behind his eyes which had not escaped his brother's attention. Jake had already begun to sense that Damian was growing tired of the public scrutiny.

"I'm already over it," said Damian earnestly. "Fame is ephemeral. This year's man of the moment is next year's fallen idol, so it's best not to get too accustomed to it."

As he paused momentarily, a short man dressed in a white shirt and black waistcoat with matching bow tie appeared from nowhere to relieve them of their jackets, before disappearing in the direction of the cloakroom.

"You see, Jake," Damian continued, "guys like me spend years climbing the so-called ladder of success. But we soon come to realise that life at the top is not nearly as exciting as the journey up. Now that I have fulfilled all of my goals, I have no more dreams, only nightmares of falling from grace. Every time I stop to enjoy all this fame, my fragile ego is reminded of the fact that one day soon, I am destined to return to obscurity. Only the most epic deeds can ensure that our names live on long after we are dead, Jake."

Damian's profound statement was cut short, when a tall slender woman dressed in a cream silk gown complemented by a white pearl necklace walked out from the restaurant into the lobby, and greeted them both with a forced smile. She had short peroxide blonde hair and big blue eyes, but her cherry red lipstick contrasted so dramatically with her pale complexion, that she looked cold and somewhat unapproachable.

"Welcome back to 18 Red, Mr Burgundy," she said in an eastern European accent, shooting Damian a brief and frosty glare, before turning to offer Jake a more pleasant greeting. "I'm Giovanna, and it is my pleasure to introduce you to our delightful restaurant. I will now show you to your table, where one of our capable waiters will ask you to select drinks from our cocktail bar, and talk you through our mouth-watering menu."

The devious smirk on his brother's face told Jake everything he needed to know. Damian had obviously charmed and seduced the attractive young host. But like so many women who had considered themselves fortunate enough to find their way into his arms, the harsh reality that she had been nothing more than a one-night stand would have brought her crashing back down to earth with a thud, and left her choking on the bitter taste of rejection.

Giovanna invited both men to follow her before leading the way through the mirrored doors and into the dining hall. The restaurant had earned its name after its owner Albert Roach made a small fortune betting big on the number 18 red, while playing roulette at a high stakes table of the Las Vegas Wynn Casino. Roach had spared no expense on the lavish cocktail and piano bar. Yet his most valuable acquisition was that of revered French chef, Jean-Pierre Lafontaine. The Parisian master chef swiftly earned the restaurant a three Michelin star rating and helped to secure its status as the most exclusive eatery in Manhattan.

"What do you think to the décor?" asked Damian casually.

"Impressive," replied Jake, as he observed numerous rotating projectors beaming a kaleidoscopic rainbow of moving shapes and colours onto several white partition walls, which were strategically positioned around the room. Each wall was no more than six feet in height, and as the two men followed Giovanna through the maze of tables, Jake noticed that these walls shifted and rotated at timed intervals, obscuring or revealing a new view of the restaurant to the seated guests. "Whoever designed this place is extremely creative."

"Thank you," said Damian, proudly confirming that he was behind the decorative composition. "The moving walls turned out even better than I imagined."

Jake recognised a great many faces, as they both took their seats at a circular table in the centre of the restaurant. In one corner, the district attorney was sat dining with senior politicians, while in the other corner various heads of the city's leading crime family were remonstrating loudly over the champagne menu. The whole place throbbed with the collective energy of a hundred over inflated egos, and the smell of money almost overpowered the aroma of quality cuisine. Jake could not help but smile at how figures from totally different worlds had come together under one roof, united by their love of fine food.

After the furore outside the restaurant, Jake was beginning to understand the attraction of spending over the odds to dine and socialise in such exclusive venues. The only time Damian could truly relax and be himself was when he was surrounded by people whose wealth or fame mirrored his own.

"Surely when you reach the top of that mountain of success, it's all about enjoying the view right?" said Jake, settling into a comfortable velvet cushioned seat and trying to force him to continue the discussion they had started in the lobby. Damian was only too happy to oblige, picking up a carafe of ice-cold mineral water and filling his glass before continuing.

"I've seen every corner of this planet twice over," replied Damian. "I've satisfied my appetite for speed in every Italian supercar you can think of, dined in every fancy restaurant, and slept with every supermodel to grace a Milan catwalk. So, there's very little left for me to do except die, while I'm still young and famous!"

Jake's expression was one of confusion, and Damian immediately became aware that he was giving too much of himself away to the perceptive detective. Sooner or later most serial killers would seek to reveal their identity and take the credit for their evil genius, happily forfeiting their lives to set their notoriety in stone. This misplaced sense of martyrdom would be well known to an experienced cop like Jake. If Damian continued to lack caution, it would not be long before the trail of breadcrumbs he was scattering led Jake to his door. Tell me, Jake, what is this theory you have regarding the Ladykiller?" asked Damian, shifting the discussion back to the case.

Before Jake could reply, the expression on Damian's face changed to one of great excitement. A wall which had previously obscured his view had slid to the right, revealing a beautiful brunette in a figure-hugging red dress. She was being led through the restaurant by Giovanna, and was heading in their direction.

"Now there's a girl with as body built for pleasure," said Damian, casually pointing at the woman. Jake was sat with his back to the entrance and had not seen her approaching, but as he turned to see who had sparked Damian's interest, the woman in the red dress smiled back at him. Jake stood up, and as she walked up to the table and kissed him on either cheek, he turned to introduce her to his shocked and confused brother.

"This is Dr Felicity Monroe, an exceptional psychologist who has been helping me with the case," said Jake cordially. "Felicity, I am sure my brother needs no introduction. Please meet Mr Damian Burgundy."

Damian gave Felicity a brief smile before recoiling back into his seat with a look of utter distaste. Jake had neglected to mention the fact that he had invited Felicity to join them and Damian was clearly annoyed at her unexpected arrival at their dinner meeting. He had intended to unsettle Jake with more of his cunning mind games, but Felicity added a whole new dimension to the evening, and threatened to derail his plans to scupper Jake's progress with the investigation.

"So, Dr Monroe," said Damian, trying hard to appear amicable, "Have you ever been to 18 Red before?"

Felicity shook her head. "No, I haven't, but I've heard the food here is the best in New York, so thanks for inviting me."

"I didn't!" replied Damian, smiling insincerely to take the sting out of his deliberate attack. "But since you are here, I can recommend the champagne and cream Pappardelle with Chanterelle mushrooms. It's to die for."

In the awkward silence that followed, both Jake and Felicity contemplated raising the issue of his blatant displeasure. However, when the waitress arrived with the wine menu, the prospect of alcohol seemed to lighten Damian's spirits. He ordered two bottles of Laurent Perrier Rose, and while the three of them enjoyed their drinks and some non-confrontational conversation, the tension soon lifted. It was not long before the discussion reverted back to the Ladykiller case.

Both Damian and Felicity listened intently as Jake explained the first of two theories he had gleaned from the most recent crime scenes. He was convinced that the killer was not quite as unique and creative as they had first thought, and that the last three murders were more like a tribute to the work of convicted serial killer, Randolf Kemp.

"I think we are dealing with a copycat killer," said Jake excitedly. "I've got the Real Time Crime department trawling back through the archives for any similarities between the Ladykiller's first two murders, and any other old cases."

Damian's eyebrow twitched nervously. The balance of power was shifting and the mist that had obscured Jake's vision and hindered his progress was beginning to clear.

As Damian observed the interaction between Jake and Felicity, he soon became convinced that the beautiful Dr Monroe had played the role of saboteur in his evil game, by revitalising the focus and resolve of the faltering detective.

"Very interesting," replied Damian. "But even if the killer has taken inspiration from other notorious murderers, how will this help you track him down?"

"Well that part is simple," replied Jake. "The Ladykiller clearly has a taste for the sensational. If I'm right and he is mimicking past murders, then it's likely that he is referencing a shortlist of the more shocking and dramatic of cases."

"Exactly!" said Felicity, interrupting Jake mid-flow. "By going back through the archives, maybe we can uncover a pattern, and work out who he might try to emulate next."

Damian rubbed his temple with his index finger. He was trying hard to remain calm, but inside he was a blazing furnace of fury. Jake seemed buoyed by the presence of the meddling psychologist, and Damian did not like it one bit. He was desperate for the control to shift back in his favour, but he felt outnumbered and outgunned by the collective momentum of Jake and his make-shift partner.

"What about your second theory?" said Damian, keen to hear what other damaging facts Jake might have un-covered.

"I think that our artistic killer has a muse," replied Jake. "I believe that at some point in the past, he suffered a deep emotional injury at the hands of a woman, probably a so called 'socialite', who shares the same physical characteristics as his victims. Whoever this woman is, he sees her as the very personification of evil, which might explain why he leaves the triple six mark of the beast on or near each victim. I think that his vicious works of art are inspired by wrath. They are his way of exorcising the demons of his past."

Damian clapped loudly. As nervous as he was about Jake's proximity to the truth, he had to applaud him for his keen attention to detail and diligent detective work. How ironic it was, he thought to himself, that Jake was convinced that he was edging ever closer to discovering the killer's identity, while at that very moment he was sitting just a few feet away.

"Bravo, brother," said Damian. "But what if it's a whole lot simpler than that? Let's take your socialites for example. Surely these women are more of a burden than a benefit to society, right? They attach themselves to rich men and then drain them of their time and money like parasitic appendages, before moving on when a bigger and better host comes along. Perhaps the Ladykiller just sees it as his duty to rid the world of a few more worthless leeches don't you think?"

Jake turned to look at Felicity and noticed that her face was burning red with anger. She was clearly incensed by Damian's inflammatory comments, and Jake knew that he could not afford to show support for such a controversial argument, and risk giving her the wrong impression about his own feelings towards women. However, he could see how Damian's suggestion complemented his own theory.

"Perhaps you're onto something brother," said Jake. "I still believe he has suffered some serious emotional trauma, and maybe it was at the hands of one of these 'leeches' as you call them."

"Exactly, Jake," replied Damian, pleased that he had successfully broadened the narrow line of thought that was leading Jake straight to him. "Now you are starting to think like a killer. Perhaps the killer's heart has been hardened to the point of hatred, by the type of woman he now hunts and butchers. Maybe somewhere in his dark past, he's been deeply wounded by a forked tongued poisonous parasite."

Felicity slammed her flute down on the table, shattering the stem and spilling champagne over her dress. Just a few days ago she had been overwhelmed by the revelation that the great Damian Burgundy was Jake's brother. The story of their childhood and their silent feud that had lasted over a decade had fascinated her, and the prospect of meeting him had left her feeling dizzy with excitement.

However, her first impressions of Damian had left her convinced that he was little more than an arrogant chauvinistic snake. While Jake seemed oblivious to his true nature, she could see that Damian was not just playing Devil's Advocate with his contentious comments. He clearly sympathised with the killer, and the hostility he had displayed since her arrival was no doubt the result of his own aversion to the opposite sex.

"Are you okay?" said Jake, moving the broken glass to one side. He dabbed at her thigh with his napkin, soaking up the moisture from her dress. His gesture was not intended to convey any passionate intent, but for a split second, Felicity melted as he touched her body. There was a brief pause as their eyes met in a glow of desire, and Damian caught his first glimpse of a relationship that was anything but professional. He knew that Jake would be desperate not to suffer the same fate as his former partner, and make his new love a target for the killer. Yet while they had concealed the truth so convincingly, a single careless glance was all it took to expose their hidden intimacy. The connection between them added a whole new dimension to Damian's twisted plot, and breathed new life into his malevolent designs.

"It's funny," said Damian, staring into Felicity's eyes while Jake fussed over her. "The stem of a flute is crafted so that we can hold the glass without gripping the bowl and warming the champagne with our hot hands. Yet the stem is the most delicate part of that pretty little glass. Wrap your hand around it too tightly, and it can easily snap."

Felicity could feel her composure rapidly slipping away. Had the alcohol gone to her head, or did she have a genuine cause to feel threatened by Damian? Was she mistaken, or was his comment regarding the champagne flute a subtle metaphor for snapping her pretty little neck?

Before she had time to respond, the waiter arrived to replace her broken glass and take their order. While Damian sat describing in detail how he wanted his bloody Wagyu filet mignon, Felicity sat picking apart his character in her head.

It was not long before her thoughts led her to the startling similarities between Damian and the profile they had constructed for the Ladykiller. He was extremely wealthy and moved in the same high society circles as the victims whose identities had been confirmed so far. He was also artistically gifted, and he clearly disliked women. She assumed that Jake had also identified these comparisons, and had sought Damian's council because he was the one person who could truly relate to the killer in almost every way. As her brilliant mind processed a host of chilling possibilities, Felicity noticed a small but very unsettling detail.

As their waiter slapped the menu shut and prepared to walk back towards the kitchen, he gave a quick glance around the restaurant, checking that none of the other staff were watching before placing his notepad down on the table in front of Damian.

"Mr Burgundy, I just have to tell you that my mom is a huge fan of yours." The waiter smiled enthusiastically as he handed his pen to Damian. "It would be out of this world if I got your autograph for her."

"Name?" said Damian, smiling as he took the pen and prepared to write.

"Randy," said the waiter, beaming with excitement. "Randy Kimble." He must have met countless celebrities during his time at 18 Red, and although Burgundy was not a rock musician, athlete or movie star, he had some strangely hypnotic power over most of the people he met, including the nervous young Randy.

"I meant your mother's name," replied Damian. As everyone including Randy laughed at the comical error, Damian gripped the fountain pen and scribbled a short message across the front of the pad, followed by his signature, a single capital 'D' with two small horns sprouting out of its peak.

It was not the childish signature that caught Felicity's attention. She was more alarmed by the hand he had used to write with. Damian was most definitely a lefty, and as he wrote, she noticed that he smudged his words in several places.

Felicity knew that Jake would be blind to the signs. He would not have considered the possibility that his brother may be a key suspect. But in reality, he only knew Damian Cannon. What did he really know about Damian Burgundy? There was over ten years of unknown history in which some awful truth could be buried. A truth so despicable that it may have altered the very essence of the brother Jake once knew, and driven him to change his name to Burgundy in an attempt to escape his past. Unlike Jake, Felicity was not looking at Damian through rose-tinted glasses. She simply saw him for who he was, and now questioned who he might be when the eyes of the world were not upon him.

She concluded that it was time to place him under the microscope, and see whether he gave away any more clues that might support her theory.

"Tell me, Damian," said Felicity, swilling the champagne in her flute as she spoke. "What made you choose the name Burgundy?"

Damian smiled with the smug satisfaction of a master storyteller who had just been asked to entertain his audience.

"I was sat one day researching the Art Nouveau movement and I came across a gifted yet virtually unknown French painter by the name of Francois Burgundy. His skill in copying the work of other great artist's stroke for stroke was unparalleled, but sadly he never made a name for himself. He was a master mimic."

Damian paused to take a sip from his flute, and smiled to himself. It was as though he knew something they didn't. Some important piece of information that was right under their noses, that they were too blind to detect.

"I was sat painting a few months later, mixing colours on my palette and it came to me. When you combine brown, the colour of earth from which all life springs, and red the colour of the blood that courses through our veins, you get the colour burgundy. Burgundy represents life itself, so I chose that name to mark my own re-birth. As Burgundy, I can be someone else, a different person entirely."

"That's a nice touch," said Jake, raising his glass to toast Damian's grand gesture to his great inspiration. "You've definitely put the name Burgundy on the map."

Felicity also raised her glass, but she did not speak. With his brief explanation, he had given her far more insight than he had realised. She was convinced that Damian Burgundy was a fraud. He had used the creativity of other talented artists to make a name for himself within an industry that had previously rejected him as a painter, no doubt due to his own lack of originality. The revelation that he had also stolen his name, left her in no doubt that he was a man who was not afraid to take whatever he could from others and pass it off as his own. He was a sophisticated thief, but was it also in his nature to kill? If so, then it seemed extremely likely that he would have taken inspiration from former serial killers, which would fit in with Jake's theory of a copycat murderer.

Suddenly, the ceiling lights slowly began to dim, creating a more intimate ambiance. The table candles were complemented by soft beams of multi-coloured light that shone from the projectors, casting beautiful mottled patterns on every person and surface in the room as they floated by.

Felicity stared at Damian while he sliced and slashed at the bloody chunks of flesh on his plate with surgical precision, and noticed how blotches of blue and yellow light gently danced over him, softening his features and revealing the face of an innocent young boy. Was this the forlorn expression of his youth, when his parents were lost and he was abandoned by his grieving older brother?

Before she had time to reconsider the possibility that he could be a killer, the projectors shifted again casting the infernal shades of red and orange across his face and illuminating his features in a more devilish light. His piercing dark eyes penetrated her just as Jake's had so often. However, Damian's eyes were full of malice. It was as though he had somehow read her thoughts, and was concocting some devious plan to remove her from the picture.

The thought sent a shiver down her spine. Felicity knew that she would have to share her concerns with Jake, but it was neither the time nor the place to have that discussion. Jake had neglected to mention that the third Witch Hunt victim had survived, probably due to his reluctance to court praise. But the fact remained that he had saved her life, and although she was in a critical condition, she may well hold the key to the killer's identity.

Felicity was an expert in analysing human emotion and she knew that Damian would find it hard to maintain his poker face if the survivor became the topic of discussion. Should she throw the cat amongst the pigeons and mention the survivor?

Despite the almost overwhelming temptation, she decided that she would use the next twenty-four hours to investigative Damian's murky past. She did not want to risk rousing his suspicion, or upset Jake, until she had something more concrete than co-incidence and speculation to go on.

As the evening drew on, several guests from a nearby table left their seats and made their way towards the exit. A tall heavy-set man with olive skin and thick black hair broke away from the group, and began walking in their direction. The creases on his large forehead told the story of a man who had lived a hard life, and the two narrow slits of his eyes, peered menacingly over the high peaks of his puffy red cheeks. His baggy ill-fitting suit, barrel chest and broad shoulders gave him the look of a comic book caricature mob boss, but although neither Damian nor Felicity knew who he was, the look on Jake's face as the man approached their table suggested that this would not be a comical encounter.

"Like a rose between two thorns!" bellowed Tony Russo, pointing at Felicity, and smiling as he waved his white handkerchief at Jake to demonstrate that he meant no harm. "Who's this hot little dame?"

Jake did not smile back at him. Relations between them had never been amicable, and he did not appreciate the attention he was giving to Felicity. It was well known that Russo was a relentless predator when it came to females, and once he had a woman in his sights, he would walk all over anyone to get what he desired. However, before Jake had time to mark his territory, Damian offered a response.

"Never mind who she is," said Damian confidently. "Who's your tailor?"

"Why the fuck do you wanna know?" barked Russo. He was as intimidating in the flesh as his violent reputation suggested, yet Damian did not show any sign of fear. If anything, his tone was one of defiance, and Russo was incensed by his lack of respect.

"Because I want to make sure I never make the mistake of visiting him!" replied Damian, smiling as he casually sipped champagne. He would not be bullied, and wanted rid of this unwelcome guest.

"Who the fuck is this asshole, Cannon?" snarled Russo, his mouth tightly pursed in an unpleasant grimace.

"This is Damian Burgundy," said Jake. He glanced momentarily around the room at the two or three men in white shirts with less-than-discrete earpieces curled over their right lobes. He knew that Damian always had plenty of security on hand who would react swiftly at the first sign of distress. However, while Damian sat grinning back at the hulking brute of a man, they would have no clue that things were about to get heated.

Russo placed two massive fists down on the table, and leaned over Damian, like a gorilla asserting his authority.

"Ah, Mr New Money!" he said, in his distinctive deep voice. "Now listen up you little prick. We got a lot in common you and me. We both made our money by tramplin' on the little guys to get to the top. So just because yer cash is clean don't be thinkin' that yer shit smells like cotton candy! And definitely don't make the mistake of thinkin' that yer can't be touched. My dough is long too pal, and so is my fuckin' reach!"

He picked up Damian's flute, and eyeballed him as he guzzled down its contents in one gulp. Russo could not have known that Damian was Jake's brother, and was just as handy with his fists as the fiery tempered detective. So, he did not feel threatened when Damian suddenly leapt from his seat, and squared up to him with his fists clenched.

"Hold on fellas!" yelled Jake, jumping in between them to diffuse the situation, grabbing Russo by both arms. "I'm sure the next time your paths cross, you guys will share a drink and laugh about the first time you met. But right now, I think it's time you left Tony."

Damian lowered his hands and waved away the members of his security team who were scrambling towards the scene. The whole restaurant had plunged into a nervous silence, and all eyes were on the three men, waiting to see what would happen next.

Jake released Russo from his grip, while Damian returned to his seat and calmly poured himself another glass of Champagne.

"You might be right, Cannon," said Russo, pointing at Damian. "The only beef here is on this prick's plate, but he needs to watch that cute little mouth of his. If he ain't careful he might get dragged outta here and taught a lesson in concrete politics."

Russo turned and apologised to Felicity for almost exposing her to an act of violence, before turning his attention back to Jake.

"Listen, Cannon, you and I ain't always seen eye to eye. Let's just say, I ain't never liked no cop I couldn't buy, and you ain't never been for sale. But riskin' yer life to save those kids from that Hangman character showed guts, so I gotta take my hat off to yer. I just wanna make it clear that there ain't no bad blood between us. If you ever need anythin', anythin' at all, then you come talk to me. I owe yer one, Cannon. My whole family owes yer."

Despite his dopey punch-drunk appearance and his inarticulate street talk, Russo was not as stupid as he looked. He had managed to evade prison time, despite being the publicly visible head of one of America's largest Mafia families. He was old school, gangster 101. The roots of his family went all the way back to the beginning, when 'their thing' first blossomed in the lemon groves of Sicily.

Back then they started out offering protection to local farmers in return for cash, to avert the attention of thieves. Today, the capo of the feared Russo Famiglia sat at the head of a multi-billion-dollar empire that reputedly branched out into every aspect of organised crime which no doubt included contract killings. However, even Tony Russo had a code of ethics. Despite his many unscrupulous deeds, he still considered himself a man of honour, and in his opinion, killing innocent women and children was totally unacceptable. This was possibly the only thing the two men agreed on, and while Jake did not fraternise with known criminals unless they were on the police payroll, something told him that one day he may need to call upon Russo's immeasurable power and influence.

As Russo bid Jake farewell and left the restaurant, Felicity excused herself from the table and headed off to the ladies room. Her first visit to 18 Red had been a tense affair that she would happily soon forget, and a trip to the restroom would provide her with a brief moment to recover.

"There are some people your money can't protect you from," said Jake, eager to explain to Damian how he had dramatically underestimated Tony Russo.

Damian did his best to feign interest, but Jake's words were nothing more than a distant whisper, drowned out by the vivid visions of blood and torture that filled his head. The secret love that Jake and Felicity had tried to conceal, had only served to galvanize the hatred he harboured for his brother.

As his evil eyes followed Felicity's flawless figure as she glided towards the restroom, his frown slowly turned into a malevolent grin. An opportunity had presented itself. One that would alter his plans for the better. Even before the altercation with Tony Russo, while he had sat devouring his steak, Damian had already decided that Felicity Monroe was going to die.

Chapter 14
Magnum Opus

Felicity was still on cloud nine when she returned home after an evening alone with Jake. She had been invited to his apartment for dinner, and while she watched him work his magic in the kitchen, he had transformed linguine, soft shell crab and some chilli-infused olive oil into a dish worthy of a chef's table.

After their meal, Jake had taken her breath away with a stunning performance of Brahms Rhapsody in B Minor. As he sat stroking the keys of his grand piano with effortless skill, she sat watching him in awe, mentally undressing him with her lustful gaze. Then finally, out on his balcony they had undressed each other for real, and made love under the blanket of stars. They were blissfully content in their own private paradise, oblivious to the fanfare of noise in the busy streets below.

There had been no mention of Burgundy or the investigation that evening, even though Felicity had spent the whole day looking into him in more detail. She had been relieved to discover that on the night of the first double murder, Damian had hosted the grand opening of his New York Gallery. The grape vine confirmed that two attractive young women had been seen accompanying him to his apartment that night, and had not left until the following morning. Furthermore, Damian had a similar alibi for the night of the abattoir murder, when he was photographed leaving the high-profile Goldberg wedding with the beautiful young actress, Gabrielle Franco. Felicity swiftly concluded that while he was guilty of being a shameless Lothario, Damian Burgundy was no serial killer.

Her evening with Jake had been like a fairy-tale, and she could not help but contemplate what the future might hold for them. However, the night was cut short when a call from Abrahams saw her lover summoned to a crime scene on the other side of town. Felicity decided that she would much prefer the comfort of her own bed if she was to spend the night alone, and so she left Jake's apartment and returned home.

A short time later, Felicity entered her apartment and placed her cell phone and keys on the small telephone stand in the hallway, before heading into the kitchen to pour herself a large glass of wine.

"Chester," she said playfully. "Chester! Where are you my little muffin?"

She smiled to herself as she considered the possibility that the scruffy grey cat, which had kept her company on so many lonely nights, may soon have to fight for her affection with the delectable Detective Cannon. However, tonight her beloved Chester, who normally ran to greet her in the hallway, was nowhere to be seen.

"Chester," she whispered, tip-toeing down the hall and peering into her bedroom. "Come out you little monster!"

Before she had time to turn on the light, she noticed that her bedside lamp was still on. The lamp was only ever used for reading last thing at night, and she was certain that it was off when she left the apartment that morning.

She walked back down the hallway into the lounge to discover that there was still no sign of her cat, and began to panic at the possibility that he may have climbed through a window that she had carelessly left open. As she stood trying to work out where he could be, a strange feeling came over her. It was as though someone had walked up behind her and was breathing softly down the back of her neck.

She let out a short sharp scream and spun around, half expecting to see her Landlord standing in the doorway. He was the only person who had a spare key to her apartment, and he would only ever use it in cases of emergency, such as a burst water pipe, or when a mischievous tabby cat had somehow escaped and was running free in the vicinity of the apartment block. However, when she turned around, there was nobody in sight.

The air around her felt dense and morbid, like some shadowy entity was loose in her home, constricting tightly around her, suffocating her with its eerie energy.

For the first time ever, she was afraid of being alone. She thought about calling Jake. He would not mock her vulnerability and would come to comfort her in the early hours, when his night's work was done. Until then she could use coffee and a light-hearted novel to keep her from falling asleep.

She scurried nervously back to the hallway table to grab her cell phone. But before she could dial Jake's number, her heart stopped. The spot on the table next to her phone was bare. She was certain this was where she had left her keys, but they were nowhere to be seen.

In a moment of panic, she retraced her steps, and ran back into the kitchen desperately scanning the counter, before returning to her bedroom. Everything that had transpired since she had returned home suggested she was not alone in her apartment, and without her keys there was no means of escape.

She slammed the bedroom door behind her and stood gathering her breath, but as she looked around the room, the sight of her keys nestled on the bedside table brought a smile to her face.

"Get a grip, you crazy woman!" she said to herself, laughing at how she had allowed her imagination to run away with her. She threw the cell phone down on her bed and began to undress, deciding not to place a late-night distress call to Jake after all.

"Your loss, Chester, wherever you are!" shouted Felicity. She switched off the lights and climbed into bed, and with the covers pulled tightly over her, she soon began to feel comfortable and secure.

A few peaceful minutes passed in the silence of her room, but before she could slip into a satisfying slumber, something sinister jerked her back into consciousness. Either her imagination was fooling her yet again, or someone was whispering her name, as they hid in a dark corner of the room.

Felicity's arm shot out from beneath the covers, fumbling in the dark for the light switch. Finally, she felt the tiny button at the base of the bedside lamp and flicked it on. There was no sign of life in her room, but she had to be sure. She climbed out of bed and grabbed a heavy bottle of perfume from her dresser. Like a child seeking the security of knowing that there was no monster lurking in her closet, she abandoned rational thought and walked slowly and cautiously over to her wardrobe.

As her hand gripped the circular door knob of the wardrobe, she took a deep breath and closed her eyes. Then, counting to three in her mind, she raised the perfume bottle above her head and swiftly tugged the door open. Relief swept over her as she was greeted with the sight of nothing but cleanly pressed and neatly hung clothing.

Felicity turned again and looked around the room. It all seemed so ridiculous, but she would not be satisfied until she was certain that lights turning themselves on, moving keys and voices in the dark were nothing more than the combination of exhaustion and too much red wine. There was only one place left that she had not yet checked, and she would not sleep easy until she had pulled the covers back and looked underneath her bed.

She walked over to the edge of her four poster and lowered herself onto all fours, before yanking back the covers and peering into the black void. A moment of silence was followed by a gasp of despair, as she realised that a pair of eyes were cutting through the darkness, and staring straight back at her!

Felicity panicked, panting uncontrollably as she scrambled backwards trying to create as much distance as possible between herself and whoever was hiding beneath her bed. She did not know whether she wanted to scream or feint, but as she opened her mouth to shout for help, Chester ran out from under the bed and pounced into her arms.

Tears were already streaming down her face, as she pulled him close to her chest and hugged him tight.

"Chester those bright eyes of yours scared the hell out of me you little rascal! Don't you ever hide from me again little fella, you frightened me half to death!"

She was still laughing to herself as she walked across the hall and into the bathroom. "What a mess," she said, looking at the teary and distressed face staring back at her in the mirror. She turned on the tap and began splashing ice cold water over her face. It had certainly been a strange end to the evening, but she was determined to put it all behind her, and could not wait to snuggle up with Chester and enjoy a good night's sleep.

However, as she looked into the mirror once more and her eyes caught sight of the shower behind her, the awful truth finally revealed itself in an image of pure horror. The dark silhouette of something terrible had begun to move behind the thin white shower curtain. Whatever was lurking behind the curtain was the reason Chester had been hiding beneath the bed, and the reason she had felt so uneasy since returning home.

Suddenly everything seemed to happen in slow motion. A black gloved hand gripped the curtain and pulled it to one side, revealing a man dressed in a well-tailored pin stripe-suit of exceptional quality. The menacing looking gas mask which covered his face was stained with the blood of many diabolical deeds. Inside her mind, a hysterical frenzy was rapidly spinning out of control. But as the figure in the mask emerged from the shower and rose up behind her like some ghostly shadow, Felicity stood frozen, unable to move, her entire body rigid with shock.

Fear to her had always been an unsettling sensation that induced panic. Yet this new emotion was unlike anything she had ever experienced. It paralysed her like poisonous venom. Her mouth hung open but she could not scream, and while her body had begun to tremble violently, she could not move to escape. As she stood trapped in the spider's web of her own despair, she knew at once that the man standing behind her was the Ladykiller.

The masked figure gripped Felicity from behind, causing her to snap out of her trance and launch into the most deafening scream.

"Screaming won't help you now," he said viciously. The voice distortion device in the mouth piece of the mask made his voice sound unnaturally deep. "But if you don't stop, I'll have no choice but to slit your throat from ear to ear!"

He placed his right hand over her mouth, while his other slipped over her left shoulder revealing a razor-sharp blade. Felicity's eyes widened as she saw the mirror image of the knife edge pressed against her neck, and she stopped screaming immediately.

"That's a good girl!" The mask turned the sound of his evil laughter into a sickening cackle.

"I can almost taste your fear," he continued. "In our lifetime we are fortunate enough to experience many genuine emotions. Anger, hatred, joy and those who are truly blessed will even sample the sweet rapture of love. Many people go through life believing that they have also experienced fear. But trust me when I tell you that I will show you fear like you've never known."

As Felicity tried to look away, he tugged at her neck and turned her face back towards the mirror.

"Look at me!" he shouted ferociously. "Look at my image and know that you will die by my hand. There is nothing you or anyone else can do to change that. Embrace this reality Dr Monroe. Embrace true fear!"

As the hand holding the knife slipped out of sight, Felicity felt a sudden sharp prick of a needle at the back of her neck. Then, within just a few seconds her eyes glazed over and she slid quietly out of consciousness.

*****

Jake could not have known what a blessing it would be to get a good night's sleep when he returned to his apartment later that night. The murder he had been called to was a clear case of jealous wife exacting bitter retribution against her cheating husband. After just ten minutes at the scene, Jake had spotted enough clues to set his colleagues on the killer's scent. Then he had returned home for some much-needed rest.

He woke the next day feeling well rested, and went through his usual morning routine. He made himself a full breakfast of oatmeal, followed by a slice of toast with two hard boiled eggs, washed down with a glass of fresh orange juice and a double espresso. It was going to be a busy yet productive day he told himself, so a big breakfast would help him keep up with the pace.

Jake left his apartment and went straight to the hospital where Cassandra Lacey, the witch hunt survivor was being treated for her injuries. She was still unconscious, but the doctor's prognosis was that she was showing signs of recovery. Sooner or later she was going to wake up and when she did, Jake was determined to be the first person to interview her.

After following up on a couple of loose leads, Jake returned to headquarters just in time for the mid-day briefing. It was well known that during major investigations, Abrahams liked to hold his briefings at noon, when the minds and bodies of his team had warmed up and were ready for action.

Jake took the stairs up to homicide, and strolled through the open plan department floor and into a packed meeting room. Since saving the life of a would-be victim, the energy amongst the team was extremely positive. If his hunch was correct, the Real Time Crime division would confirm that the Ladykiller's first four outings also mirrored the details of other homicides within the criminal database. This news would set the men and women of NYPD homicide into motion, with fresh hope and renewed purpose.

However, when Abrahams finally walked into the room and took to the podium, the positive energy suddenly took a nose dive. It was clear that something terrible had happened, and the Captain's grave expression suggested that he was not looking forward to sharing the bad news.

"I'm afraid there's been a last-minute change to the scheduled briefing," said Abrahams in a sombre tone. "A short while ago I received a package sent by courier and marked for my attention. The package contained a recording which I've just watched and which I'm about to show you all."

As Abrahams paused and looked up at him, Jake sensed that whatever they were about to see was not going to be pleasant, and that he in particular would find the contents of the footage particularly disturbing. Before he had time to speculate further, Abrahams confirmed his fears.

"Jake, I have to warn you that information concerning your private affairs have been revealed in this recording. Information that I assume you've not yet shared with anyone here, myself included. But despite your personal involvement in this latest turn of events, I want you to know that we're all in this together. We are a team and we'll all combine our efforts to catch this son of a bitch and put an end to all of this madness."

Abrahams handed the disc to a junior officer to set up the visual, while he walked over and stood next to Jake. He placed one of his heavy hands on Jake's shoulders and leant forward to whisper in his ear.

"I want you to know that you're the best damn detective I've ever seen, Cannon. The killer obviously knows it too, that's why he's done this. So, don't let this asshole get inside your head and take you out of the game. Just stay strong and you'll get through this!"

Jake did not respond. His heart sunk as he realised what Abraham's was implying. He pulled his cell phone from his pocket and hastily checked the log for missed calls. Felicity had not tried to contact him. On any other day she would have called him by lunchtime, and he had assumed that her reluctance was due to him cutting their evening short the night before. Now he began to suspect that her failure to call was due to some terrible incident that had prevented her from making contact.

The interim screen of the television crackled and fizzed for a few seconds, adding to the heavy tension in the room. Then finally, the first image appeared and was met with a chorus of gasps. Six women lay naked and unconscious, their lifeless bodies strewn about a cold metallic room with no means of escape. Their faces were not visible, and it was impossible to tell whether they were alive or dead.

Suddenly an image flashed up on the screen for a fraction of a second, causing several officers to jump nervously, while others braced themselves for whatever distressing scenes were about to follow. The image vanished almost as quickly as it had appeared on the screen, but Jake's sharp eye had taken a snapshot of the white wall with the number 666 smeared upon it in blood.

When the screen returned to the prison room, the bodies which had been lying on the floor where now sat upright, their arms and legs strapped tightly to six chairs. They were definitely alive, and most of their heads swayed with a lethargy that suggested they were heavily sedated. None of them had been blindfolded. Instead, the killer had edited the footage so that the eye-line of five of the women appeared to have been scratched out. Only one woman had not required any such detail. She sat motionless in her chair, her long hair draped down over her face.

One of the women had been gagged and although he could not see her eyes, Jake already knew every contour and curve of her beautiful body. The woman struggling to free herself was Felicity.

Jake clenched his fists and looked away. His eyes became glassy as he fought against his tears, but he was not weeping with sorrow. These were tears of rage. How had he been so careless? He should never have allowed himself to be seen in public with her under any circumstances, and as a result of their constant coffee meetings at the Blue Bean and their very public dinner date with his brother, her connection with the case had not escaped the killer's attention. If she died as a result of his lack of caution, the shame he had felt over the death of Marnie Gant would be nothing compared to the guilt he would feel over the loss of Felicity.

Another frame flashed up on the screen, this time the series of numbers was different, and held no obvious meaning. But when the image of the prison room returned, a tall figure dressed in a pinstripe suit brandishing a chef's blade and wearing a gas mask was standing in the foreground. Now only the woman with the long-matted hair remained placid. The other five women had all been gagged and looked incredibly distressed as they sobbed and wriggled like snared rabbits. The sight was all too much for one young officer, and as he ran out of the meeting room with his hand clasped tightly over his mouth, the rest of the department winced as they continued to watch the harrowing footage. Finally, the haunting tone of the Ladykiller's voice, distorted by his blood-stained mask, began to relay his terrible message.

"What I have done…what I am about to do…is going to change everything….forever!"

Between each sentence there was a dramatic pause. The Ladykiller slowly paced around the room, stopping every so often to hold the blade under the neck of each of his prisoners. While the women panicked at the killer's touch, Jake understood why he had not blindfolded them. He wanted them to see everything. He thrived on his victim's anguish and by heightening their fear he was enhancing his own experience of the impending kill. Jake gritted his teeth as the recorded message continued.

"You are fascinated by death and destruction, and when you see it…you simply cannot look away! You tune into the Worldwide News for your daily dose of devastation, and when reality does not satisfy your lust for blood. You turn to fiction to curb your craving for violence. Look at you now! Shamefully aroused by the images I present to you. Images of pain and suffering. Images of imminent death! I am combining man's two greatest passions, art and bloodshed. I

207

*am the world's first homicidal artist, the first Gladiator of my
kind, and this city is my Colosseum...New York is ready...you
are ready...for the Art Homicide movement!"*

The Ladykiller stood pointing his knife at the motionless
woman with the long-matted hair for what seemed like an
eternity, before holding it beneath Felicity's neck and
addressing Jake directly. Every few moments, more frames
containing various number sequences flashed up on the screen
for a split second, before returning to the image of the killer
and his captives. There was something deliberate about every
last detail of the recording, and Jake was more determined
than ever to decipher the killer's message.

*"Jake Cannon! You are the champion of your cause, and
I am the pioneer of mine. But only one of us can win this
twisted game of fate. Right now, it seems I am holding the ace
in the pack...namely your precious Dr Monroe."*

Jake snapped in an angry outburst, yelling at the image on
the screen.
"If you harm a hair on her head, I'll rip your heart out!"
said Jake. The Ladykiller responded, as though he had
anticipated Jake's fiery reaction.
*"Anger and malice will not solve this puzzle. You cannot
catch what you cannot see Jake, and to see me, you must first
see the painful truth. This game ends tonight at 1800 hours,
with my stunning Magnum Opus! You and the rest of your
team have approximately six hours to save six lives. At 1800
hours, I will kill the last of these women, Felicity Monroe. You
have less than six hours to save her Jake. Tick tock, tick
tock..."*

As the screen went black, officers who knew Felicity were
already weeping, while others stared at Jake, hoping he had
the answers that would help save all six women.
It was all too much for Jake. He lost control of his senses
and stormed out of the meeting room into the hallway, and

began pounding his fists on the wall. Abrahams gave chase, following him as he tore down the hall like a tornado. He knew that Jake's emotions would run away with him, but he had not expected such a wild reaction. He grabbed him by both arms and pulled him into a small office, slamming the door shut behind them both.

"Why didn't you tell me, Cannon," said Abrahams. "I could have helped you Goddammit. Now I have a team player held captive and my best cop forced off the field and onto the bench."

Jake's menacing low eyes stared back at him. It was a look Abrahams had seen before when he had wrestled the gun out of Jake's hands up on the roof terrace on the night they captured the Hangman. It was also the very same look that his old partner Bobby Gant had given him, after the tragic loss of his wife. He knew at once that Jake no longer wanted to catch the Ladykiller, he wanted to kill him, even if it cost his badge or his own life.

As valuable as he was to the manhunt, Abrahams was not willing to let Jake throw everything away. His personal involvement with Felicity was the ace in the killer's pack, and unless he was taken off the case, it would be Jake's undoing.

"I'm pulling you off this investigation, Cannon," continued Abrahams. "I'm sorry, but you've left me no choice."

Suddenly Jake's expression changed. He took a deep breath and closed his eyes as he fought to recover his composure.

"With respect, Captain, if you pull me out now then you are playing right into the killer's hands," said Jake convincingly. "I am the only person who can crack this case and save these women. You know it, and so does he. That's exactly why he's done this. He's found my weakness and he's using that to take me out of the game. But you have to believe me when I tell you that I'm strong enough to deal with this. I promise I won't let you down, but you've got to trust me, Captain."

Abrahams stared long and hard at Jake. Despite his a tendency to bend the rules, he rarely failed to deliver results. However, this was his second major manhunt in just a few months. The Hangman case had taken it out of him and now the Ladykiller investigation looked like it could finish him off. Yet something told the Captain that although it was a gamble putting Jake him back out onto the streets, it would be worth the risk.

"Okay, Cannon," said Abrahams. "I'm gonna go with my gut here and let you go. Just tell me what you need."

Jake gave a deep sigh of relief. He could not afford to let emotions cloud his judgement, and he had to remain focussed to the finish. There were a host of clues in the killer's recorded message, and he needed answers.

"First off, we need to know what the numbers in those flash frames mean, Captain," said Jake assertively. "Can you get a team on that right away, and get Real Time Crime to report back on their archive analysis urgently. We need to know whether any of the other killings show signs of copycat behaviour. But right now, the most important thing I need you to do, is get me in front of Sebastian Bronson."

Abrahams looked at him with a confused expression. Bronson had pleaded guilty to several counts of murder, and was currently locked up in the maximum-security wing of the State Penitentiary awaiting sentencing. Abrahams was certain that the Warden would not agree to allow access, especially on such short notice.

However, Jake had noticed the startling similarities between the Ladykiller's threat and the Hangman's final act. Six multiplied by three was eighteen, and it was no coincidence that this was the number of children that Bronson had tried to kill on the sixth day, of the sixth month. The mark of the beast was also hidden between the lines of the Hangman case, and Jake kicked himself for not seeing the signs sooner.

As he listened to Jake's reasoning, it began to make sense to Abrahams. If it meant saving the lives of six innocent women, then it was worth a shot. He would have to speak to Castilian, and call in some very big favours, but once he pointed out the obvious connection, he was certain that he would have the necessary clearance to get Jake in front of Bronson.

"I'll get right on in, Cannon," said Abrahams. "I'm not making any promises, but I'll do what I can."

"Thank you, Captain, but there's just one more thing," replied Jake. "I have to meet him face to face. I will explain why on the way but for now you just have to trust me. You've got to get me inside Bronson's cell."

Chapter 15
Satan's Asylum

On the east bank of the Hudson River, the state correctional facility was a picture of inescapable doom. From a distance, it looked more like the hub of some archaic industrial enterprise, but from close quarters it had the unmistakably glum appearance of a penitentiary. The tall, grey walls which stretched up towards the skies were dotted with watch towers, where armed guards stood surveying the grounds below with eagle-eyed intensity. Every fence was topped with razor sharp barbed wire, and the occasional yap of a German shepherd reminded each of the prison's three thousand inmates that any attempt to escape would be futile.

Jake had been responsible for sending many of New York's criminal fraternity on the 50-kilometre trip north, to see out their sentences. However, with little over four hours left to save Felicity and five unknown women, his thoughts were focussed on only one convict.

Bronson was being held in the dreaded 'D-Wing', the brand-new maximum-security facility. The wing was built on the grounds of the original 1825 jail house which had stood abandoned since the 1940s. The surge in crime during the recent recession, meant that plans to turn the old site into a museum were scrapped in favour of the new prison blocks. D-Wing soon became known as 'Satan's Asylum', as it was said to house men whose crimes were so abhorrent, that even the Devil himself would question their sanity.

Satan's Asylum consisted of a series of subterranean chambers. Each chamber comprised of a solid steel door with a twelve-digit combination lock, which would not have looked out of place on the vault of a Federal Reserve Bank. Behind each door was a room lined with security cameras and artificial lighting. Positioned in the centre of the room was a raised circular platform. When prisoners were alone in their quarters, they were free to roam about the room and use the reading desk, bed, and a host of rudimentary sanitary provisions. However, when the siren sounded and a small light above the door turned red to signal that the prison guards were approaching, thick iron bars would rise up from the ground and form a secure perimeter around the circular platform, allowing anyone who entered the room to maintain a safe distance between themselves and the monster imprisoned within the cage.

Any convict who refused to retreat to the platform when the alarm was raised would incur the wrath of specially trained and heavily armed prison guard known as 'Bisons'. They would descend down to the asylum in teams of three via a password protected elevator, dressed in riot suits complete with stab resistant padding, wire ribbed gloves, steel throttle proof neck braces and heavy-duty helmets with blackout visors. Each Bison carried an electrified prod known as a 'lightning rod', capable of delivering a high-voltage, low current shock powerful enough to knock a man off his feet and cause considerable pain.

Of all the dangerous individuals residing in Satan's asylum, Bronson was the only prisoner who even the Bison guards feared. When one guard made the mistake of calling him a sick paedophile on the day of his arrival, Bronson had snapped. In an intensely violent episode, he had wrestled the Bison to the ground, and pounded him with heavy blows while twisting his helmet ferociously, in an attempt to break his neck.

The report which landed on Prison Warden Douglas Finegan's desk had chronicled the incident in detail. One Bison described how he and another guard had stunned him with enough voltage to kill a bull, yet Bronson refused to loosen his grip on the guard's helmet. So, it was little wonder that Warden Finegan had protested so vehemently against the suggestion that Jake Cannon would be attending on short notice, and not only did he want access to Bronson's cell, but also insisted that the security bars separating him from the beast himself were not raised.

At precisely 14:47 pm, the siren inside Bronson's cell alerted him to the imminent arrival of the guards. He placed a book that he had been reading down on the table and walked over to the circular platform.

"Three...two...one," he muttered to himself, counting down the seconds before the holes in the ground spat out several large steel rods which would rise like beanstalks around him until he was completely caged in. However, the bars did not emerge and when the red light on the wall turned green, the door slowly slid open and three very nervous looking Bison guards edged their way inside, followed by a sharp suited Detective Cannon.

Jake strolled confidently into the room before turning to the three guards, who were stood against the wall, brandishing their lightning rods in Bronson's direction.

"Leave us," said Jake sternly. The guards stood for a moment, their blacked-out visors hiding the disbelief on their faces. "Leave us now!"

"We'll be right outside," said one of the guards, as they backed out of the door and shut it behind them, leaving Jake alone with the convict.

Jake walked over to the table and took a seat, gesturing to Bronson to join him. However, the hulk of a man stayed rooted to the spot in the centre of the platform.

Suddenly, Jake noticed a chill in the air. It was not the high-tech air-conditioning system designed to help regulate both the temperature and the mood of the inmates. This was something completely different. This was the cold chill of death. He had felt it before, around men who had taken many innocent lives. But today, sitting in a cell just a few feet away from the Hangman himself, the bitter chill of evil deeds was colder than ever before.

Jake refused to be intimidated by the killer's sinister glare. There was a long and awkward pause as both men stared at one another, trying to work out their next move, until Bronson finally broke the silence.

"You're either very brave or incredibly stupid, Detective Cannon," he said, smirking hatefully as he slowly walked over and took a seat opposite him. "Why would you choose to put yourself inside my cell? What's to stop me reaching over this table right now and breaking your neck?"

"Let's get one thing straight Bronson, I'm not afraid of you," said Jake defiantly. "You may be twice my size but if you make a move, I'll put your jaw on the wrong side of your face before you can blink. So, let's not waste any more time measuring dicks here. There's another psycho on the streets killing innocent women, and I'm pretty damn sure you and him are pals. I suggest you do the right thing and make amends for all the evil you did out there in the world, by telling me who the fuck he is!"

Bronson's eyes widened. By paying him an unexpected visit, the cock-sure cop had presented him with an opportunity he had long craved. There were things he wanted Jake to see and understand, and now he finally had the chance to bear his soul.

"You're very clever, Jake," said Bronson. "Very clever indeed, but sadly you're also very predictable. You assumed that by sparing me the indignity of talking to you from the other side of those prison bars that you would earn my respect, and in turn, I would tell you what you want to hear. But it doesn't work that way. I look into your eyes and I see nothing but contempt. You hate me, so how can you trust anything I tell you?" Bronson slid the copy of the book he had been reading across the table, so that Jake could see the cover. "The truth is that you will never trust me, unless you try to understand me."

He was right. Jake despised him and regardless of what was at stake, he simply could not bring himself to feign empathy for a man who bore the tattoos of the children he had killed like a trophy. As Jake searched deep within himself for some false statement of reassurance that might convince the killer to open up to him, Bronson began to plant the seeds of his warped sense of morality.

"Do you know what the piece of art is on the cover of that book?" said Bronson pointing down at the paperback. Jake took a long hard look at the image. The picture showed a horrid scene in which a mother knelt in the street, clutching her wounded child in her arms. In the background, several women battled to protect their babies from men carrying daggers.

"It's the Massacre of the Innocents," replied Jake, still staring at the book. "Herod was afraid of losing his throne to the new-born Christ. The asshole gave an order to slaughter every male child in or around Bethlehem. It's a sick piece of art, so I can see exactly why it would appeal to a twisted freak like you."

"You're right, Jake, I'm a killer," said Bronson, angered by yet another attack on his character. "But I am no more a killer than you are. The difference is that only one of us has a truly righteous cause."

"Screw you, Bronson, I'm nothing like you!" yelled Jake, seething at the suggestion that he could possibly have anything in common with the creature sitting opposite him.

"Nothing like me?" replied Bronson, questioning Jake's reasoning. "So, you don't carry a gun?" Jake leaned forward ready to attack once more, but Bronson held up his hand in a gesture of indignant dismissal of whatever distinction that Jake was about to make.

"Please save me the sanctimonious bullshit about carrying a weapon to defend yourself and others," continued Bronson. "That doesn't change anything. It just means that you walk the streets with a loaded gun and a 'kill or be killed' mentality. Either way, you've taken lives, Detective Cannon, so that makes you a killer."

Jake did not respond. He knew that time was slipping through his fingers but Bronson was clearly not prepared to give up the Ladykiller's identity until he had voiced his justification for murdering seven children, and attempting to kill a further eighteen.

"Okay, Bronson," said Jake calmly. "Tell me what makes you so different from every other psycho I've sent to this place?"

Bronson was pleased to finally have Jake's ear, and gave him a smile of appreciation before continuing.

"We live in a world full of killers, Jake. We kill in the name of religion, we kill for territorial superiority, we kill for sport and some of us even kill for pleasure. But if you think that I am the type of guy who just kills for kicks, then you've got me all wrong."

Bronson turned to the book once again, and pointed at its cover. "I first saw the Massacre of the Innocents when I visited Rome years ago to study Renaissance art. The piece was exhibited in the Vatican, and when I saw it hanging there in all of its shocking beauty, I was filled with shame, because those soldiers represent you and me. We were born naked and innocent like the children in the picture. But as we became adults, our minds were corrupted by evil and our spirits infected by the disease of moral indifference. Now we are like the guards in that picture, Cannon. So, you see, if those eighteen children had died by my hand, their pure and perfect souls would have been delivered into God's kingdom. Now they will grow up to become sinners just like we did. You think you saved those kids, but you just condemned them to a life of shame, beyond which only eternal hell fire awaits them."

Jake sat back in his chair and nodded his head. He would never accept Bronson's decision to play God and decide the fate of so many young children, but he had to admit that there was an element of truth in his extreme ideology. In a world where it no longer seemed possible for righteousness to flourish, he wondered how many of those eighteen children might grow up to become just like the monsters he had fought so hard to protect them from.

For the first time since the start of the Hangman investigation, the bitter hatred he felt towards Bronson was finally beginning to subside. As he stared back at the giant sitting across the table, Jake was certain that somewhere, buried beneath the wreckage of so many unforgivable deeds, was a microscopic trace of good intention which would compel Bronson to reveal the Ladykiller's true identity and prevent any more innocent bloodshed.

"I think I understand," said Jake. "The world sees you as the wolf, but you consider yourself to be the shepherd, a devoted servant of God. But surely you must see that righteous intentions alone won't balance your account with the man upstairs. You've broken the most sacred of all the commandments. I know that a good deed today won't be enough put you back in God's graces, but it might just set you on the path to redemption."

The gaping hole of Bronson's wide mouth opened up to display two rows of decaying yellow teeth, as he laughed out loud.

"I'm afraid my sins outweigh my virtues by a great margin Jake," he said. "I will never walk through Heaven's gates. I am destined for the one place where my wickedness will be rewarded."

Jake was certain that he was alluding to the realm Jabula, just as Damian had explained when they met at his Gallery. If this was the case, then he was almost certain that both Bronson and the Ladykiller had been brainwashed by the same perverse school of wisdom. Jake sensed that he was edging closer to the truth.

"That's not true," replied Jake. "You can save the lives of six women. Six innocent women, who don't deserve to die Bronson. I'm begging you, just give me a name. Tell me where I can find him and I can still save her. She doesn't have to die!"

The pupils of Bronson's eyes dilated as the corners of his mouth arched into a smile. The Ladykiller was holding six women captive, but it was clear that Jake was particularly interested in one. In a foolish lapse in concentration, he had slipped up, and tipped the balance of power in Bronson's favour.

"Oh dear," said Bronson, stroking his chin with his thumb and forefinger. "He has taken someone you care about, hasn't he? Someone you love?" He shook his head sympathetically, sending a shiver of dread pulsating through Jake's body. Bronson knew exactly who Jake was up against, and with the odds now stacked so heavily against him, he did not fancy his chances.

Jake was tired of Bronson's games. He fought the urge to leap over the table and grab him by the throat. He slammed both fists down on the table in a fit of rage. "Tell me who he is or so help me God…"

"You must understand that God can't help you now Jake!" yelled Bronson, interrupting Jake mid-sentence. "You have played right into his hands, and now they have you exactly where they want you!"

"What do you mean '*they*'?" said Jake. The word echoed through his mind like a chilling mantra.

"*They* are men who promote death and create chaos for their own dark agenda," replied Bronson. His voice was monotone and emotionless, but his unblinking eyes were wide and fixed firmly on Jake. It was as though he had fallen into a dream state, induced by some unpleasant recollection. "They are a brotherhood of powerful and ruthless men. Forget secret societies with strange handshakes and archaic rituals. Forget everything you think you know about men of power, because none of that is real. The truth Detective Cannon…is far more terrifying than you could even begin to imagine."

"A sadistic cult?" asked Jake, desperately fishing for clues. "Are you one of them?"

"No, I'm not one of them," confirmed Bronson. "I'm just a pawn. But the man you hunt is one of them. He's a demon, trapped in the body of a man, and he's here to do the devil's work."

Jake glanced at his wrist, and remembered that he had been asked to remove his watch upon entering the building. His mind was a blurry haze and a look of sheer confusion was written all over his face. There would be no point in beating it out of Bronson. He would most certainly give just as good as he got, and the Bison guards would be on top of them in seconds. They would remove Jake from the room, and the opportunity to extract any valuable information from the prisoner would be lost.

As Jake considered opening up to him about Felicity, it suddenly dawned on him. Mimi Chandler! There was something about the little girl they had found hiding in Bronson's apartment that had prevented him from trying to kill her along with the other children that night at the school house. Of all the nineteen kids he had kidnapped, she was the one whose face he had chosen to have tattooed on his back, on the night he visited Ronnie's tattoo studio. Her memory might not be enough to convince him to help, but it was worth a shot.

"I know there's still good in you, Bronson," said Jake. "That's why you spared Mimi Chandler. You saw something in that little girl that touched you, and you just couldn't bring yourself to kill her. She was the light in your dark world."

Jake leaned across the table so that there was only a matter of inches between the two men. "My light is called Felicity, and right now that animal has her. She used to be just like Mimi, and now she's a good woman who lives her life trying to help others. You saved Mimi, and you can save Felicity too."

Bronson's expression turned to one of sorrow and shame. His eyes welled up as though he was about to cry, and for the first time, Jake saw weakness in the man who had once fuelled the fear of the entire city.

"Wrong again, Jake," said Bronson, looking up at the ceiling as though he was recalling the little girl's face from the archives of his memory. "I would have taken her life along with the others, but it would have been pointless. Unfortunately for poor Mimi, she was robbed of her innocence long before I found her."

He had indeed intended to hang Mimi, but shortly after abducting her less than a mile from her school, Bronson came to realise that there was something different about her. Unlike the others, Mimi was not afraid of him. She soon revealed that being kidnapped was a welcome relief to the ordeal she faced almost every night, behind closed doors, at the hands of her deviant father.

"I'll help you, Jake," continued Bronson. "I'll tell you enough to put you on the right track, if you do something for me in return."

"Anything," replied Jake enthusiastically. "I'll do anything you want, just tell me what you know."

"Okay, Jake," said Bronson. "Mimi Chandler is not safe. You took her from me and put her right back in the lion's mouth. Despite what you think of me, I'm no pervert, but her father is. Promise me that when this day is over, you'll do what I ask. Promise me you'll protect her from that bastard!"

"You have my word," said Jake. He need not have replied, as his expression alone told Bronson that he would pursue justice.

Bronson gave a brief nod of appreciation, before glancing up at the camera in the corner of the room. It was as though he was afraid that someone, somewhere was watching him with deep disapproval. Someone from whom not even the Asylum could provide safe sanctuary. He lowered his voice until it was little more than a whisper, and began revealing what little detail he could to Jake.

"I don't have a name," whispered Bronson. "I don't have a face either. I only have voices from beyond the shadows, messages and instructions from a faceless master. I have a truth that will most certainly destroy you, Cannon."

Bronson looked up at the camera once more and then down at his open palms.

"What truth?" yelled Jake "What truth, Goddammit!"

"That all of this is for you!" shouted Bronson. He stood up, sending his chair tumbling across the room, and as the door opened and the Bison guards rushed in, Jake turned and raised his hand, urging them not to come any closer.

"Back off!" screamed Jake. "Don't touch him!" If the guards intervened, then it was all over. He was so close, all he needed was one small clue that could help him unmask the killer. "Please Bronson, tell me what you mean!"

"I don't know what you did to anger him, Jake," replied Bronson, "but you're the reason he's here. They didn't choose this city by accident. Everything they are doing, the whole fucking game, it's all about you!"

Jake leapt towards him, but was restrained by two Bison guards. The third guard waved his lightening rod at Bronson, ushering him backwards, and as soon as he was safely on the platform, the bars crept up around him. As Jake was led out of the room, Bronson offered one final clue.

"Who have you crossed, Jake? Who have you betrayed? Find the man who considers you to be his enemy, and you will find your killer!"

The heavy steel door slammed shut behind them, and Jake was escorted through the series of elevators and security checkpoints until he was back on the outside. The helicopter that had transported him to the prison was stood on the concrete platform, shimmering in the afternoon sun like a huge black beetle. As soon as Jake walked through the gates, the propellers slowly began to rotate, as the pilot prepared for the return journey.

The Bison who had greeted Jake on his arrival, returned his watch, gun, belt and shield and wished him a safe flight.

"My cell," said Jake in a stern manner. "You took my cell phone, where is it?"

The guard apologised before handing him the device, and shut the gate behind him. Jake waved in the direction of the chopper, signalling that he needed a few moments to make an important call before they departed. His head was still a scrambled puzzle of information.

"Talk to me, Cannon," said Abrahams, finally answering the call. "Tell me what you know."

"Not much, Captain," Said Jake. "He claims they've never met, and I believe him. But they definitely studied at the same school of villainy. They are both part of some sort of cult, but it all got too heated before I had the chance to get any real details, so the Warden pulled the plug."

"Ah shit!" yelled Abrahams. "I really thought we might strike gold with that asshole."

"There's still time," replied Jake, looking at his watch. It was 15:13 pm and the Real Time Crime team would have come back to the Captain with some vital information. "What did the guys at Real Time say about my copycat theory?"

While Jake listened, Abrahams relayed the detailed report which confirmed beyond a shadow of doubt that his assumptions were correct. Each of the Ladykiller murders bore a clear resemblance to murders dating all the way back to the late 1930s.

In 1937, a butcher by the name of Roger Fitzgerald killed his wife when he discovered that she had been having an affair with his brother. Her badly butchered body was found in a meat locker, and her heart had been removed. Fitzgerald later revealed that he had cooked the heart in a pie, which he and his unsuspecting brother had eaten for supper the night before her body was discovered.

Then in 1979, Steven Jenkins, a construction worker from Queens was found in his car with a bullet in his head. It transpired that Jenkins had taken his own life, after killing his wife following the discovery that she had been having an intimate relationship with another woman. Overcome by rage, Jenkins broke all of her limbs before nailing her to the floor of an apartment he was renovating. Her vagina had been sewn shut in a savage act of revenge for her shameful betrayal.

As Abrahams continued to relay the details, Bronson's final words began to run through Jake's mind over and over again. How could this all be about him? What had he done to offend someone so wicked?

Then in a flash, Jake was struck by the bitter truth. If Bronson was right and this was all about him, then there was no better way for the copycat killer to stage his final multiple murder, than in the very place where Vladimir Volkoff had introduced him to the world of the serial killer.

"Captain, I think I know where he's taken the women!" said Jake confidently.

"Where Jake?" replied Abrahams. "Where are they, and how the hell do you know all of a sudden?"

"Bronson said that this whole thing was all about me," Jake confirmed. "I will explain in detail later but right now you need to send a tactical team over to Water Street. I think he's going to try and re-create the Brooklyn Bridge massacre."

Chapter 16
Apartment No. 16

"Do me a favour buddy, just shut up and fly!" yelled Jake.

Between the deafening swoosh of the propellers as they cut through the air, and the pilot's inaudible small talk, Jake had reached his last nerve. He was in no mood for conversation. His mind was preoccupied with thoughts of capturing the Ladykiller, and causing him unimaginable pain.

The killer clearly harboured a grudge towards Jake, but by abducting Felicity and threatening to take her life, he had taken the mysterious vendetta one step too far. Now it was more than a homicide investigation. It was a private war between two men, which looked destined to end in a bloody showdown.

As they drew closer, Jake could see that the small narrow section of Water Street, between Dover Street and the Peck Slip had already been cordoned off, and was deserted save for a few armed Police officers. There were large crowds gathering behind the barriers at both ends of the street, no doubt members of the public who had been evacuated from the buildings surrounding the crime scene, and others who had stopped to get a look at the drama unfolding. From his aerial vantage point, Jake observed a handful of officers shepherding a group of inquisitive onlookers back towards a nearby car park, to make room for the countless police and emergency vehicles that were streaming into the large open space in the cross roads between Water Street and the Peck Slip.

Jake felt his stomach rise uncomfortably, as the nose of the helicopter dipped and the aircraft dived into a dramatic descent. His eyes scanned the streets below, looking for a spot where the pilot could land safely.

"Hover at thirty feet," yelled Jake. "They'll soon clear the area and you can set her down." The pilot nodded his head and did as he was instructed. Sure enough, the crowds below who had been slow to retreat, began scurrying towards the car park, and away from the helicopter. There was a loud thud as the pilot touched down on the uneven cobbled street. Jake leapt out, and marched through a maze of squad cars towards the familiar yellow tape.

Water Street was lined with grey and red brick buildings ranging from four to eight storeys high, casting their shadows down the long narrow cobbled lane. At the far end of the street, a section of the suspended bridge to Brooklyn was alive with the constant stream of traffic, as drivers made their daily commute.

He ducked under the barrier and made his way towards building 272. It was a red-brick eight storey apartment block with a metal fire escape running down the front face, and a green painted entrance door on ground floor level.

For many months after the Impaler killings, the building had been a tourist attraction for homicide historians and fanatics. They had travelled from every corner of the country to see where the infamous Vladimir Volkoff had made his last stand. But in the years that passed, the allure had faded, and the nightmares that had kept the block unoccupied for so long, was now all but forgotten.

Jake could not help but ponder the irony. His battle with the memories of building 272 had begun so many years ago. Now, he was stood in front of the green door once more, trying to save the life of the woman who had finally helped him put those demons to rest just a few days earlier.

"It's not six o'clock yet," he muttered to himself. He had to hold onto the possibility that Felicity was still alive. The killer's deadline had not yet come to pass, so whatever harrowing scenes awaited him on the eighth floor, he prayed that Felicity's lifeless body would not be among the mayhem.

"Who was the first cop on the scene?" asked Jake as he approached a group of officers standing by a van in front of building 272.

"I was, sir," said a fresh-faced patrol officer. "Me and Officer Randone were grabbing a coffee just across the street, when the call came in over the radio."

"Don't call me sir," snapped Jake. "Call me Cannon, and you are...?"

"Pearce," replied the energetic young cop. "Donovan Pearce."

Donovan was stood with three other officers, who were all staring sheepishly at the ground, avoiding eye contact with the intimidating detective. But Donovan was obviously a different breed. His bright blue eyes were unblinking and full of excitement as they connected with Jake's. He had not been overwhelmed by the sudden call to action. He reminded Jake of himself, back in the days when he was a new recruit eager to prove his worth.

"Okay, Donovan," replied Jake. "I'm sure you know who I am. I'm also assuming that if the killer had been apprehended at the scene, I'd know by now. So, I'm guessing there was no sign of him by the time you came over here?"

Donovan nodded his head in a gesture of affirmation.

"I don't have time to go into detail right now," continued Jake, "but what I can tell you is that we are working against the clock. So, is there anything you can tell me that might help us close in on this asshole in the next few hours?"

"I hope so, sir!" replied Donovan, disobeying Jake's request not to refer to him as 'sir'. His thick curly blonde hair gave him the appearance of a thrill-seeking adrenaline junkie who would have been more at home surfing the wake in Malibu, than working a New York beat. Yet when he spoke, he sounded every inch the dedicated and diligent cop.

"I approached building 272 with my partner, and we noticed that this van was parked outside. The keys were still in the ignition, so we assumed that the perpetrator might still be inside."

"You knew who you might be dealing with here right?" said Jake. "Didn't you think it might be a good idea to wait for the special weapons team?"

"With all due respect, sir, if there was a chance that we could have saved some lives here today, we weren't about to stand around and wait for the cavalry."

Jake did not press the issue. He would have done the same, so it was not his place to preach tactical procedure.

"We made a clean sweep of the whole building and found them on the eighth floor," continued Donovan. "Well I'm sure you don't need me to spell it out, sir, it ain't pretty up there!"

Jake's heart sank. His fears had been confirmed, lives had been lost. His mind was a haze of images and details as he contemplated what he might find inside. He took a deep breath and prepared himself for the worst.

"Were there any witnesses?" asked Jake, trying his best to control his emotions.

"Yes, there was, sir," said Donovan. "By the time we got back outside, other officers had arrived. We briefed them on what we had seen, and then teamed up to evacuate the buildings along here. I managed to speak to the lady who owns that café across the street."

"Go on!" said Jake, urging him to divulge what the woman had told them.

"She said that a guy drove up here in this van at around 12.30pm. He was definitely alone, and he started unloading some large items from the back of the vehicle. According to her they looked like human bodies, all wrapped up in sheets. There were four in total."

"A strange man carrying packages which looked like human bodies into 272?" asked Jake. "Why the fuck didn't she call the police?"

"I asked her the same thing," replied Donovan. "But she said that after that, he started pulling mannequin limbs out of the back of the van, so I guess she assumed that's what was wrapped up in those sheets."

"Did she get a good look at him?" asked Jake impatiently.

"No, sir," replied Donovan. "He kept his face pretty well hidden, but I got a pretty good description of his frame. She said he was about six-two, with a slender athletic body. In fact, the guy she described had a build pretty similar to yours, sir."

Jake looked at the van once again. It was a jet-black GMC day van. Why had he left his vehicle behind? Had he been interrupted?

"Did she see him leave?" asked Jake.

"No, sir," answered Donovan. "But I'm guessing he left in a hurry, and on foot too. He must have known it wouldn't be long till someone raised the alarm, and he sure as hell wouldn't wanna be pulled over riding around in that van anywhere near here."

Donovan was right. Once the killer drove up here, he would have known someone might be able to place him and the van at the crime scene.

"Excellent work!" said Jake, praising Donovan for his attention to detail. The young cop lacked experience and was clearly under pressure, but he had reacted more like a seasoned detective than an inexperienced patrol officer. "Keep it up and you'll make a great detective one day kid!"

Jake left Donovan and the other officers and turned back towards the building. He was well known for his steely temperament when working the scene of a graphic murder, but for the first time in years, he was genuinely afraid. He felt a deep, dizzying nausea as he placed one hand on the green entrance door and pushed it open, before walking inside.

The hallway was just as he remembered it. A narrow entrance with several small mail boxes on either side of the wall and a communal payphone which looked like it had seen better days. On the right-hand side was a door leading to the two ground floor apartments, but to the left, just a few feet from the front entrance, was a flight of stairs which led to the first-floor landing.

Jake walked cautiously towards the stairs. Every step was slow and laboured, as though his feet were set in blocks of concrete. The hall was dark and everything was covered in thick dust. The whole building smelt like death.

As he climbed each storey towards the summit, Jake could feel his chest tightening and his breath shortening, like a mountaineer battling against the effects of high altitude. Onwards and upwards he climbed, until finally he reached the mahogany door to apartment 16.

"You're an iron cast hero," he whispered to himself, remembering the words of his old partner and mentor. "This is what you do Jake, now man the hell up and work this crime scene!"

He pulled a toothpick from his breast pocket and put it into his mouth, before putting on a fresh pair of rubber gloves. Then he gently turned the small brass door handle, pushed the door open, and edged his way inside.

The familiar metallic odour of human blood immediately filled his nostrils. It was a stench so rich that he could taste it in his mouth. Just like the crime scene at the Italian restaurant, there was blood everywhere, cloaking the studio apartment in a blanket of vivid vermilion.

The room was almost bare. There was no furniture aside from a single burgundy Chesterfield button back armchair in front of a row of large panel glazed windows. The chair was facing back towards the room, no doubt positioned to allow the killer to sit and admire his work. He had picked the perfect backdrop once again, thought Jake. The high ceiling was lined with criss-cross wrought iron beams, the brickwork on many of the walls was exposed, and the floors were all bare polished wood. The familiar features of factory-converted apartments always proved popular with the 'arty' types, who loved their raw appeal.

Directly opposite the windows, on the only white plastered wall in the room, the killer had painted a huge mural of the Brooklyn Bridge. The brushwork was wild and frenzied, but it was not the style that captured Jake's attention. The piece had been painted in blood, which had streamed down the wall and gathered in pools on the floor.

Jake began to tremble as he stood staring at the painting for what seemed like an eternity, deliberately avoiding the elephant in the room. Finally, he closed his eyes and took a deep breath before slowly turning to look at the bodies of the killer's victims, suspended lifelessly in mid-air, impaled upon four large iron steaks which had been nailed firmly to the floor.

Jake's legs buckled sending him crashing back into the armchair, paralysed by the overwhelming relief that none of the four bodies belonged to Felicity. Lives had indeed been lost, but he felt no shame in taking comfort from the fact that she may still be alive.

Jake looked at each of the victims in turn, and his thoughts flitted between past and present as both the original crime scene and its contemporary counterpart merged inseparably in his mind.

"Keep it together, Jake!" he said to himself.

There were four bodies in total, and just as with the original Impaler murders, the killer had taken photographs of the victims in their final hours and scattered them around the room. However, just as they had been in the Ladykiller's recorded message, the eyes of each woman had been scratched out of the photos. For some reason, the killer did not want to share his victims' terror with anyone. It was as though their pain was his pleasure, and his alone.

Their tall slender frames, their pretty and well-proportioned faces, and their long, flowing brown hair. Once again, the women were all strikingly similar in appearance to each other.

The Ladykiller had painstakingly replicated the original Brooklyn Bridge massacre while adding a few new touches of his own, but there was one disturbing detail which puzzled Jake. All four woman were missing a single limb. Either an arm or a leg had been savagely severed from each of their bodies, and although the original body parts were nowhere to be seen, there were mannequin limbs laying on the floor beneath each victim.

The painting on wall made perfect sense to Jake. Vladimir Volkoff had hung a canvas of the bridge on the very same wall seven years ago. Yet the mutilations confused him. What did it all mean?

"You were right again, Cannon!" The familiar voice of Captain Abrahams shook Jake from his deep contemplation, and brought him back to the present. Abrahams entered the room, and stood next Jake, surveying the carnage. "I knew I could put my faith in you to connect the dots, but I'm afraid we are just too late."

"No, Captain!" replied Jake defiantly. He was concerned by the pessimism in Abrahams' voice. Four victims had lost their lives, but two still remained. Felicity was still alive, and Jake would not give up hope until he had found her. "We still have time to save her."

"No, Cannon. I fear that time is the one thing we definitely don't have on our side," said Abrahams. "The Ladykiller has played his last card. I've just been informed that he's gone viral with everything. The recording he sent us, these photographs, and recordings of every single murder he's committed so far. He's posted them all over the internet Cannon. The press and public are all over it."

"Holy Christ!" yelled Jake. He knew instantly that this had always been the killer's intention. Like every artist, he sought critical acclaim, and now it was time to reveal his wicked work to the world. "How did we not see this coming?"

"I've already asked myself the same question a thousand times, Cannon," said Abrahams, grimacing angrily. "I guess money just isn't enough for some folks. This guy must have wanted something more. Recognition and notoriety perhaps? Either way, I'd bet my last dollar that he'll hand himself in when the clock strikes six, and take a bow while the whole world watches. So, all we can do now is pray that killing Felicity was never part of his plan. You're our best detective and he knows it. The son-of-a-bitch must have found out about you and Felicity, and brought her into the game just to throw you off track. He would have figured that bringing you back to this place might break you. But you're stronger than that Cannon. You're holding it together, right? "

Abraham's eyes searched Jake's face for any sign of weakness. It had been a risk putting him back on the streets after showing him the killer's recorded message, and he would never forgive himself if Jake fell apart under the pressure.

"I'm all good, Captain," replied Jake, offering a half-hearted nod of reassurance. However, Jake was far from fine with the situation. The Captain's words had triggered something in the deepest caverns of his mind. An unwanted idea that he was reluctant to contemplate, was now pounding away at the walls of his consciousness with such force that it was no longer possible to ignore it.

There was only one person who might have seen him interacting with Felicity in a manner that was not strictly professional. Damian had watched them both like a hawk when they had all met at club 18 Red. Jake had tried not to show any affection towards Felicity that night, but had he inadvertently let his guard slip? A single glance or a careless compliment may have sealed her fate, if the predator himself had been watching.

Suddenly the floodgates of suspicion began to open. Jake's mind was overwhelmed as the similarities between his own brother and the murderous monster began to mount, pointing a finger of unquestionable suspicion in the direction of Damian Burgundy. He fit Jake's profile of the killer in almost every way, from his wealth and the social circles within which he moved, to his knowledge and talent as an artist.

"That mess with your old partner, what was his name...Gant? Yeah that was a real bad time for you."

Jake recalled his brother's words when they met at Labirinto. Damian had known all about the Impaler case and its climatic conclusion in the very building where he now stood. His comments had all seemed so innocent at the time, but now they seemed more like the blatant mockery of a guilty villain, hiding in plain sight, and feeding off the information Jake had foolishly divulged about the investigation. Was it possible that in sharing important case details with Damian, Jake had inadvertently given the killer the edge he needed to remain one step ahead of the police?

"Did you notice he left the same triple six tag on the left hand of each victim?" said Abrahams. Jake spun round to see the Captain crouched down, trying to avoid stepping in a pool of blood while inspecting the bodies. "Real Time intelligence came back to me about those numbers that kept flashing up on the screen in the Ladykiller's recorded message. Turns out they all relate to passages in the bible that refer to the Devil."

Jake looked back at him with a blank expression, as though he was unaware of the relevance of the Captain's last statement. But Jake was fully aware of what this all meant. The mark of the beast symbolism and the numerical references to the coming of the Devil were all marks of respect. The killer was paying homage to his dark Lord and master, and staking his claim to a seat at Satan's table.

As Jake reflected back to the meeting with Damian at his gallery, he remembered the look on his face as he described Jabula. Damian had shown such passion for the subject. It was as though he himself believed in the concept of the third realm.

Jake was certain that Bronson had fallen under the influence of evil men while studying art in Rome. Damian had also spent time in Europe, and Jake was now convinced that his mind had been corrupted by the same powerful brotherhood during his time in Italy.

"There's very little left for me to do except die while I'm still young and famous!"

Jake had raised an eyebrow when Damian had made the comment, but on reflection, there was something haunting in his brother's expression that night at 18 Red. A disturbing sense of sincerity in his voice. These were not the casual ramblings of a billionaire who had grown tired of the high life, they were the words of a sadistic serial killer who believed that his despicable deeds in this life, would soon be rewarded with eternal bliss in the next.

As Abrahams muttered to himself in the background, Jake continued meticulously piecing together the clues in his head.

"Surely these women are more of a burden than a benefit to society...perhaps the Ladykiller just sees it as his duty to rid the world of a few more worthless leeches."

Damian's words continued to flood Jake's memory, and as he looked back towards the impaled bodies, the relevance of the false limbs became clear. To the killer, women were empty, worthless vessels. Like mannequins, their sole purpose was to remain silent and look pretty. By removing some of their arms and legs and replacing them with fibreglass limbs, he was comparing his victims to hollow and inanimate dolls.

Jake felt sick to his stomach. He was certain that Damian was the killer, and their family connection had clouded his judgement. He cast his mind back to their childhood, searching for images of Damian at an age when he was still innocent and pure, but even Jake's memories painted a picture of guilt. As children they had spent many hours in their father's training ring, sparring together. Unlike Jake, who took after their mother, Damian had fought Southpaw like their father. Just like the Ladykiller, he was left handed!

Jake searched his mind for any excuse not to pursue his brother until finally, he remembered his alibi for the first two murders. Damian's high-profile liaisons with women on both occasions had placed him beyond suspicion. He could not possibly be guilty of murder if he was in his apartment having sex when the killings took place.

Suddenly, Jake's heart sank once again at the realisation that there was one in particular clue that he had foolishly overlooked. In the opening scene of the Ladykiller's recording, none of the women had been bound or gagged. They had laid unconscious on the floor, and within just a few swift frames, they appeared strapped to chairs, drowsy and lethargic, as though they had been sedated.

Of course! If Damian had lured anyone back to his home, then a strong sedative would have been enough to send them into a deep sleep, long enough for him to leave the apartment and commit murder. When his guests woke the next morning, they would have no idea that he had ever left their sides. The alibi was a stroke of genius, but the clues that Damian had intricately hidden in his recorded message told Jake that he wanted to be caught. Damian would have known that he would be the only person sharp enough to uncover the truth, so while logic told Jake that he should inform the Captain, his instincts told him that he would have to confront his brother alone, if he wanted to save Felicity's life.

"You okay there, Cannon? You look like you just saw a ghost!" said Abraham.

"I'm fine, Captain," replied Jake. "I was just thinking I'd head over to Felicity's. I know you sent Gibbs there while I was with Bronson, but I know that apartment like the back of my hand. So, I think it's worth me taking a look at the place."

"Great idea, Cannon," said Abrahams, clearly pleased that Jake still seemed to be holding it all together. "If you're done here, let's get out of this hell hole and let forensics take over!"

As soon as they were outside the building, Jake watched the Captain disappear into the crowd of officers who were standing in the street. Since he'd been inside, the number of spectators behind the police barriers had increased considerably. The familiar site of news crews scrambling to set up their recording equipment, and the din of several helicopters overhead had become the common hallmarks of a Ladykiller crime scene.

Jake took another swift glance at his watch. It was 16:27 pm and he was faced with the dilemma of how to get from Water Street to the Galleria Labirinto in the shortest time possible. His car was still at headquarters, and relieving an officer of their squad car and using the siren to clear a path to his destination would only rouse suspicion. He could not afford to risk Felicity's safety, by being followed by anyone else with a badge.

In normal traffic, it was a fifteen-minute journey to 36 West 53rd Street. But with the roads full of people travelling across town to get a glimpse of the reworking of the Brooklyn

Bridge Massacre, he could not risk jumping in a taxi and getting stuck in traffic.

Jake decided that he would head underground. The walk to the subway on Fulton Street would take less than five minutes, once he was past the barricade and the crowds. The 8th Avenue Express on Subway A, would get him to 42nd Street. One quick transfer at 42nd, and six minutes later he would arrive at 5th Avenue Station. From there, it was only a four-minute walk to the Gallery. The whole journey would take almost half an hour, but he had no real alternative. Jake was ready for the final showdown. In a few seconds he would march off in the direction the Subway, but first he took a long deep breath, and closed his eyes.

*****

Somewhere across town another pair of eyes slowly opened. Felicity rubbed her head and rolled over onto her back. What a terrible nightmare her mind had concocted, she thought to herself.

She reached over to grab the alarm clock on her bedside table. She had forgotten to set it the night before, and judging by her pulsating headache, she guessed that she may have overslept. But as her hand searched in the darkness, there was no sign of either her clock, or her table. As she rolled over and reached out further, her heart skipped a beat as the unmistakable texture of silk caressed her skin. These were not her bed sheets. This was not her bed! A sudden panic came over her as she realised that the masked killer emerging from her shower had not been a dream. She had been abducted, and the nightmare was real.

Felicity leapt up out of the strange bed and stared frantically into the darkness. She could see neither the walls nor an exit as the entire room was pitch black. Suddenly she paused, and stood rooted to the spot in perfect silence. There was the feint sound of breathing coming from somewhere in the room, as though someone was stood watching her, waiting to pounce. She was not alone!

"Hello?" said Felicity nervously. "Is there someone there?"

"It's me...death! I have come for you!" The voice cut through her like a knife, and sent her into a blind panic. She began screaming, and scrambled around the room in search of a way out. As she did so, the voice spoke once more.

"Lennox...heavy metal!"

At once the thrashing, aggressive music filled the room. The fusion of electric guitar, thunderous drum beat and a coarse, intimidating vocal were intended to amplify her fear.

Felicity stumbled and fell to the ground in shock. She was still dazed and disorientated from the effects of the powerful sedative, but she refused to give up hope of escaping. She crawled on all fours until she came to a wall. Climbing to her feet again, she felt her way along the wall until her hands reached the unmistakable texture of wood. She had found a door! As the dreadful sound of her captors laughter grew louder and louder, she searched wildly for a door knob. He was close, and she had to find a way out.

At last she found a cold, metallic handle and yanked it down, before opening the door and running into a long, narrow corridor. It was dark once again, but now the awful music was complimented by high intensity light pulses. The strobe effect flickered rapidly, lighting up the hallway in brief flashes of red which revealed several doors.

Felicity ran down the hallway rattling each handle in turn, but they were all locked. Behind her, she could hear the door through which she had just escaped slam shut and a quick glance over her shoulder confirmed that the killer was right behind her.

Screaming and flailing her arms wildly as she ran, she finally reached the last door at the opposite end of the hall. As she turned and pressed her back up against it she could see the killer, storming menacingly towards her, drawing closer with every flaming flash of light. She turned and gave the handle a tug and to her relief, the door flew open.

Felicity ran out into the next room, but her legs gave way beneath her and she tumbled onto the hard-tiled floor. Still locked in a high-pitched scream, her eyes took just seconds to adjust to the blinding light of a large and well-lit apartment. Directly in front of her, a mannequin stood covered in black paint and doused with splashes of red. On its face was a mask which she had seen before. It was the same mask worn by the Ladykiller. She had never been inside the apartment, but as she glanced around in every direction at the opulent décor, she knew at once exactly where she was.

"Lennox…silence!"

The voice behind her was soft, and familiar. As the music stopped, she spun around and saw the killer standing behind her. He was no longer wearing the pin-stripe suit. Instead, he wore tight fitted jeans and high-top sneakers, both of which were stained with paint. He was naked from the waste up, and his toned, tattooed body was also covered in a rainbow of pastel paint.

"Oh my God, Damian! How could you do this?" yelled Felicity. If only she had trusted her instincts and warned Jake that night at the restaurant, then she would still be safe, and the killer might already be behind bars.

Damian did not respond. He walked over to the window and stood in silence, staring out across the city.

"Why Damian?" said Felicity, still lying in a heap on the floor. "Please tell me why you did this."

"Power!" shouted Damian, turning back towards her. Pearls of sweat were running down his face and body, and he had a look of crazed excitement in his eyes. "When you can have anything in the world, you begin to search for new drugs. New ways to feel alive. I can't explain how powerful it makes you feel to take someone's life."

"But what about all those women, Damian? All those young, innocent girls you killed, and their grieving families left to pick up the pieces. They didn't deserve what you did to them."

As Felicity tried to make sense of it all, she remembered the recording. His words were clear in her mind, a deadline had been set and by now Jake would be looking for her. She was certain that Damian meant to kill her, but if she could just buy herself some more time, then Jake might be able to get to him first.

"Why did you choose those women, Damian?" continued Felicity. "Why did they all look so alike? If you tell me I can help you to get over whatever anger you have stored up inside you, but you have to let me in. You have to tell me how this all started. Who hurt you, Damian?"

"All of you!" He yelled angrily. "Every single woman I have ever met owes me an apology. You looked through me like I didn't exist, but that all changed as soon as I became rich. You all threw yourselves at me, with promises of love and companionship. But not one of you saw the real me, you just saw how happy my money could make you."

It was clear to see why Damian was so bitter. Felicity had met plenty of wealthy men who had turned sour after being used and emotionally abused by one too many women. But it wasn't enough to drive them to murder. She was sure that he was holding something back. Just like Jake, his demons were hidden somewhere in his mind, and he was not ready to share them with her. All she could do was try to be the voice of reason.

"You must know that your brother will find you, Damian," said Felicity. "If you harm a single hair on my head, Jake will never forgive you. He'll figure this all out, and then he'll come for you."

Damian turned to the window once again. He knew that his brother was out there, somewhere in the vast metropolis, connecting the dots that would lead him to Labirinto.

"I hope so, Felicity," he said, smirking villainously. "In fact…I'm counting on it."

Chapter 17
Unforgivable

"Welcome back, Mr Cannon. Mr Burgundy has been expecting you."

As Quarter greeted him with a beaming smile and warm embrace, Jake swiftly concluded that Damian's loyal right-hand man had absolutely no idea about his employer's disturbing double life. He accompanied Jake through the liquid lounge and down the hall to the elevator.

"Head straight up to the Penthouse suite, sir," continued Quarter. "Mr Burgundy assures me that you know the entry code."

Jake did not answer. He simply nodded and looked down at the elevator control panel. Next to the standard dials for the first 35 floors was a label marked 'Penthouse', beneath which there was a smaller panel of numbered buttons. Why would Damian be so confident that he knew the code for his private apartment? There was an awkward silence as Jake studied each number, racking his brain as to what the code might be. Finally, the answer came to him.

He reached down and punched the same digit into the panel three times. 6...6...6. The tall figure of Quarter disappeared as the doors closed and the elevator began its ascent towards the top floor.

Jake pulled his gun from its holster and gritted his teeth. His eyebrows felt like lead weights, pulling his forehead down over his eyes and fixing his face into a fierce frown. As the lift finally jolted to a halt, he bucked like a bronco ready to be unleashed.

Like some insidious serpent releasing a slow poison into his mind, Damian had deceived him right from the start. He had remained close to Jake, offering his council while all the time seeking to sabotage his investigation, and disguise the fact that he was the killer. He had tormented and murdered several young women, driven by his twisted sense of artistic relevance. Furthermore, he had tried to cause Jake pain by threatening Felicity's life. For this, Jake would show him no mercy. He was determined to extract the facts he needed to close the case and bring down the brotherhood of evil that Bronson had alluded to.

The doors opened and Jake stepped cautiously onto the bejewelled black tiles, which sparkled under the feint light of the elevator. Seconds later, the doors closed behind him, leaving him standing in complete darkness. Had he just walked into another grisly crime scene? Jake inhaled deeply, testing the air for the odour of blood and flesh, but the air was cool and fresh, scented with a hint of expensive cologne. It was a fragrance that Jake knew well, and it told him that Damian was close.

"Damian!" he yelled, pointing the nose of his gun towards the floor. As much as he wanted to put a bullet in him, he could not risk letting off a shot in the dark. "Show yourself!"

"I'm right here, brother! I've been expecting you!" Damian's voice slithered through the darkness towards Jake, who spun around aimlessly, desperately trying to place the direction from which the words had travelled. Damian laughed at the sound of Jake's leather soles clapping across the tiles as he stumbled around the apartment in search of him.

"I can almost taste your hatred, Jake," continued Damian. "This is going to be even more fun than I had imagined!"

"You can't hide from me forever!" screamed Jake. "I will find you, and when I do I'm going to tear you apart!" He had lost all sense of reason, and the pursuit of justice was now a distant notion. Jake was completely out of his mind with rage, and all he could think about was violent retribution.

As Jake tore across the room like a tornado, he crashed into something solid. Still holding his gun in his right hand, he inspected the object with his left. Its rigid frame was covered with coarse bristles that felt like the hide of an animal. He had found a chair.

"You've found us at last!" said Damian, mocking him with derisive applause. Jake listened to each thunderous clap, convinced that he was no more than a few feet away. As Jake quietly coiled like a Cobra ready to strike in direction of the sound, Damian's voice rang out again.

"Lennox, lets heat things up a little!"

Suddenly, a huge burst of flame leapt up from the fireplace, startling Jake, and rising to a crackling blaze. The yellow glow of the open fire gave him his first glimpse of Damian, and the unpleasant scene he had created.

Damian was stood facing him, at the opposite end of a long banquet table. He was in character, dressed in his pin-stripe suit and black leather gloves. However, the vintage gas mask was nowhere to be seen. Jake guessed that the disguise was now surplus to requirements. The Ladykiller's identity was no longer a mystery.

Jake instinctively raised his gun. However, as he looked down at the table, he immediately lowered his weapon. Sitting in the chair in front of Damian with her head slumped down over the table, was a motionless figure cloaked in a hooded red velvet robe. The hood was pulled over her head hiding her face from sight, but Jake guessed that the person in the chair was Felicity. Although the sight of Damian holding a knife to the side of her neck unsettled him, his threatening actions suggested that he had not yet killed her.

"I swear, if you've hurt her…" Jake's sentence was cut short by Damian's sick laughter.

"Don't worry, brother!" he replied. "I promise you that Dr Monroe is still very much alive."

A solitary red apple had been placed on a silver platter on the table in front of her. Besides this and a matching silver goblet, the table was completely bare.

"What's this all about?" asked Jake. "Your fifteen minutes of fame? Your name up in lights at the top of the all-time sicko serial killer list? Why the fuck did you do it? You had everything a man could ever want, Damian!"

"You're absolutely right brother," he replied. "Everything a man could ever want right? Well I'm more than just a man!"

Damian was becoming increasingly animated as he spoke, and while Jake's eyes followed the hand holding the knife, he noticed that the edge of the blade was never more than a few inches away from Felicity's head. As much as Jake wanted to get his hands on Damian, he was not willing to put her at risk by making any sudden movements.

"A guy makes a million dollars and he's a millionaire!" continued Damian. "He's made more money than most people will ever see, and he can live a life of luxurious excess. But you could put a thousand so called 'millionaires' in one room, and together they couldn't match my bank balance. Do you have any idea what that kind of money does to a man's mind, Jake?"

"Your success is no excuse for what you've done!" yelled Jake. "You've murdered innocent women, and for that you'll get the death penalty and all the money you've made will be lost."

"You really don't get it do you?" replied Damian. "This kind of wealth can't be earned Jake. It can only be given to you by men who control everything, and only to those who they deem worthy."

Damian began waving his arms around frantically as he spoke, and Jake winced as the knife sliced through the air, dangerously close to Felicity.

"Fate! Destiny! Call it whatever you want," continued Damian. "When you abandoned me all those years ago, I fell into the arms of a new family. A powerful family who not only welcomed me into their house, but offered me a seat at their table. I was fortunate enough to be given that opportunity for one reason only. They identified a rare and passionate darkness in me. They showed me how to channel the bitter and vengeful hatred burning within me, and with their guidance, I became more than just a man. I became a God!"

Jake was finally beginning to understand what Damian was trying to tell him. When Jake had left home in search of his mother all those years ago, he had left behind a vulnerable and naïve younger brother, who was susceptible to manipulation. Now he was part of a powerful and persuasive group of dark thinkers. Men who had no doubt given him access to unlimited wealth in return for his mind, his body and his soul. Damian had left New York swathed in the innocence of youth, but he had returned a murderous psychopath bent on revenge.

"I understand everything now," replied Jake. "You blame me for the monster you've become. But you have to remember, we were both young when dad died, and when Mom left I just didn't know how to handle it. I was nineteen years old and the two people I looked up to most in the world were gone. I didn't know how to be a brother and a father all rolled into one. All I knew how to do was be a son, and when that was taken away from me, everything fell apart."

As Jake spoke, tears began to stream down his face. His fury had been diluted by a cocktail of guilt and regret. However, Damian was not moved by his half-hearted apology, and showed no sign of breaking. His expression remained stern, and void of pity.

"I was seventeen years old, Jake!" screamed Damian. "Seventeen! All of a sudden, I was alone and my heart was filled with nothing but hurt and hatred. But it wasn't you I hated back then brother. There was someone else to blame for the way things turned out."

Without warning, Damian lowered the knife, and stepped back away from the figure slumped in the chair.

"The anger I feel towards you now is the result of years of resentment Jake," he continued. "I envy you because you never knew the truth. I've carried it around with me since the day Dad was murdered. It took my soul and drove me into the shadows, but now it's your turn to share my pain."

Jake did not hesitate as Damian motioned for him to step forward. He walked towards the figure in the red cloak and paused for a moment, contemplating what cruel twist may lay in wait for him. Was Felicity already dead? Damian had sworn that she was still alive, but was his threat to slit her throat just a cunning trick to keep him at bay long enough to make his point?

Jake reached out and took hold of her hood, before lifting it back over her head. Then he took her chin in his trembling hand and lifted it to reveal her face. Her skin was cold and firm, and the eyes that looked back at him were wide and vacant as she gazed through him without emotion.

Jake stared at her face in disbelief. He grabbed her hand and clasped it in his own, but it was limp and lifeless. She had fallen under the spell of a powerful sedative, one from which there was no return.

Jake's gun slipped from his hand and fell to the ground, and his whole body went numb. He was unable to move or open his mouth to utter a single word. It was as though he had been bitten by some exotic creature that had robbed him of his senses. Yet, he had not been drugged of poisoned. No paralysing toxin had been released into his blood. He was simply suffering the effects of a deep and traumatic shock, because the woman in the chair was not Felicity.

As her long brown hair fell down around her perfect jawline, the terrible truth hit him like a bullet between the eyes. Every last victim had been selected for their striking resemblance to the woman in front of him. She was Damian's muse, his dark inspiration. She was Elsie Cannon, their mother, and Damian had killed her!

"A poisoned apple," said Damian, pointing down at the silver platter. Jake had not noticed that a single fatal bite had been taken from the ruby red apple. "You have to admit, it's the perfect irony!"

Jake did not respond. He stood in silence, still holding her hand as the tears streamed down his cheeks. It had been over five years since the letter had arrived at headquarters, marked for his attention. He had opened it in front of Abrahams, totally unprepared for the heart-breaking news. His mother had written to him to confirm that she was dying of cancer, and although she had stated in the letter that she did not wish to be found, he had searched the city once more for his beloved Elsie.

Less than a month later, her name had appeared in the obituaries. Nobody could tell him where she had died, or where she had been laid to rest. Ever since receiving that letter, Jake had lived in the belief that he would never see her again.

"I was able to succeed where you failed brother," said Damian triumphantly. "With the help of my powerful contacts, I found her right here in New York. I pulled her out from the rock she had crawled under."

He circled the table, beaming with pride as he recalled his despicable deed. "I had her imprisoned for five long years and when I finally confronted her, she simply could not believe that I was the architect of her suffering. The truth drove her insane!"

"The letter?" said Jake, choking on his words as he spoke. "Five years ago, she wrote to tell me she had terminal cancer. She only had weeks to live. I just don't understand."

Jake's eyes had glazed over and he looked unsteady on his feet. He was still in shock from the discovery that his mother had not been dead all these years. His heart was now filled with the renewed pain of her loss, and Damian sensed that the revelation had all but destroyed him.

"It was me who sent you that letter, Jake," replied Damian. "I've fantasised about this moment for years. The brief glimmer of hope as you realise you've finally found her, only to discover in an instant that the dream is in fact a nightmare. Your anguish as you realise that she did not die five years ago, but that she died right here, by my hand, less than an hour ago. It's priceless!"

As Damian's high-pitched laughter echoed around the room, Jake finally snapped. He flew into a tempestuous rage, leaping over the table and launching himself at Damian. There was an awkward struggle as both men tumbled to the ground and wrestled frantically until Jake overpowered him. He straddled Damian's torso, pinning his arms to the ground with his knees as he began pounding his head and body with a barrage of blows.

Damian offered little resistance. He simply laughed out loud as his face split and bones shattered under the force of Jake's heavy fists. Teeth were dislodged and huge bloody wounds opened up above his right eye and on his left cheek, yet Jake showed no sign of ceasing his relentless attack. He had almost beaten Damian to death by the time he dragged him to his feet and threw him over the table.

Jake took hold of his throat with both hands and pressed his thumbs into Damian's Adams apple.

"Why?" screamed Jake. "Why did you kill her? Why Goddamn you!"

As Jake finally loosened his grip, Damian was still laughing as he fell in a coughing, choking heap on the floor.

"Oh, there's still some fight in you, big brother," said Damian. "I like that." He stumbled to his feet and wiped the blood from his heavily swollen eyes. His once flawless face was now a hideously mangled Picasso.

"She is not the woman you think she is, Jake," he continued, panting heavily as he tried to catch his breath. "She is a witch. A cold-hearted whore who made the beast with two backs with the boy who killed our father!"

Jake shook his head in disbelief, as Damian relayed the awful truth behind their father's murder and their mother's sudden departure.

"It's true, Jake," continued Damian. "I found them together one day when I returned home early from school. She was giving herself to her piano student like some cheap two-dollar tramp right there in the marital bed."

Damian pulled out a chair and took a seat, writhing with pain as he clutched his bruised and broken ribs. "She begged me not to tell you Jake, so I agreed to keep her dirty little secret when she promised to end things with Benjamin Trail. Well she kept her promise. She told Trail it was over that afternoon, but I guess he figured that if he couldn't have her, then neither could Dad."

"You're lying!" screamed Jake. "That's not true, none of this is true!"

"It's all true!" replied Damian. "Think about it. Why would a young guy like Trail with no history of violence or mental instability suddenly decide to break into our home and put a knife in Dad's chest? He was heart-broken, and Hell hath no fury like a schoolboy scorned!"

Jake looked back at his mother's lifeless body. He did not want to believe it, but he had to concede that it must be true. He had never considered Trail's motives at the time, or indeed questioned how their mother could have abandoned her two sons when they needed her most. However, through the wise eyes of adulthood, everything finally made sense to the logical detective.

"How could she do that to Dad?" said Jake, wiping away the tears.

"You already know the answer to that question," said Damian coldly. "Sex is a weapon wielded by wicked women to ensnare wealthy men! Our father was already a successful boxing champion when they met and she knew it. Elsie saw the opportunity for an easy life and grabbed it with both hands. But once a whore, always a whore Jake. It was never about love. She sold herself for money, and I'm pretty sure that if I hadn't found her with trail that day, she would have betrayed Dad over and over again. I never told the cops about what I saw. Our family was already in ruins, and the shameful scandal would have finished us all."

Damian hobbled over to where Jake was standing. "Lennox...open the blinds," he said, spitting a mouthful of blood onto the floor as he spoke.

The black-out blinds which had kept the room in virtual darkness slowly lifted and the apartment was filled with the fading light of dusk. As Jake surveyed his surroundings for the first time, he caught sight of the mannequin. Its face was still covered by the Ladykiller mask. It was an instant reminder of Damian's demonic alter ego.

"Now do you see what she did to me, Jake?" he said, pointing to the inanimate fibreglass version of himself. "My soul was demonised long before I left for Europe." He placed one hand on Jake's shoulder. His eyes were now two swollen slits in his battered visage, and as they met with his, Jake felt a cold chill dancing through his entire body.

"Now you get to be the hero and end this here today," said Damian. "You win, I lose, and good prevails of over evil. I've killed our mother, so now you can take my life without guilt."

As Jake took a deep breath and looked away, his eyes fell upon the huge canvas in the middle of the room, and all at once he knew what it represented. It was the banquet in which Satan himself welcomed the most despicable souls into his realm.

Damian was clever, but not quite clever enough. His selfless speech was a cunning trick to convince Jake that he would be justified in exacting bloody vengeance. However, Damian had posted his works all over the internet in the hope that his legacy would live on forever. 'Art Homicide' as he had called it in his chilling recording, would be his parting gift to a decaying society. The name Burgundy would live forever and his work would become the murderous blueprint for other immoral thinkers who were eager to follow in his foul footsteps. His life had been short but sweet, and now his eyes were fixed on a greater prize. Damian was a true believer in the devil's dark doctrine, and by persuading Jake to take his life for the greater good, he believed that his soul would join the rest of his wicked kind in Jabula.

Jake pushed the hand away from his shoulder, and knelt down to pick up his gun. While Damian watched in confusion, Jake reached inside his pocket and pulled out his cellular phone and made a call.

"Captain...it's me," said Jake, rubbing his temple as he spoke. "I...I have the Ladykiller secure at 36, West 53rd Street. The Penthouse apartment of the Labirinto Art Gallery." There was a long pause as the muffled voice on the other end of the line responded in detail. "Yes, Captain," replied Jake. "It's my brother. Turns out that Damian was our man all along!"

Suddenly Damian reached out and slapped the cell phone from his hand.

"You fool, Jake! Why can't you see that everything I did here was to protect you?"

"Protect me?" yelled Jake, looking down at the cell phone which lay shattered in pieces on the floor. "Protect me from what?"

"From yourself," replied Damian. "Did you think I was gonna let you make the same mistakes as Dad did, and ride off into the fucking sunset with that meddling bitch?"

Jake's heart sunk. Felicity had slipped from his mind after the discovery of his mother, and he cursed himself for the momentary loss of focus. She was still in danger, and there was still one final twist in the tale.

"That's right," said Damian, with a grin of fiendish satisfaction. "Mother makes victim number five for the day, so you are still missing one brunette!"

"Where is she, Damian?" yelled Jake. The corners of his mouth were foaming as he spoke. He was not in the mood for any more games, it was time to end the whole sick charade. He pulled his gun on Damian once more, pressing it into his chest and backing him up against the wall.

"What the fuck have you done with her?"

"That's it, Jake, release your anger! You want to kill me so much it hurts doesn't it?" Damian gripped the barrel of Jake's pistol and pressed it into his own forehead. "Do it, Jake! Pull the trigger and end it!"

Jake was shaking. He wanted to kill him so much it hurt, but somehow, he resisted the urge to pull the trigger. He lowered the gun and looked around the room, trying to work out where Felicity might be hidden. She could not be far he thought to himself. Damian had set the whole thing up to come to a heated climax in his apartment. This was his final act, so Felicity had to be somewhere within those four walls.

He turned away from Damian and ran towards the hallway. As he entered the narrow corridor, he kicked open each door in turn, scanning every room from top to bottom until finally, he reached the threshold of Damian's bedroom. He flung the door open and ran inside, stopping dead in his tracks as panic and fear took hold of his senses again, just as they had minutes ago upon the discovery of his dead mother.

There was a large wooden cross fixed to the wall above Damian's bed. It was hung upside-down in a sickening satanic gesture. Jake covered his mouth with his hand at the sight of the naked body, hanging from the cross. She was battered and bruised and her hands and feet had been tied to the timber posts with rope.

Felicity had been tortured, and subjected to a painful and humiliating inverted crucifixion. There were several small lacerations visible around her abdomen, from which blood slowly flowed down over her body, and onto the crisp white bed sheets below. It was a harrowing sight to behold, yet as he raced over to her, Jake spotted something that filled him with hope. Her chest was still expanding and contracting as she fought for breath. She was still alive!

He gripped the cross with both hands. It had been fixed to the wall by a large metal bracket and Damian had obviously tied her to the cross, before rotating it to the inverted position. Jake spun it round before heaving it off the wall with all of his might, and lowering it onto the bed.

As he scrambled with the knots to untie her, Felicity opened her bruised eyelids and looked up at him.

"Jake," she whispered softly. "You found me. I knew you'd find me."

Tears of relief poured from her eyes and she smiled through the pain at him as he fought with the knots to free her hands.

"I love you, Jake," she said tenderly. "Promise that you won't forget how much I loved you." Her head swayed and her eyes danced in every direction, as the last traces of life slowly drifted from her body.

"No!" yelled Jake. "I promise to tell you how much I love you every single day for the rest of your life, because you're not going to die here tonight. You're my light Felicity. I've never loved anyone before, but I love you. You have to fight to stay with me because I can't do this alone. Please stay with me!"

He poured every ounce of hope into her as he held her in his arms, begging her to stay alive. He wept uncontrollably, kissing her all over her face as he pleaded with the heavens to spare her life, but it was too late. Felicity's eyes rolled into the back of her head, and she slipped peacefully out of consciousness.

At that moment Damian walked into the room and stood at the end of the bed, looking down at them both.

"You made a big mistake coming back to New York, Damian." said Jake. His voice was coarse and vengeful. "You and your evil cult should have left me and my city alone, because now it's personal. I swear to you that I won't rest until every single one of you is dead do you hear me? I will hunt your so-called 'brothers' down and make them beg for their lives. But they will find no mercy at the end of my gun. Only unspeakable suffering and a merciless death!"

"Be careful what you wish for, Jake," replied Damian, still able to smile despite his badly swollen face. "Your arms are too short to box with demons! My brothers are poised and ready to finish what I've started here, so get ready, because your city is about to become the blood-soaked canvas of our dark art!"

As Jake looked at him with the low eyes of evil intent, Damian smiled back at him. He knew that his twisted game was finally about to end.

"Goodbye for now, Jake." said Damian. "I will see you in Jabula!"

Jake smiled back at him as he raised his gun and pointed it at his chest. "I hope so, Damian," he replied. "Because my hatred for you will never die!"

With these words, Jake unloaded his clip into Damian's body. He roared like a wild beast as he marched forward, firing again and again into his chest, lifting him off the ground and sending him crashing into the mirrored wardrobe a few feet behind him.

Jake continued firing until his gun was empty, and stood staring down at the lifeless body of the man he once called brother. He had just killed the only family he had left, and while he may one day regret his actions, in that very moment he felt no remorse. He was not worried about the consequences of taking his life, because justice had been served. Damian Burgundy deserved to die.

Jake turned and ran back to the bed, and held Felicity in his arms.

"Stay awake! Please stay awake with me, Felicity."

He pressed one ear against her chest, waiting, listening for the faintest of heartbeats. He was desperate for a sign, anything to tell him that she was still alive. But as he listened long and hard…he heard nothing.

Chapter 18
Brotherhood of Evil

"Citizens of New York breathed a sigh of relief this morning, as the Ladykiller's reign of terror was brought to a sudden and dramatic end. The good news came with the shocking revelation that the killer responsible for the murders of several young women, was in fact the Billionaire art mogul, Damian Burgundy! Burgundy, was shot several times during a bloody confrontation with police at his Manhattan penthouse at the top of the Galleria Labirinto building just behind me. Burgundy was pronounced dead in the early hours this morning, and although the exact details remain unclear at this time, CWC sources have confirmed that the officer responsible for capturing him was Detective Jake Cannon, the hero cop who also brought Sebastian Bronson to justice earlier this year. Captain Ron Abrahams has urged everyone to offer Detective Cannon their support during these troubled times, as it has also emerged that he and American born Damian Burgundy, formerly Damian Cannon, were in fact brothers...holy...apologies for the brief interruption to our live broadcast but some sort of violent clash has just erupted across the street here. We are being forced to take cover and as you can see...oh my God, is he okay? There are several men dressed in what appear to be white stocking masks...I'm not entirely sure where they came from, they just appeared out of nowhere and they are now vandalising the art gallery. They seem to be trying to storm their way into the Labirinto. Ladies and gentlemen the scenes unfolding here are extremely disturbing, and as soon as we can re..."

Lucian Ferone turned off his television set before Belinda Bryce was able to conclude her live action report. He had heard enough. Damian was dead, and although the dramatic climax had always been part of their grand design, his heart sank at the news of his passing.

Lucian stood up and strolled across the marble floor of his lavish private study to a cabinet in the corner of the room. He topped up a cut crystal tumbler with Henry IV Cognac Grande Champagne, before walking out onto his sun terrace. Lucian's Tuscan retreat had always been a favourite of Damian's, so it was only fitting that he returned there to pay his respects to his beloved protégé.

Lucian's slender frame cast a thin ghostly shadow across the polished tiles as he stood looking out over the port of Santo Stefano. His narrow mouth creased into a smirk of satisfaction as he caught sight of his mammoth yacht 'La Bestia'. It stood out from the other vessels like a giant shard of platinum floating on a bed of shimmering blue diamonds. With the faint sound of water crashing against the rocks and the chirpy chatter of birds in a nearby tree to soothe him, he sipped his vintage Cognac in silence, waiting expectantly for the call. Moments later, his cell phone began to ring.

"Good afternoon, Fallon," said Lucian. "I've been waiting to hear from you. I take it you've heard the latest regarding Damian?"

"Afternoon?" replied the voice on the other end of the line. "It is 10:10am here Lucian. If you had joined me in Leblon as originally planned, you would know that I am only an hour ahead of developments in New York. But how silly of me to assume that our plans for a lucrative campaign of gentrification in the favelas of Rio de Janeiro, which could dramatically expand our empire, would be significant enough to distract you from Damian and his art homicide project."

Lucian did not reply. He did not appreciate the sarcasm and Fallon understood immediately that he was not in the mood for his attempts at humour.

"Forgive me, Lucian," continued Fallon. "That was insensitive of me. I appreciate that unlike Sebastian, Damian was more than just a devotee. He was an honoured member of our sacred circle, and he was like a son to you. So, I understand that this is a difficult time and I hope you will accept my apology. But you must also remember that dying for our cause was always his intention."

As they spoke, a menacing hound which looked more like a wild wolf than a domesticated dog, tiptoed gracefully out onto the terrace and lapped at Lucian's feet.

"Heel, Omet!" Lucian's instructions were met with instant obedience from his well-trained beast.

"I always knew that Damian was different, Fallon," said Lucian. "This world was his playground for a time, but ever since he learned the truth about our circle of power, and the existence of the realm of Jabula, he was never content here."

"Yes, indeed!" replied Fallon. He was stood chest deep in the warm water of his rooftop infinity pool with his phone grasped in his left hand. He repeatedly dipped his right hand into the water and ran it through his long thick mane of black hair. "Damian truly embraced our dark doctrine, and I am certain that since his passing, Jabula has surely never received a more deserving guest."

As Fallon spoke, a young man with a perfectly formed physique and olive skin tone emerged from beneath the water and began wading towards him. Seconds later, another man who was the very mirror image of the first, also rose above the surface of the water. Fallon scowled as they approached, and dismissed them to the opposite side of the pool with a wave of his hand, while he continued his conversation.

"Right now, I am standing in the pool on the roof of my apartment, with the sun beating down on me, as I look out towards Ipanema," continued Fallon. "Rio is a truly remarkable city, Lucian, and one that is ripe for the taking. Millions upon Millions of souls, all ready to be corrupted. Ready to fall under our control, while the Redeemer himself looks on helplessly from his mountain perch."

"No!" exclaimed Lucian angrily. "We will continue our assault on New York. That was always the plan, and it's what Damian wanted. We owe him that."

"Listen, Lucian," replied Fallon. "It's obvious why Damian chose the place of his birth to mount his campaign.

The eyes of the world remain constantly fixed on the city that never sleeps. America's obsession with guns and violence makes it the perfect location for our dark art. But remember it's been seventeen years since we first tried to conquer New York, and despite our best efforts, they stood united and refused to be broken. Don't you think it's time we focussed our efforts elsewhere?"

Fallon had sensed Lucian's frustration, and tried to calm him with words of wisdom and reason, but it was no use. Lucian could not be swayed from his course of action.

"You're wrong, brother," said Lucian, his voice was deep with passion. "Our last assault was a failure because the city refused to yield to a foreign terror. The tragedy we orchestrated did not divide them and break their resolve. Instead, it united them. But this time we will attack them from within. The architect of our next wave of bloodshed will be one of their own. A native New Yorker born and bred just as Damian was, but he will strike with an immeasurable force, and ignite their fear like never before. I want to make them suffer under the weight of their own anxiety. We will plunge their world into chaos, but from that chaos a new order will rise. As New York is toppled, others will follow. Then city by city, the world's leading Nation will slip into our control. We will be free to harvest the souls of the masses as they are re-born into darkness."

"You have high hopes Lucian," said Fallon. "Can one man really bring New York to its knees?"

Lucian gave a fiendish smile, stroking the perfectly trimmed grey beard that sat on the end of his sharply pointed chin.

"Of course!" replied Lucian. "Mark my words, Fallon, when our next devotee has completed his work, Babylon itself will rise from the ashes of the world's most decadent city. Order will collapse and mayhem will reign!"

Both men laughed uncontrollably as they visualised the next chapter of their evil conspiracy unravelling.

"I hear that the cop is being hailed as a hero," said Fallon. "The irony is astonishing. Our men on the inside have already confirmed that it was Jake who killed his own brother, but no doubt the NYPD will rally to his cause and defend him to the last."

"Good," said Lucian, rubbing his hands together gleefully. "Where would our little game be without Jake Cannon?"

"Don't forget the girl too," said Fallon, waving his hand at the two young men he had dismissed to the opposite end of the pool, but this time beckoning them to come closer.

"The girl makes it all the more interesting," continued Fallon. "Now Jake has no choice but to stand and fight."

"What do you mean?" replied Lucian. He had turned off his television set before Belinda Bryce's news report had concluded, so he was completely unaware that there had been one final twist in the tale. As Lucian stood in silence, Fallon took great pleasure in enlightening him.

"You have no idea, do you?" said Fallon, chuckling with excitement as he broke the news. "The girl survived! The psychologist, Felicity Monroe is still alive!"

Lucian grinned. He could hardly contain his satisfaction. It had been Damian's intention to kill her, but now it became apparent that Felicity was far more valuable to them alive. She would add an entertaining centrepiece to the next chapter of their murderous plot.

"That is excellent news," said Lucian. "Now Jake still has so much to lose, and everything to play for. There will be those within the NYPD who will want to see him take the fall, but our men at the top will ensure that he is protected. Jake Cannon must not be allowed to buckle under the weight of the Ladykiller investigation. He must recover, and he must return to duty."

Lucian had focussed all of his anger and hatred on the detective. Jake was the reason Damian had desperately wanted to return to New York and embark on his killing spree, a task which was usually reserved for their loyal devotees, but not a sworn member of the brotherhood. Jake was also the man responsible for taking Damian's life. For this reason,

Lucian was bent on vengeance. He wanted to prolong Jake's suffering and bear witness to his agony.

"Detective Cannon thought that Damian was a troublesome adversary, but he hasn't seen anything yet!" said Lucian. "Things are about to get very interesting indeed."

Fallon stared into the eyes of the two young men with lustful intent as they swam across the pool towards him. "I cannot wait, Lucian," he replied. "The dark dawn will soon be upon us!"

The call ended abruptly, and Lucian turned and walked back into his study. He took a seat at a large desk at the far end of the room, and glanced up at a wall mounted control panel.

"Lupo…give me soothing music!"

The two speakers on the wall above the control panel came to life with the ping of piano keys, and as the melancholy melody of the Moonlight Sonata took hold of him, he leant back in his chair, closed his eyes, and allowed his mind to run wild with wicked thoughts.

Lucian Ferone was the true epitome of evil. He would not be satisfied until the streets of New York ran red with blood, and Damian's death had been avenged by their next devotee. A man who would kill viciously and without mercy. A serial killer who would embark on a campaign of murder and vengeance which would almost certainly end with the death of Detective Jake Cannon.

END